ONE LAST HIT

LINDA COLES

Chapter One

WINTER IN CROYDON was always dull. Cold, damp and dull. Rarely did it snow, rarely were there clear sunny days, and cold miserable rain fell like it owned the place. Summer could be stifling, with the density of buildings, hot traffic pollution and a lack of breeze that turned the city into an oven.

"Shame some summer heat couldn't be stored for days like today," said DS Amanda Lacey, as she and DC Jack Rutherford dodged the raindrops. "Even the smallest amount of heat would be welcome right now," she grumbled as they dashed from Jack's car towards the white mobile food van. They stood huddled together under the far-too-small striped awning along with two other hungry individuals. There was barely enough room for all four of them, and Amanda's trouser seat and legs, exposed to the elements, were getting damper by the minute.

She and Jack were on their way to see a CI, a confidential informant, and had stopped for sustenance. Amanda's stomach had been making more noise than a motorway grader levelling the road surface as they drove, so rather than treat the CI to the noise, they'd pulled over for food. Jack had his fun facts handy and as always chose that moment while they sheltered to educate her and the other two suits.

"A rumbling stomach is the sign of a healthy digestive system as well as possible hunger. Did you know that?"

"No, Jack, can't say that I did, though you've enlightened me once again." She smiled, knowing there was more to come, grateful for the distraction of waiting under the wet awning. "Do tell me more."

"It's your digestive muscles contracting and releasing little pockets of gases that build up, which is why your gut gurgles after a meal, but more so when it's empty. There's food absorbing the noises when your tum is full, so it's quieter. Then, as you get hungry it growls, letting you know it's ready to take food on board."

"Good to know. Thanks, Jack."

They stepped forward to place their order.

"Two bacon rolls and two teas, please. No sugar," said Amanda. She turned back to Jack, who was looking a little dubious. She knew exactly why. "You can't have a bacon roll *and* sugar in your tea if you're going to lose that weight, Jack. You can't have it both ways," she told him as gently as she could. "Which would you prefer to give up today – bacon or sugar?"

Jack conceded with a submissive sigh. "If it was up to me, I'd have two sugars in my tea," he said petulantly.

"Well, it's a good job it's not up to you, then. Your doctor told you to drop a few pounds for a reason and it's better you do it now than when you get much older. It's easier on your body all round."

Jack saluted Amanda cheekily, as he often did. Even though she was technically his boss, they were extremely close work partners and friends too.

"Well, I'm having a dash of brown sauce. Can't eat bacon without it."

"As you wish." Amanda turned back to watch their rolls being put together and slotted into paper bags. The man inside the caravan had heard the brown sauce conversation and slipped a sachet in alongside one roll before handing them both to Amanda.

He handed over two white cups and Jack took them both. There was no need to ask which was which.

"I'll get the car opened," Jack said, and dashed off to let himself in

Amanda followed a moment behind him. Inside, she put the bags down, shook her head and ruffled her blonde hair with her fingers in hopes of heading off a bad hair day. Her short, loose curls had a habit of looking like an angora goat once they'd got wet. Marilyn Monroe she was not, though she had the hourglass figure buried beneath her sensible work attire. As a detective, there was little point in her wearing heels and tight skirts like they did on Netflix; she was more the Doc Martens type – highly polished and just as tough.

Glancing in the rear-view mirror, she sighed at the wet angora looking back at her, then wiped her side of the windscreen with the back of her hand so she could see out to the rain.

"What's so interesting out there?" Jack asked her.

"Just watching those two over in that car, the ones who were being served when we pulled up."

"What about them? They'll be on their lunch break, same as us, probably."

"Well, that's just it. They look like they don't normally eat from a roadside van, and since they got in their car, they haven't touched their food. The bags are still on the window ledge. I can see them."

"Well, maybe they're talking or something."

Amanda didn't reply as she finished her own roll and sipped her tea. More cars pulled up, more suits bought their lunches and then hurried back to their vehicles as the rain fell. Finally, the original navy BMW pulled away, spinning its wheels on the loose wet gravel. The passenger window opened and an arm appeared and threw two white bags and two white cups out into the bushes. Then they were gone.

"Now that's odd, don't you think?" asked Amanda.

"Yeah, I'd say so. Who throws perfectly good bacon rolls away – and why?"

Chapter Two

"FANCY A SWIFT ONE BEFORE HOME?"

Duncan looked at his watch; he was one of the few men at the station to still wear one. It informed him it was just before 7 p.m. and he'd been due home an hour ago. He looked at it a moment longer, asking it for the answer: to drink or not to drink; that was the question. With no obvious clue as to what he should do, he let his own head guide him.

"Just one – why not?" he said. And that was that. DS Duncan Riley collected his few loose belongings off his desk and made his way out of the Greater Manchester police station accompanied by his colleague and friend DS Rochelle Mason. Neither of them spoke until they were clear of the building. A comfortable yet excited silence buzzed through both their bodies, though each kept it from the other.

Rochelle finally broke the silence as they approached their individual vehicles, which were parked next to one another. Duncan's car bleeped loudly as he pressed his key fob.

"Usual place?" he asked her.

Rochelle was still busy fumbling in her bag for her keys. "May as well, if it's just a quickie," she said at last. Even though he couldn't see her eyes shining in the light from the streetlight, he knew they would be; her tone had given the game away. As a detective, he didn't miss a trick, not from a criminal, and certainly not from a flirty colleague. And besides, he liked it. He watched as she slipped astride her Triumph motorbike, started the engine, and pulled her helmet on. The throb vibrated through them both. She lifted her visor to speak. Her breath floated on the cool evening air, forming a long cloud in front of her, like cigarette smoke, only far sweeter.

"I'll see you there. I'll have a lager and lime if you get there before me." She winked at him invitingly and made her way cautiously out of the car park. Duncan pushed a lustful thought away and smiled to himself as he slid inside his car.

He pressed the ignition and the engine sprang into life. Putting the car into gear, he accelerated out of his spot and then pulled alongside Rochelle's bike at the exit.

"And I'll have a pint, no lime!" he yelled through his open window. But he knew she would arrive after he did – not that she was a sponger. No, she had a different reason.

Rochelle liked to make her entrance.

At nearly six feet tall with a dirty blond ponytail, she was a real head-turner, particularly in snug jeans and a leather jacket. With a generous mouth and bright blue eyes, she'd appeared in many of her male colleagues' dreams at some point or other. And a fair few of his own, he had to admit, though nothing had ever come of them.

At the bar, Duncan resigned himself to buying Rochelle another lager and lime, and the thought of her brought another smile to his otherwise tired face. And tonight, like other nights, it was two work mates, one drink. Any more and it would be another row for sure, though not with Rochelle but with the other woman in his life – his wife Sam.

The very thought of Sam sent a ripple of depression through his body. The feeling was not new to him over recent months, but as Rochelle made her entrance into the crowded bar, the thought shimmied off back from whence it came and he enjoyed the view while it lasted. He waved her over and noted the envious looks of the other male drinkers; there was apparently a fair amount of hormonal jealousy in the room. He chuckled to himself as he watched her pick up her lager and tip the glass back greedily, the golden, frothy liquid vanishing as she half-drained it. She slammed it down on the bar and let out a satisfied gasp. A bit of white foam stayed on her top lip and she cleared it expertly away with her tongue. Watching the whole scenario play out in front of him, Duncan realized he was gawping – much like the other men immediately around them. He closed his mouth again, embarrassed. Did she know she had such an effect on men? Because if she did, she never let on or played to it, particularly – except while making an entrance, that was.

"Thirsty?" he said evenly?

"You bet. I've been dreaming of that since about four o'clock. With my nose stuck in paperwork all day, I've been dying to break away for a swift one, but alas, it wasn't to be." She waved her arms around the room as though acting in a Shakespearian play. Always the exuberant, theatrical one.

Duncan nodded and sipped at his own lager, waiting for the conversation to flow to something other than work, though what she said next wasn't really what he wanted to talk about.

"How's things at home? Are you still hiding out?" She took another long mouthful of lager. There was no malice in her voice, just friendly enquiry. It was no secret at the station that Duncan and Sam weren't getting on too well, though it wasn't discussed out loud. Sam could be a real ball-breaker at times, and a lazy one at that. How and why she'd turned out to be so was still a mystery to Duncan, and most of the time he ignored it. Until they rowed, that is. This was becoming much more frequent, and he had noticed increased venom from her side. He pushed the gloomy thoughts to the back of his mind now and answered Rochelle's question.

"That's why I'm having a swift one, and only one. Gives me chance to unwind before I get re-wound. Call it Dutch courage." It sounded sad and pathetic to his own ears. He picked up his glass and took a couple of large gulps, partly to keep up with Rochelle's consumption and partly to find the hit that came with the alcohol. "So, no, things are no better. I wish they were," he added. Their eyes met for a second or two and he could see the pity in hers. Was there pity in *all* his colleagues' eyes? It wouldn't surprise him. He felt her arm around his shoulder and made no move to change it. It was welcome, and he knew she was being a mate, that there was no ulterior motive at play. He forced a smile before draining the last drops in his glass.

"Thanks for your concern, Rochelle. Let's hope today was a good day for her or else I'll be back here drowning my sorrows in an hour."

"I won't wait for you, then. Let's be positive."

She pecked him lightly on the cheek, and he got to his feet to head home.

Home. Could he call it that? It didn't feel like it much.

Chapter Three

THE AIR WAS as cold as a snowman's ear as Duncan pulled up outside his house. The street was quiet, too cold for even the hardiest of kids to be loitering outside or kicking a ball around their back garden. Dogs had been walked, owners tucked up in the warmth back inside until nearly bedtime, when the back door would be opened briefly for toilet emergencies and final calls before the household retired for the night. Duncan was glad he didn't have a dog to worry about, something else to be left up to him to look after.

He stayed put in the driver's seat, the last remaining heat seeping out of the metal to meet the cold and evaporate into the night like a ghost. The lights in the lounge were on, curtains closed so only a chink of gold shone from the top where the two curtains joined in a thin wedge shape. The only other rooms with a light on were the girls' bedrooms, the light reflecting down onto the small grassy garden below. He opened the car door, and the frosty air enveloped him as he grabbed his bag from the seat next to him and headed for the side entrance and warmth. Inside, he closed the door quietly and stood listening for a moment. The only sound was the TV. He heard the familiar notes of *Coronation Street*'s theme music playing out before news of yet another caramel biscuit you simply couldn't do without filled the gap. Maybe she'd come out to greet him, get his dinner out of the oven, make a hot drink, even, he thought, but so far, the only warmth greeting him was from the central heating.

No surprises there, then.

Duncan placed a smile on his face and pushed open the door into the lounge. Sam was spread out on the sofa, a mug of tea on the small table next to her, spilled crumbs from a half-finished packet of biscuits beside it. Not caramel, as the advert had suggested; just chocolate. Without turning to look at Duncan or greet him properly, she said simply, "Hi." That was the sum of it.

"Hi, Sam. Had a good day?" he enquired, struggling to keep the aggravation from his voice.

Still without turning, she replied, "Not bad." She couldn't have sounded any more nonchalant if she'd tried. Duncan noticed she was in her nightdress and robe, her hair all mussed up. That in itself wasn't a problem; it was evening, after all. But it was what she had been wearing when he'd left her that morning to go to work – except then she'd been under the bedclothes.

Sam hadn't bothered to get dressed all day.

All. Sodding. Day.

Stay calm, Duncan.

"I'm guessing you've eaten already?" he said evenly.

"Yes. Me and the girls had fish fingers at five o'clock."

The kids must be sick of fish fingers by now.

She still hadn't taken her eyes off the TV; he might as well have not been there.

"Right. Okay, well, I'll make myself something to eat, then." He waited a moment, in the unlikely event she might just oblige and be helpful, just for a change. After all, she'd been home all day, as she was every day, and he'd been out grafting for the last eleven hours. While he didn't expect her to serve him, he did expect some sort of a meal in motion; she didn't have much else to do. But it was too much to wish for; he knew that. This was the same thing that happened most nights now, so why was he surprised? Why he hadn't stayed on and eaten at the pub or grabbed a takeaway on the way home he'd no idea; at least he'd have had a hot meal and a smile for his trouble.

Duncan headed for the kitchen and pulled the fridge door open; the bright light glared into his eyes in the otherwise dark room. Milk, cheese, two eggs and half an open can of baked beans. Slipping his jacket and tie off and dropping them on to a kitchen chair, he busied himself beating eggs and grating cheese, then shoved two slices of bread into the toaster. The smell gave him comfort; at least his meal would be hot and tasty. He sprinkled salt and pepper into the egg mixture and heated the beans in the microwave. Within a couple of minutes, he had a decent cheese omelette, toast and beans. He set the food down on the table ready to eat. He was exhausted, and even though he was famished, he felt totally deflated as he sat down.

That was when Sam walked in, shuffling in her too large slippers. She bent and took a piece of his toast.

"Didn't think to make me any, then?" she said, her voice full of hatred as she bit into the slice.

Duncan sat still, breathing evenly. "You've already eaten, you said."

"So?"

"So, it's gone seven p.m. and I have just finished work and made myself something to eat. I'm knackered and hungry, so if you don't mind, I'll eat first, and we can argue later." He picked up his knife and fork again and started on his omelette, scooping a forkful into his mouth to stop himself from getting into another argument with her.

"Selfish pig," she hissed in his ear.

Duncan's stomach rolled. Here she goes – here *we* go again.

He heard her put more bread into the toaster. He stayed quiet, eating and hoping she wasn't going to kick off.

But he was wrong.

Chapter Four

Spittle flew from her mouth as she ripped into him. Duncan had barely eaten half of his meal but he downed his cutlery to add his side, hurling his fuel onto an ever-burning fire between them. Some couples thrived on their own heat and enjoyed make-up sex afterwards, but not Sam and Duncan. They'd gone way past that and there was no going back. There was not a day went by now that they didn't have crossed words, unless they weren't physically in the same place.

"What are you getting so upset for again, Sam? Eh? What I have done now to piss you off so much? Tell me, because I'd love to know!"

"You didn't ask me if I wanted some toast, you selfish pig," she spat at him. Specks of spittle landed on his face.

"Really? That's what this is all about? You've been home all day, not even got showered and dressed while I've been at work, and you want *me* to make *you* toast?" He stopped himself short of adding what he really wanted to add.

"Would it have been so hard to ask?" she yelled back.

Duncan shook his head in disbelief and sat back down to finish his meal, though eating in such a wound-up state was virtually impossible.

"Well? Aren't you going to answer me?" Her voice pierced the air.

"Keep your voice down, will you? We don't need the whole street hearing our senseless row again, nor the girls, for that matter."

"Well, you started it!" But Duncan was no longer listening. He was simply trying to swallow what was in his mouth, his stomach constricting in temper. What the hell was wrong with her? What had happened to the mother of his children, the woman he'd married, the woman he'd loved? But he couldn't hold back any longer. He leapt to his feet, chair scraping noisily like a Gatling gun firing round after round into the small space, momentarily shocking her into quietness. Duncan lunged at her face first, his turn to let spittle fly.

"You're a lazy cow, that's what you are!" he yelled. "I'm sick of it. Look at you, just look at yourself, will you?" He snatched a deep breath before carrying on with the tirade within him, one that had been wrestling to get out. "You're a slob! The house is a mess and I'm more than sick of it. I've had it up to here," he said, motioning to his temple with a stiff forefinger, "so either you sort yourself out, or I'm off. And don't think I won't take the girls away with me because I will. And right now, you're not a fit mother to have them around anyway. Get some help, get whatever it is that puts some sense and pride back inside you, and do it quickly, because if there is no change, if you've not got yourself sorted in the next two weeks, that's it. I'm done, finished."

The remaining air in his lungs drained out in a rush before he sucked a fresh breath in to refill them. Neither of them said a word. The sound of Coronation Street played out in the other room. Apt, really, their row playing out with the credits. If only it were that simple.

Duncan was the first to move. He headed straight upstairs to his two daughters, who had more than likely heard every nasty word, leaving Sam looking stunned and speechless where she stood. He knew the waterworks would be starting round about now, but that had stopped working on him when he'd stopped caring any more. He gathered himself as he approached the children's rooms. Jasmine's door was ajar, her light shining into the hallway, so he pushed at it gently and stuck his head around the corner. Both girls were sat together on her bed; both their faces were full of sadness and worry. Jasmine had a stuffed rabbit on her lap and was stroking its felted-up ears. She'd had the toy since she was a toddler and no amount of her parents' 'losing' it had worked, though one day she knew it would fall to pieces and Mr. Rabbit would be no more. Duncan did his best to fix a bright smile and lighten the mood. Seeing them visibly upset broke his heart. He kneeled down on the floor to their level, scooped them both into his arms, and kissed them both in turn on the soft part of their necks, their favourite thing.

"Mmm, you two both smell good," he quipped, trying to make them smile, but on this occasion, he was way off the mark. Sensing their distress and knowing his daughters were no fools, he sat back on his heels and tried to explain.

"I'm guessing you heard Mummy and me shouting again, and I'm sorry you had to hear it." Two sets of quiet, sad eyes looked at him. Jasmine nodded.

"Sometimes, grownups don't agree on things," Duncan went on, "and we get noisy rather than talking about it properly. Like you get noisy with each other on occasion. But a few minutes later, everything is okay again and not so noisy. That's all that Mummy and I were doing. We weren't agreeing, so we got noisy. And we're sorry. Okay?"

Victoria nodded this time as Duncan leaned back in to give them a squeeze.

"All right, then," he said briskly, determined to restore order and happiness. "Let's have a race to see who can get into their PJs and into this bed, and I'll tell you a true story about the dragons that used to live in the woods by the park."

That did the trick; their parents' shouting was almost forgotten as Victoria and Jasmine scrambled for sleepwear and then jockeyed for position in the one bed. Duncan helped by fetching another pillow from Victoria's room and smiled as they both sat up ready for the best story two young girls could ever hope for.

Duncan was going to have to make it a good one, he knew, and a long one. Maybe by the time he went back downstairs, Sam would have had time to think about his ultimatum and switch the tears off.

He could only hope.

Chapter Five

For a change, Duncan was pleased that Sam was still asleep this morning. After their unholy row last night, they'd avoided one another for the remainder of it, she slinking off back to the sofa sulking, he reading exaggerated dragon stories to the girls. The thought amused him as he shaved in the bathroom – the two sad faces turning into bright little ones as the story had got more exaggerated and unbelievable. Maybe he should have recorded it for future use, something to draw on again and extend on for another night. He'd been tempted to let the girls sleep in one bed together and take the other himself, but he'd never been one for sleeping separately like other rowing couples did. So, after he'd tucked the girls into their beds, he'd climbed dutifully into the marital bed, keeping to his own side. Sam had kept to hers, and nothing else had been said.

He rinsed his shaver blade under the tap and turned the shower on. As water tumbled over his head and rinsed the remaining shaving soap from his face, he rubbed his hands roughly up and down his face and pondered the day ahead. The case they were working on had taken its toll on many of the detectives; cases involving children always did. Had that been the catalyst for his outburst last night, he wondered, or was he right in his observations of how his wife had become? Calling her a slob had been mean, but deep down he knew it was true. She wasn't ill, after all; she had become lazy, and not showering and dressing all day was not what most people did, home all day or not.

The smell of citrus filled the shower cubicle as he lathered his body in soap and rinsed, feeling more awake than he had a few moments ago. While it was still early, he planned to have a quiet breakfast on his own then stop for a takeaway coffee and muffin on his way in. Working such long hours on the case, all he wanted was some peace and quiet, some time to himself, some time to think. In a perfect world, a weekend away – on his own – would do him the world of good, but there was little chance of that anytime soon. Maybe he'd get some respite on the tactical training course he had coming up – if it didn't get cancelled beforehand. With all resources being thrown at the missing children case, he wouldn't be surprised if they couldn't spare him to go. And of course, the child was more important than his tactical training and a cheap hotel overnight stay.

He stepped out of the shower and dried himself off quickly. Wearing only his underpants, he tiptoed around the bed to his wardrobe and fetched the clothes he needed. There was no sound from Sam as he took his clothes downstairs and finished dressing in the lounge. He poured cereal into a bowl, added milk and sat in the near darkness – again. It hadn't been that long ago he'd been sat in the same place trying to eat his omelette during a screaming match. At least it was peaceful now.

His phone vibrated on the tabletop. The screen said it was Rochelle.

"Morning, early bird. What's up?" He listened while he crunched.

"You sound like a cement mixer. What are you eating?"

"Muesli. It's good for you."

"I'll take your word for it. Prefer a bacon sandwich myself with plenty of ketchup, but I didn't ring to discuss breakfast options."

"Oh?" *Crunch, crunch, crunch.*

"Thought you might like to know another child went missing last night. Another girl, seven years old, so similar in age to the others. She was playing with her friend in their back garden and then suddenly she wasn't anymore. Mother reported her missing at about eight p.m. after she'd searched and called her friends."

"Eight p.m.? Why so late? It would have been dark long before then."

"Let's just say the mother was out of it. Poor kid probably wasn't even noticed as missing until she'd been gone a couple of hours. Fat lot of help the mother is going to be, I'm afraid. You nearly ready to leave? I'll fill you in properly." Duncan was draining his bowl as she spoke.

"Just leaving now. Want a coffee on my way in?"

"Always."

They hung up. It wasn't just on American cop shows they did that. Rochelle did it all the time and Duncan had found himself copying, though not intentionally. It really pissed some people off, including Sam. He shook his head to dislodge the thought of his sleeping wife and all that meant. He grabbed his jacket and left through the side door, closing and locking it behind him. If she was going to lie in bed a few more hours, at least the girls would be safe from potential intruders.

The outside was drizzly and cold, the slate-grey sky hanging heavily with no chance of the smallest chink of blue to ease the oppression of the coming day. Duncan turned the car's heater on full; tepid air blasted at the windscreen and he willed the engine to warm it quickly. When a small, round space had been cleared on the glass, he pulled out into the road and headed off for coffee and then the station.

Watching from the bedroom window, Sam stood gazing down as his car drove off into the wet, grey distance. Her face was blank. There were no tears; there was no emotion. Nothing registered on her face. Apart from dislike.

Chapter Six

THE COFFEE SHOP was her local and looked like any other chain of coffee shop. Red or green logo – you choose; it was about all that was different. The same food, the same coffees, the same featureless service and the same unsmiling people, customers and staff. There really must be a nicer place to meet.

Sam nursed her latte and filled Anika in on the previous night's events. Anika listened with some interest, making relevant noises at pertinent times to let Sam know she was still paying attention. Anika had heard her friend's grumblings about Duncan on many occasions but stuck it out anyway. What else was a friend supposed to do?

Sam whined on. "And when he said he was off if I didn't change, it put the fear of God into me. He's been no support whatsoever while I've been trying to get another job and it's really upsetting me. Why can't he come home one night, just once, and hand me a bunch of flowers or a box of chocolates or something nice? Maybe wrap his arm around me? Why not, eh?"

When Sam looked up from her drink, she had tears in her eyes. Anika put her arm around her shoulder in comfort. Sam let the tears spill over and trickle down her face. Her nose started to run and she blew it loudly into her serviette. Snuffling, she scrunched it up and tossed it onto the table for the staff to clear away. Anika bit back a grimace of distaste.

"It's not nice when you have a row, I know, but you've got to clear the air Sam," she said. "Tell him how you feel. He might not know that you feel unsupported and stressed. If he did, he might cut you some slack, help you around the place, do his bit, like. It's worth a go, isn't it?"

Sam nodded. "I'll have a chat when he gets home. But he's always late back in the evenings now, and knackered, so it might not be a good time." The whine was back in her voice again

"There's never a good time," Anika said, willing herself to be patient, "but you have to try. No one ever wants to talk about their issues, but you can't fix things if you both don't accept they need fixing."

"I've tried to get another job, I really have, but there's not a lot out there. Not one that doesn't pay peanuts, anyway, and I'm not going flipping burgers somewhere. I'm better than that. I had a decent job twelve months ago. It wasn't my fault they downsized. I liked it there."

Anika felt the sting of the burger comment but kept her face carefully neutral. Sometimes Sam could be so thoughtless, but Anika was stronger than people gave her credit for.

"I know, Sam, but getting another job, whatever it is, will at least get you out the house again, give you a purpose. More than the girls, I mean. It will be good for your spirit."

Sam rolled her eyes at the word *spirit*. Anika was a believer and Sam wasn't, but that didn't stop Anika mentioning it.

"There's loads of jobs you're qualified to do, Sam. I think you need to get a bit more active on it, though, be proactive even. Send your CV on spec, see what comes back." Sam nodded half-heartedly and Anika took a deep breath. Sam's lack of interest was beginning was to rub on her and she could feel her exasperation simmering.

Gathering her things, she fixed a smile on her face. "Look, I've got to get off now, as much as I'd like to sit drinking coffee all day. Give me a buzz tomorrow and let me know if you talk to him and get things sorted. But do try, won't you? And take another look at your CV, see if you can beef it up a bit. Make a list of where you'd like to work and I'll help you if you like."

Sam had her head down, finding a stray piece of cotton on her thigh of immense interest.

"Sam?" Anika prodded. "Give it a go, yes?"

"Yes. I'll give it a go. And thanks for listening."

Sam sat with her coffee dregs, watching as her best friend left the café, headed outside into the light rain that had yet to let up. The remaining cold froth in the bottom of her cup looked uninviting, and she'd had enough coffee for one day. She gathered her phone and her bag and trudged out of the café through the same exit, leaving the soiled serviette in the middle of the table.

The cashier glared at her back, knowing full well what was inside it. The gall of her, she thought, and headed off to the storage room for a pair of rubber gloves.

Once outside, Sam walked towards the newsagents to buy a newspaper. Maybe Anika had been right; maybe getting herself a job, even a basic one, would make her feel better, a bit more upbeat, until she found something more suitable. She didn't have to stay there forever, did she? Just until she found something better, at any rate. And she'd spruce up her CV, spend the afternoon on the job sites. The more she thought about it, the more energy she gathered for the task ahead. If she was going to save her marriage, she had to do something.

She selected the local paper and a packet of chocolate Hobnobs.

'By the end of the day', she told herself, 'I'll be ready to roll.'

After she paid the cashier, she unravelled the top of the packet of biscuits and stuffed half of one into her mouth in one go. The sweet, oaty chocolate biscuit soothed her nerves, and she chewed contentedly as she walked back towards her house.

The walk took her twelve minutes. The packet of Hobnobs was fully devoured within ten.

Chapter Seven

IT WAS NO USE. They needed more working capital; there was no getting away from it. As Luke thoughtfully scratched his designer stubble chin, he knew they'd exhausted most of their options. The banks weren't interested in yet another underfunded, bright but wacky startup idea; nor were the few investors they'd approached. It seemed unless you were a tech startup, you weren't trendy enough to warrant the interest. And even then, it was tough going, but at least you were taken a bit more seriously.

Their venture was food – mobile food vans with a trendy take on traditional foods: gourmet organic burgers and mouth-watering pulled pork in BBQ sauce. But while it was a sexy idea, to the moneylenders it was also a huge risk. Everyone knew the food business failure rates were catastrophic, but Luke and Clinton felt otherwise. They'd had the idea, made their plan and were hell bent on making it work – not becoming another depressing statistic.

Luke was aware Clinton was talking to him and pulled his mind back to the present.

"Sorry mate, I missed that last part."

"I think you missed most of it, didn't you? Were you listening at all?" Clinton said indignantly. Luke had the good judgment to apologize.

"Sorry, Clinton. My bad. I was just thinking about not being that failure statistic – drifted off for a moment. But I'm back in focus now." He slapped his thighs noisily. "Tell me again?"

Luke sighed loudly and pushed his specs back up his sweaty nose.

"I said, maybe we should revise our presentation. Maybe it's too dull, too many figures in it or something. Whatever it is, it's not doing us any favours, is it? Either that, or it's how we *ourselves* are presenting the info when we get in front of prospective lenders and investors. Maybe we should look at the whole thing again with fresh eyes, or, better yet, ask someone else to give us their educated opinion. It's got to be worth a try, has it not?"

Luke rubbed his stubble again in thought. "I *am* thinking as I sit here. I heard every word that time," he said, smiling easily.

"Yeah, yeah. I know. When you're ready, do tell me your thoughts, won't you?"

Luke tapped his chin with two fingers now. "Well, aside from doing something dodgy to raise the money, like becoming hit men or drug dealers, I guess we don't have much of a choice. I can't see what we're doing wrong, but there's obviously something not hitting the spot, because I feel sure the idea itself is sound. We're just not explaining it well enough or succinctly enough, maybe, or perhaps the offer itself needs adjusting."

"You mean like the percentage on offer for the investment? You want to give more than ten percent away?"

"I don't want to, no, but if ten percent is not attractive enough for the money we're after..." He paused. "Think *Shark Tank* or *Dragon's Den*. They barter on the percentage given away for the sum invested. The contestants rarely get what they go in for. I'm saying we have perhaps been a bit too optimistic."

"I'm happy to negotiate, but we have no one to negotiate with yet. We're not even close to either. It's like selling your house – you've got to have someone interested in it first to talk price with, and we have no one."

The small room fell quiet as both men sat deep in thought. After a few minutes, Clinton got restlessly to his feet. Even though it was a cold, wet day outside, the space was stuffy and he needed some air.

"I can't think straight in here. It's too warm. Want a coffee? I need a walk."

"No, thanks. Want me to come with you?"

"No, I need to think. I won't be long." He headed out.

Luke stood and walked across to the window. Raindrops ran down the glass, and he watched people scurrying through the street below, most wielding brightly coloured umbrellas, indicating that there were women under them. Men never carried coloured ones, usually sticking to black, blue or grey. Why was that, Luke wondered?

He watched as Clinton emerged from the front door and made his way towards the small green park area and the coffee shop just past it. Luke knew his partner well; he needed his air and space. He even had a favourite seat in the park where he'd escape each day with his packed lunch, weather permitting, and watch the world go by. It was where Clinton did his best thinking.

Turning from the window, all Luke could do was hope Clinton had a brain wave while he was out because, right now, they were out of ideas.

Chapter Eight

CLINTON SAT LOOKING at no one in particular. Traffic chugged by in the light drizzle, hot exhaust fumes from buses rising like steam from a New York city underground vent. Clinton didn't usually sit on a wet seat, but with little in the way of shelter in the little parkway, it was either that or sit indoors. The appeal of steamed-up café windows and equally steamed-up second-hand air was zilch – he needed to breathe. He'd purchased a newspaper from a vendor on his way there and used it as a seat cover, which at least kept his bum dry. There was no one else sat nearby; no one else was stupid enough to sit out on such a wet day without an umbrella. He'd probably regret it later, but that was later. He watched an older man shuffle past with a white woolly dog in a damp tartan jacket; the old man himself wore a matching deerstalker hat. Was that intentional, Clinton wondered? Matching outfits was something women with expensive handbags and huge diamond rings did, not elderly men in overcoats. Now there was a market, he thought: people spent silly money on their pets these days. As the man shuffled on, the small dog with its nose to the ground behind him, Clinton tried to focus on what he'd come out of the office to think about.

Clinton was the sensible one of the two partners, the calm one, the one with the thinking brain, the logic. He needed data to back up his decisions, not just gut instinct like Luke did, because without data, without evidence, anything they came up with was only opinion. And the wrong opinion could lead you into a whole lot of trouble. He liked to be the thinker, the balance to Luke's creative side, but at the same time, he felt the pressure of being the one to come up with the right answer all the time – and of being to blame if things went wrong. That was what being a partnership was all about, though: knowing your strengths and weaknesses. If creativity was needed, he had none; that was Luke. If confidence was needed in an important casual meeting, that was Luke too. But if it was a suit meeting, then Clinton was the man for the job. It made things interesting when their areas of expertise crossed over, and they were careful not to come across as a double act.

Clinton smiled outwardly at the double act reference; he was too young to remember the chocolate caramel biscuit advert, but his mother referred to it regularly. Something about chewy caramel on the inside, delicious with a cup of tea, and the whole thing was portrayed as a double act. But thoughts of biscuit adverts were not going to solve the problem, so he decided to leave his relatively dry seat and walk a while. He sauntered along, taking shelter where he could from overhanging store fronts, until he came across a shop that had cheap umbrellas on a stand. He selected a black telescopic one, thinking he'd use it again at some stage. It would fit nicely in his bag, but really, there was no chance he'd ever remember it. He gave the cashier a £5 note and carried on up the pavement, knowing he wouldn't get any wetter though his head was already soaked. Funny how light rain seemed to soak through so quickly.

Luke, however, was warm and dry back in the small office space they shared with a couple of other small companies. It was the trendy thing to do. There was a perfectly good coffee machine in the kitchenette and Luke preferred that rather than spending cash on a fancy latte while they were desperate for money. He waited for the brew to finish, poured a dash of milk on the top and added sugar. He took a thoughtful sip and savoured the taste before swallowing it down.

There was no view to speak of from the tiny kitchen window, nothing of note, nothing to stand and stare at while waiting for inspiration to strike. Just a few wet rooftops, glistening slate grey, some with disused chimney stacks left over from before gas and electric heat, when people took the time to actually light a fire. He'd always enjoyed the smell of a coal fire; it reminded him of his gran's house, the brass coal scuttle sitting ready to top up the dying ashes when the need arose. There was always a smoke that went billowing up the chimney when damp coal was first thrown on, and as a boy Luke had been mesmerized by the wonderful smell it produced. He missed his gran. He even missed the coal smoke, but he could see why people chose the speedy way to heat their homes.

He took his mug and wandered around the communal area looking at nothing in particular, trying to find inspiration in the mundaneness somehow. A voice caught his attention: it was Russell, a partner in a small accountant's that also worked in the space. He was also their landlord.

"Sorry, Russell, I was someplace else."

"So I see. Was it warmer and sunnier than here, perhaps?" Russell always had a cheery face, much like a butcher, though more likely from too much whiskey. Noses as bulbous as his rarely came from anything other than drink, and since Russell had the stomach to match, alcohol was the obvious culprit. And lots of it over a long time.

"I wish, but no. Deep in thought trying to sort a problem." He added, "The same problem as always." His voice and enthusiasm were lower than a slug's stomach.

"No luck then, I take it?" Russell knew the boys were desperate for funding and had offered his own advice for what it was worth.

"No luck, no. There will be an answer somewhere; there's one for every problem. Our job now is to find that answer. I wish it were simple." He sipped his coffee and rubbed the rim of the mug absent-mindedly with his thumb.

Russell patted Luke on the back as he passed back to his own office, leaving Luke to drift off back to where he had been before Russell had interrupted him. Absolutely nowhere.

Chapter Nine

By the time Clinton had returned, Luke was hard at work with his head buried in his computer. Even though they hadn't yet got a firm plan of how to sort their cash issue, he figured he might as well spend some time researching what others had done before him.

What had the world used before Google came along?

There were all kinds of articles on generating funding, as well as forums and blog posts, and he began scrolling in the vain hope that something would stick out for him, something he'd missed during their first research. On a pad next to him, he wrote down a few key points to talk to talk to Clinton about. He also had a list of people to contact through his extended business network, see if he could buy them coffee and pick some brains or garner an introduction or two. If they could just get in front of a few more investors, that would be a start. Clinton himself was looking at the presentation content, though it would be down to Luke to recreate the data into something more visual. Sadly, he had few ideas at the moment.

There was one other item on the pad, a word he'd written cryptically a few days earlier. *Hit.* He knew what it meant, but nobody else did. It was the last item on his list of things to research. He opened a new browser tab. He'd do the research, he told himself, then make a decision on whether it was something he could actually do.

"It's a fall-back option, nothing more," he muttered out loud.

"First sign of madness," said a sing-song voice. It was Russell, who happened to be passing on his way out.

"What is?"

"Talking to yourself, though I hear answering yourself is far worse." Russell smiled good-naturedly and gave a quick wink as the door swung shut behind him. How did he always manage to be so upbeat? Luke wondered. Maybe he needed to stew in as much whiskey as Russell did each evening.

And some afternoons.

He dropped his head back into the article he'd been reading before being distracted by the word *hit* on his pad.

Chapter Ten

TWO HOURS later and Luke was still hard at it when Clinton approached his desk, rubbing his eyes, specs in his hand. He stretched his jaw and brows out and replaced his specs.

"Shit, those figures are heavy going but I think I'm about there. Want to take a look?"

"I'll pass on the detail, thanks. Give me the main points." Luke pushed his chair back, snagging a caster wheel on a rug just behind his desk. Annoyed, he pushed back a little harder than necessary and ended up rolling at speed across the room. It was what he needed to reawaken himself and focus on something else.

"Steady on, Luke, you'll do yourself a mischief," Clinton said, laughing, as Luke rolled back towards his desk and stood. He stretched like a puppy preparing for a walk after a nap, quick and lithe.

"So, what have you got, then?"

Clinton pulled out the relevant pages from his folder and recited the figures.

Luke looked at him blankly. "So, what does that mean exactly?"

Clinton stared. "You don't know what that means?"

"No, not exactly. That's why I'm asking." Luke looked thoughtful for a minute and it was obvious he was pondering something.

"Luke?" Clinton prodded him.

"Hang on." Luke was looking at the floor, deep in thought. Thirty seconds or so passed before he spoke. "I wonder if that's it?"

"What? What are you talking about?"

"We need to change the way we present this data. We need to make it more relatable, so it means something more, something they can visualize easily rather than a bunch of numbers."

"I'm listening. Go on."

"Do you remember when the iPod first came out and Steve Jobs showed it to the world?"

"Yeah, I guess."

"Well, he said having an iPod was like having one thousand songs in your pocket. He didn't say 'It's got a five-gig hard drive.' He related it to something people understood straight away – one thousand songs in your pocket. People could instantly see that." Luke was suddenly excited. "Do you get what I'm saying?"

"I do, yes, I do. Do you think that's what we need to do then, before we present this to anyone else?"

"I'm certain of it. It worked for Steve Jobs. Why wouldn't it work for us? We just follow the same concept, keep it clear and easy."

"Well, we've got to present this on Friday. Do you think there's enough time? It makes sense to change it beforehand."

"Yes, it does. What we've been doing so far hasn't worked, so let's not waste another meeting doing it that way. Let's make this happen for Friday."

They stood quietly for a moment longer contemplating their new direction. Could they pull it off?

"This is what I suggest we do." Clinton took charge. "I'll pull out the main points, then together we'll see how they can be turned into something more recognizable. Then we'll work on finding the right way to present the data."

"I'll see if I can find that presentation he did and take it a step further."

"Right. You start on the look and feel, and I'll get the data and main points."

Clinton looked at Luke and said, "Do you think we have something now?" His tone was almost timid.

"I hope so," Luke added.

In the back of his mind, the cryptic word *hit* blinked at him.

Hit.

Hit.

Chapter Eleven

LUKE AND CLINTON nursed bottles of lager, but neither was drinking. An unopened packet of crisps sat between them along with the silence. The only conversation came from other drinkers in the pub on a Friday lunchtime. A slot machine in the corner clanked out coins to a lucky winner, a burly man by the bar laughed heartily at his mate's joke, and the sound of music playing in the background was a quarter turn too loud.

The boys couldn't have cared less anyway. Their revised presentation had also fallen flat. The slug sure had a low belly.

"On the positive side, the new *style* of presentation went down well, don't you think?" Luke was ever the optimistic one.

"Doesn't matter too much now, does it? They still said no." It was a statement rather than a question, and it sounded petulant. The fact of the matter was it had been an important meeting, because they'd exhausted their list of contacts and prospective investors. This last group had been their remaining hope. Now that hope was gone, and in its place was 'What next?' They'd both invested all they had personally, which wasn't much, and cut corners at every opportunity. Their credit cards were maxed out, overdrafts at their limit. The added coincidence of its being Friday seemed to accentuate the fact that they had driven to the end of the road. There was no more money to be begged or borrowed. It was a good job they both still lived at home and had roofs over their heads.

The barman turned the volume up yet more on the stereo system as Sam Smith crooned *Stay with Me,* adding to Luke and Clinton's depressed mood. To the lovers in the opposite corner of the pub sharing fries and sandwiches for lunch, the song was perfect; to the two deflated men, it was far from it. Clinton took a swig from his bottle. The golden liquid held no real interest for him; it might as well have been lemonade.

"So, what's next then, do you think? Time to give up?" Clinton looked at Luke. He was the creative one – surely he'd think of something?

"Hell, no. We've come too far and invested too much to let it drift off with the next tide. I'm not doing that."

"Then should one of us get a job, to bring some cash in? We've got rent due in a couple and Russell has already been great with us. I don't want to overstep things."

"Maybe we should move out from there, operate from a café like other entrepreneurs. All we'd need is an internet connection."

"True enough, but what about the rent coming due? How are we going to fund even that?" Clinton reached for the bag of crisps and opened it. There was no point wasting food at a time like this. He pulled out a small handful of cheese and onion fried potato and handed the rest of the bag to Luke.

"Getting a job – one that pays enough, that is – won't happen overnight, though. It will take months. Unless you want to scrub floors, which is about all either of us would get in the next forty-eight hours, realistically. Even then, they'd say we were overqualified and probably not take us on," said Luke morosely.

"Well, at this rate, we might have to try. At least if we worked in a chippy we'd get fed into the bargain," said Clinton gloomily.

Sam Smith finished his song and Adele piped up.

"Oh, for heaven's sake! What's with the depressing music? It's like the last dance on a Saturday night in the sad part of town." Luke slammed his hand on the table and the barman glanced over, although he left the music as it was. Luke shook his head solemnly. Maybe the guy was feeling depressed himself – or if he wasn't before, he sure would be now. He turned to Clinton and said, "Come on, let's get out of here before I set fire to the damn rain myself."

That at least raised a smile on Clinton's face and he quickly drained the rest of his lager in one. Grabbing his jacket, he caught up with Luke, who was already nearly at the front entrance, and they went back out into the cold street. The rain had stopped, at least.

"Where to, Boss?" It was Luke's way of being a little submissive when he needed to be. If Clinton was the serious data guy, that made him the boss man, at least for today.

"Better tell Russell we can't pay the rent, then I'm off home. Maybe a change of scenery on a cold Friday afternoon will do some good. I'm not doing much else here. I suggest you do the same."

"I'm not letting this mean it's all over. Rover," Luke said firmly. "It's another setback, but that's all. I'm hopeful we can carry on, aren't you?"

Clinton stopped walking and turned to meet Luke's eye. "I'm really not sure, to tell you the absolute truth. I don't see how, beyond prostitution or drug dealing."

"What happened to hit man, and where did prostitution come in?"

"Whatever, smartarse. You know what I'm saying. They're all illegal or dangerous." Clinton started to walk off again and Luke sped up to meet his pace.

"I hear you. Look, you're right. Let's tell Russell, then head home. The break will do us good."

So that's what they did. Russell knew it was coming but didn't seem to care too much.

"Glad to have been a desk or two while you needed it," he'd said. "See you around."

Luke and Clinton had gathered up their scant belongings and left the building, each with their laptop in one hand, plastic carrier bag filled with odds and sods in the other. No one claimed the begonia; it stayed in place on the windowsill, where it had sat for the last few months.

Chapter Twelve

As soon as Sam got back to the house, her good intentions were left on the pavement. She turned the key in the door and went inside, heading to the back and the kitchen. She tossed the biscuit wrapper in the bin and flicked the kettle on as she passed it. Her coat hit a chair by the table, and then fell to the floor, where it stayed. Full of chocolate biscuits, Sam slumped down to wait for the water to boil. Her newspaper lay unopened; her fingers drummed the tabletop in thought. The clock on the cooker said a little after 12 o'clock, lunchtime, and even though she wasn't hungry, she craved something, anything to take away the depression of the situation, of her morning. Even for Sam, it was too early for a glass of wine, so she pulled her bag towards her, reaching for the inside pocket. There was little point, really; Sam knew it was empty. She'd taken the last ones yesterday.

Being married to a detective had its drawbacks. It was hard to keep your secrets safe even in the inner sanctum of your handbag, and she had the girls' safety to consider too, the responsibility of making sure that they never found her pills. But right now, the pills were what she craved, what she longed for – the promise of what they could take away for a short time, until it was necessary to return to reality and all that came with it.

The kettle flicked itself off. She stayed put, not really that interested in another hot drink at all; her thoughts were on something much more desirable. Standing, she picked her coat up, grabbed her keys and headed back out, slamming the front door behind her. Her Ford Focus was parked in the drive of their red brick house, gleaming blue in the ever-present rain. It started the first time, but then it always did. The car was only a few months old, bought brand new as a gift from Duncan for her last birthday. She'd been so pleased, so happy back then. She gunned the engine and her tyres squealed as they tried to catch a grip on the wet concrete. Praying she wouldn't see anyone she knew, she headed down Clumber Road towards the A57 and across to Beswick.

And what she needed.

While she steered with her right hand, her left rummaged in her bag, fingers seeking and finding the soft pink leather wallet that had also been a gift from Duncan, though some years back. Flicking it open deftly as she drove, she fingered the stiff new bank notes, hoping they all added up to £50 so she could get the hit she so desired. Anything smaller wouldn't do, not today. The familiar anxiety crept into her body, making its way across her chest like a heavy-limbed giant spider, grabbing at her shirt, twisting the cloth together and tightening its grip until breathing was hard work, almost impossible. And so was driving. Her windscreen was fogging up with her panting as she fought to control herself and not have a full-on panic attack. Not at the wheel, at least. Not again. She practiced taking deep breaths as she drove, telling herself slowly, "In. Out. In. Out," her chest rising and falling as air drained away and refilled. Up ahead, she saw the road sign for the turning she needed and she indicated right, though in reality the road sign was superfluous to her requirements: Sam knew exactly where to head and could have probably done so blindfolded. Right again, then left and the house she sought was visible up ahead.

It wasn't the nicest part of town, but drug dealers rarely operated from big houses on the affluent side of Manchester. Of course, someone would be servicing the celebs – they wouldn't be slumming it in Beswick from an old semidetached house with grubby net curtains and weeds two feet high out front.

The house looked quiet. She hoped someone was in to process her transaction and take the pain away, take her to somewhere more relaxing, somewhere that cushioned her, like covering her in bubble wrap, helping her through the day unharmed. Then the side door opened and a tall, willowy, well-dressed blonde woman came out. She wore a pale pink skirt suit with fine stilettoes on her feet and looked rather out of place. The woman walked towards the street and Sam watched her as she crossed the road and got into a racy little high-end red Mini, not a car you'd associate with these parts either. Maybe she was a customer too, one who hadn't found a dealer closer to home that serviced the more affluent. Or perhaps she liked the drive out here.

There was no point sitting in the car, so Sam made her own way to the side door and knocked, then waited a beat or two before knocking again. Through the opaque glass she saw movement, and the silhouette of a woman approaching. The door opened slowly. The woman, a bit older than Sam, said nothing, but beckoned Sam inside into the pokey kitchen area and motioned her to take a seat. She smiled a little and flicked the kettle on to boil, though it was all for show, in case she needed a cover story. Sam couldn't help noticing the woman's roots needed bleaching; there was a good four inches of dark regrowth streaked with grey in a wide stripe down the centre of her head. She was otherwise tidy in her dress, though, wearing fitted black pants and a pretty blue blouse with a tiny flower print. Her gold bangles clinked together as she busied herself. Funny the things you noticed even when you were nervous, Sam thought.

"What sort of tea would you like?" the woman enquired as she brought a shallow wooden tea box out from the pantry. Sam stared at the box like she'd never seen it before. It was made out of a fine balsa wood, stained and decorated with an intricate pattern. It looked like something you might have found in a Moroccan bazaar, and Sam wondered, as she did each time, where the woman had bought it. Maybe she had been to Morocco. Sam worked on finding her voice.

"I'll know when I see it. I can never remember what it's called."

The woman opened the lid, revealing several small compartments, and lifted out the top layer that contained individually wrapped tea bags. Underneath, of course, was anything but tea. Sam scanned the compartments for what she wanted. Each little bag contained an assortment of tablets, and Sam instantly spotted the ones she preferred.

"I like it quite strong, please," she said as calmly as she could, keeping to the code they used.

The older woman picked up bag of 80 mg tablets and showed it to Sam.

"That should be strong enough, do you think?"

Sam reached greedily for the baggy between the woman's fingers, but the woman deftly withdrew her hand. *Of course*, thought Sam, mentally smacking herself. She wanted to see the cash first. Sam pulled out £50 in notes. The woman shook her head. Eighty milligrams was going to be more money. Sam pulled out the last note she had, another £20, and the woman handed over the pill.

"Perfect," Sam said, and slipped the pill straight into her mouth. The woman passed her a glass of water, which she downed nervously.

"Actually, I'd better get going, but thanks for the offer of tea," Sam said, and stood ready to leave. Inside she was climbing the walls, desperate to get out of the small kitchen and back into the familiar confines of her car, away from the woman, and away from the house.

She wanted to be home when the effects fully kicked in.

Chapter Thirteen

DUNCAN PULLED INTO HIS DRIVEWAY. The house was in darkness again, save for the familiar chink of light showing through the curtains. A flicker of blue light accompanied it sporadically; the TV was on. He sat in his car; the interior was toasty warm after the drive home with the car heater on full. The kids would be in bed and Sam would be stuck in front of the television, he knew. He hoped she was at least dressed today. As for something warming and tasty to eat after another long day, he doubted it. Perhaps he should have stopped off at the chippy and eaten there, but he hadn't fancied the grease overload.

He opened the car door and the cold, damp air clung to his face as he took the few steps towards the side door and inside. He'd told himself on the drive over that he wasn't going to be angry or disappointed, that he was to be positive and upbeat, pleased to see her, pleased she was okay, pleased the children were fast asleep. After a day working a missing children case, there were more important things to be thinking about than arguing with your wife. Everyone inside this house was safe and sound, and he thanked God for that.

"Hi Sam, it's me. I'm back," he shouted through from the kitchen, but there was no reply. He sighed and collected himself as he opened the door into the lounge. He tried again.

"Hi Sam, I'm home."

Sam turned towards him and smiled. "Hi, Duncan. I didn't hear you drive up. Good day at work?" She muted the sound on the TV, a good start.

"Ah, you know, it's always tough when children are involved," he said with a weak smile. "What's for dinner? Is there anything made?" He was hoping, just not expecting.

"I'll put some soup and toast on for you. You sit down – you look done in."

Well, that was the truth. As for soup? At least it was hot and quick and reasonably nutritious.

"Thanks, love. Four slices, please. I'm ravenous." He began undoing his shoes and flicked them both off, wiggling his sock-covered toes, then flopped down on the soft sofa and closed his eyes for a moment. Sam headed into the kitchen and Duncan could hear the soup pan hitting the stove, the toaster springs creaking as bread was pushed down into it, the clink of a bowl being retrieved from the cupboard.

And humming from Sam.

Still with his eyes closed, he tried to figure out two things: the last time he'd heard her hum, and what the song she was humming could be. He didn't have a clue to either of them. He opened his eyes and stared at the TV. The set was still silent; the screen showed judges scoring a batch of scones made by a group of hopefuls. He pressed the mute button again and voices filled the room. He let the mundaneness of it wash over his body while he waited.

Sam put her head around the door. "Who won the challenge?"

"Sorry, Sam, I wasn't paying much attention. I didn't hear."

Sam flitted back into the kitchen to pour the soup and Duncan sensed that she was on edge again. He cringed; the slightest thing could end in a row, he knew, and he desperately wanted to avoid one. Not only that, he hadn't the energy left to defend himself. He closed his eyes again and only opened them when the soup and toast arrived on a tray. Sam placed it roughly on the coffee table in front of him; some of the liquid slopped over the edge of the bowl. He said nothing, and neither did Sam. Instead, he stood and went to get some paper towel from the kitchen to mop it up. He was careful not to meet her eyes.

"I've missed the end now. I don't know who won," she whined accusingly.

Duncan concentrated on his toast, crunching loudly. Crumbs dropped into his tomato soup, his favourite. He heard her huffs and puffs of exasperation at missing the end of her program, but he carried on eating, willing her tension to drop back to a near normal level.

The last couple of days at work had been tough, and the nights at home were not much better. Their house wasn't what you'd call a relaxing environment to come home to. And he hadn't seen his two girls in three days. They were always still in bed when he left and fast asleep when he returned. He'd look in and kiss them anyway when he'd finished his supper, but it wasn't ideal. If he got some down time at the weekend he'd make it up to them, but that depended on the case. Leave had been suspended and everyone was expected to join in the search; the department was throwing all available resources at this case in the hope that the two missing children would be brought home alive and well, and quickly. They all knew the first twenty-four hours were crucial, and that deadline had passed, meaning the chances of the children's safe return had slimmed down considerably. Nobody voiced the reality, of course, but everyone doggedly kept their hopes up.

He was aware the volume on the TV was back up and Sam was talking.

"You didn't hear a word of that, did you?"

Here we go.

"Sorry, Sam, I was miles away. What did you say?"

"Oh, never mind! You're no different when you are here to when you're not here. I'm talking to myself either way." She got up and stomped towards the stairs in an obvious huff, but Duncan called her back before she had chance to disappear.

"I said sorry, Sam. What did you want to ask me?" He stood up to make his point, hands on his hips. He really didn't want to go there again – not another row, not tonight.

"Oh, just fuck off, would you?" she yelled, and thumped up the stairs. There was little point Duncan saying anything or going after her; it would certainly turn nasty while she was in such a foul mood. He flopped back down, deflated, muted the TV again and tried to finish his soup and toast, but the food stuck in his throat. It was like eating balls of cotton wool dipped in ketchup. He dropped his spoon onto the tray, stood, and took his things to the sink where he rinsed his dishes. He opened the dishwasher door. It was still full of dirty dishes from earlier in the day.

"Dear Lord," he said to himself. Sighing, he put a tablet in the soap dispenser and switched the machine on, leaving his tray on the kitchen bench until the morning. Exhausted, he quietly slipped upstairs, avoiding the bedroom he shared with Sam. Instead, he tiptoed to the girls' room and kissed his two sleeping beauties on their foreheads, being careful not to wake them. Leaving their door open just a crack, he tiptoed to the bathroom and brushed his teeth, then slipped into the PJs that hung on the back of the bathroom door, grabbed a couple of blankets from the hall cupboard, and settled himself back down on the sofa for the night. Within ten minutes of lying down, he was fast asleep, the TV still flickering.

Chapter Fourteen

Sam lay alone in the double bed seething inwardly. She'd heard him climb the stairs and go into see the girls, but then he'd surprised her and gone back down to the TV room. When she'd crept to the bathroom shortly after, Sam had noticed his PJs, which normally hung on the back of the bathroom door were gone. He must have collected them with the intention of staying well away from her for the rest of the night, and that was a first for them both. The thought depressed her. But really, what did she expect after telling him to do one and then storming upstairs, closing their bedroom door behind her? It was hardly an invitation for some love and affection, now, was it?

The digital clock read 12.15 a.m., and sleep eluded her as usual. She knew it was going to be a long night. Perhaps she could get through to the kitchen unnoticed and make herself some tea, though she didn't want to face him if he awoke. She felt a twinge of guilt for her overreaction this time, but she knew her short temper was a symptom of how their relationship had deteriorated over the last six months or so. There was little love between them now.

Love. Where had it gone?

Sam flipped the bedside lamp on and the room glowed a pale peach colour, not bright enough to read by but just bright enough to fall asleep by. On the cabinet next to her pillow sat a wedding picture of the two of them. They would be ten years married next anniversary round, and Sam stared at the picture, dissecting herself ruthlessly. How she'd changed over the decade from that day. Her sun-kissed hair had been styled in an attractive and romantic up-do with tiny flowers woven through. Her figure had been slender in the full-length creamy silk slip dress, and she had looked radiant. Duncan for his part had looked happy and handsome. His cravat matched her dress and those of the two tiny bridesmaids. The sun had shone gloriously as the photographer had snapped away in the church gardens; the roses had been in full bloom. Where had those two happy people vanished?

Sam looked at the young bridesmaids again. They had been the same ages then as her two girls were now, and she stroked their bright little faces through the glass. Thoughts of that day, their vanished happiness and the two little girls fast asleep in the other room made her eyes brim with tears. But she caught herself, wiped them away with the hem of the bedsheet and climbed out of bed, headed for Jasmine's room next door. The handle creaked a little as it turned and she slipped inside, closing the door quietly behind her. She heard the light sounds of a little body breathing peacefully, unaware there was someone stood by the bed, watching and listening. She knelt down beside the bed and whispered what she wanted to say, knowing there was no way anyone could or would hear her.

"You know how much I love you, both of you, don't you? I hope you do, my love, because I'll do whatever it takes to keep my two precious girls safe from harm and always happy. Whatever it takes, understand? You'll always have me, your mother, looking over you, no matter what. I just want you to know that. No matter what."

Standing, she kissed Jasmine lightly on the cheek and headed to Victoria's room, to check on her and kiss her goodnight. Once she was satisfied both were settled and fast asleep, she went out to her own room and the empty bed and climbed back in. The sheets were now cool and the temperature in the room seemed to have dropped a few degrees, so she burrowed down under the covers, pulling them up over her head, and finally let the tears fall freely.

Eventually, Sam fell into a deep, undisturbed sleep. She slept so soundly, in fact, that she slept through the alarm the following morning. When she finally did come to, it was gone nine o'clock. Her first thought was the girls.

"Oh, hell!" she groaned, scrambling out of bed. "The girls!" She grabbed her robe as she flew from her room. Unsurprisingly, the girls' door was open and the bed was empty. Victoria's room was empty as well. Calling their names, her heart pounding, she catapulted herself down the stairs at speed and flung the lounge door open.

"Jasmine! Victoria! Where are you?"

That room was empty, too, but she noticed two folded blankets on the arm of the sofa. Duncan must have stayed there all night and tidied them away earlier this morning. She dashed through to the kitchen, expecting to see two small faces eating Cocoa Pops at the table, but it was empty.

"Jasmine! Victoria! Where are you?" she called again. But it was obvious the house was empty.

The girls were gone.

Perhaps Duncan had got them ready and taken them to school? But why hadn't he woken her? She looked around the work surface for a note, but there was nothing. If Duncan had taken them to school, he wouldn't have been so heartless to not leave a note, would he? There was only one way to find out. She'd have to call him.

Then a thought hit her. What if he had taken them? He would know she had only just got up and would be furious with her for oversleeping. But what if he hadn't taken them? That would be far worse. There was no choice: she dialled his number and waited for it to connect.

"Hi," he said evenly.

Sam blurted out her question. "Did you take the girls to school?"

"What? No, I left around seven a.m. Why, was I supposed to today? Have I forgotten something?"

"No, you weren't. It's just, well I overslept and when I woke up, they were both gone. I figured you had taken them, but there was no note." Her voice rose in panic as the tears came.

"Oh my God! Where are they?"

Sam disconnected the call and raced back upstairs, calling her children's names, but the house was still eerily quiet. She knew they were gone.

And now Duncan was heading back home.

"My babies, where are you?" she wailed as she threw on jeans and a sweater. *Oh God...* Tears blurred her vision. She'd finally done it. She'd screwed up and lost them forever. How the hell had she managed to oversleep and not hear them? How long had they been gone? Stuffing her feet into her old trainers by the front door, she grabbed her jacket from the banister rail and fled the house.

It was freezing cold outside, but at least it wasn't raining. Calling for Jasmine and Victoria, her eyes flitting frantically from side to side, she zipped up her jacket as she trotted along, trying to keep from screaming. No, that wouldn't do. They had to be close by. Maybe they were playing in a neighbour's yard. Had they got coats on? she wondered. Why hadn't she checked that before legging it out in a rush? Picking up the pace, she rushed down the street, still calling, stopping everyone she passed to ask if they'd seen two little girls out on their own.

Nobody had.

After circling the immediate streets and looking over garden hedges calling their names, she slowed to a walk again and then stood still, a heavy feeling of dread settling in her gut.

What the hell had happened to them?

What the hell had she done? She was to blame, and now she had no choice but to call Duncan again and update him. With shaking hands, she punched his number into her mobile again.

"I'm nearly home now," he said. "Meet me back there and we'll form a plan."

He didn't sound mad at her, only concerned. But she knew his anger at her stupidity, her carelessness, would come. The blame game would start all over again, and she'd get to be the loser this time for sure.

But another question entered her head. How had they actually got outside if they'd gone under their own steam? Duncan always locked the door behind him when he left so early – always. Though if the door had been left unlocked, it would have been all too easy for an intruder to enter.

And help themselves.

She couldn't bear to think about that.

So, had the door been left unlocked while she slept? That would be the first question she'd asked Duncan when he got home.

She was rounding the corner at the end of the street when she saw his car pull up outside their house. She broke into a run and called out to him. "Duncan!"

He stood and watched as she slowed to a stop, breathless after the short distance.

"I've looked around here locally – nothing. I can't think where they'd have gone." She bent and put her hands on her knees, gasping.

Duncan, always the calm one, asked, "Have you checked their school? Maybe they just went on their own."

She shook her head. "I just panicked and went out to look, and then I called you. Oh, Duncan! Where can they have got to?"

But Duncan was busy dialling the school. He spoke to the secretary and then listened gravely, nodding. He asked her to call if she did see them and then ended the call. He shook his head at Sam.

"I'm taking that as a no, then?" she said, her mouth dry.

"That's right." His voice tightened. "Where the hell were you?"

"I overslept. I didn't hear a thing."

Slowly, his next words scraped through his teeth. "You have one job and one job only, and that is to take care of our girls and the house. And you can't even do that properly." He paused and took a breath, visibly controlling himself. "You are aware there is someone taking children out there at the moment, I assume? Two young girls are already unaccounted for. I hope to God you haven't doubled that."

"Did you lock the door after you when you left this morning?" she asked.

"What? Of course I did." Then he got her meaning. "Oh, so you think I'm to blame, then, do you, for leaving the door unlocked?" His voice rose several octaves, incredulous. "Well, I locked it. I *always* lock it. It's what I do to keep my family safe. But I'm not the one they're left in charge with. That falls on you − but you were too busy *sleeping,* and now look!"

Sam hadn't got the words to fight back. She knew she'd screwed up. The girls were her responsibility while she was at home all day.

Duncan could see the fight had left her and calmed a little as tears filled her eyes again. The detective in him took over from the father.

"Look, this is getting us nowhere. Tell me where you've looked so far, and I'll get a couple of the lads to give us a hand. If we haven't found them in the next two hours, we'll make an official missing persons report. I need you to make a list of all of their friends and favourite places and we'll start there. Okay?"

Sam nodded her agreement, glad he was taking over, giving them a plan to work to. She went back inside to get a pen and paper and make the list. When it was complete, she sat and began calling the parents of their daughters' friends.

Chapter Fifteen

HIS HEART IN HIS MOUTH, Duncan drove the local streets looking for his two little sweethearts, fighting down a rising sense of panic. How far could two little girls go on their own? Heavens, they were only seven and eight and, to his knowledge, not particularly street-smart. The streets worried him, particularly the busy main A57 road that led into the city. If they'd gone anywhere near there... It didn't bear thinking about. He'd called Rochelle and she'd organized a couple of uniformed officers to give them a hand. Right now, four units were actively looking. In another hour, he'd pull out every stop that he could to bring them home safely. Sometimes being in the police had its perks, though he hoped he never needed to use his colleagues again.

Disappointment in Sam stabbed his heart again. Try as he might, he couldn't get her out of his mind. The last few months had been hard to watch, hard to understand, and hard to deal with. And now this. It couldn't get any worse than this. What his future with Sam was he was unsure, but he knew one thing. If he left, if they split up, he would take the girls with him, because no judge in the world would let her have custody of them after this. He'd see to it. These cases were usually stacked against the male parents, he knew, but not this time. His phone rang. Rochelle.

"I'm guessing nothing at your end?" she asked him.

"Sadly, no. I can't see how they could have gone so far away. Even if they left right after me at seven a.m., which they wouldn't have, they're on foot." He didn't want to think about them getting a lift with a stranger. "How far can two sets of tiny feet go?"

"We'll find them, Duncan," she told him determinedly. "It's really early on. They're probably playing somewhere, unaware of the commotion going on to find them. And when they get hungry, they'll be back up your front path before you know it."

Duncan knew she was trying to be optimistic; he'd told many parents the same story. But he knew the statistics; that was the downside to being a detective.

"I'll call you later," he said, and clicked off, returning his focus to the street he was cruising down. His stomach felt like someone had filled it with cement. His thoughts circled back to Sam and her lazy ways, lying in bed while his girls wandered out of the house. Were they warm enough? Had she checked if their coats were gone? He didn't remember asking her, and the point was important. He called her using the hands-free and she picked up almost instantly.

"Found them?" she blurted.

"No. No, not yet." *Keep positive.* "Have you checked if they took their coats with them?"

"What? Oh, no – hang on. I'll run and look." The car was silent while he waited for her to check the hall cupboard. Then she was back.

"Both coats are gone. That's a good sign, isn't it?"

"I'm not sure if there is anything good here, but yes, it could mean they went under their own steam. I'll keep looking."

He rang off, not bothering with goodbye, and let out a heavy sigh of relief that their coats were in fact gone. What predator would kit them out before snatching them? No, on the surface, it looked like they had let themselves out and gone on an adventure.

So where the hell were they?

Chapter Sixteen

Back at the house, Sam had called everyone she could think of, but nobody had seen her two girls. She then called Anika and told her the full story, big wet tears falling down both cheeks as she talked.

"What can I do to help?" her friend asked her.

Anika wasn't one for sitting around in a crisis, and Sam welcomed her strength. While Duncan had strength, their relationship was at breaking point and she was unable to draw any reassurance from him.

"Duncan is out searching the streets, as are some officers. Can you come over? I could do with a hug."

Anika agreed, though she thought it odd that her friend wanted her for a hug. Surely, she could be more productive elsewhere? Sighing, she grabbed her purse and said she'd be right over.

"Thanks. I appreciate it."

Sam rang off and reached for her own bag. She pulled out the painkillers she'd bought from a pharmacy on the edge of town yesterday. She stared at the half-empty blister pack; there were only six left. They'd have to do. She pushed all six Paramol into the palm of her hand and threw them all to the back of her mouth, then washed them down with the remainder of the almost-cold tea that was in her mug.

That should take the edge off for a while. She tossed the empty packet into the pedal bin in the kitchen cupboard and closed the door.

On any other day, she would have shredded the packaging into tiny pieces to make it invisible amongst the other bin contents. Half the problem of taking as many painkillers as she did was destroying the evidence. She had almost bought a small garden incinerator from the hardware store for the job, but she knew Duncan would have asked her what it was for, since she did no work in or out of the house.

She heard the front door open as Anika let herself in and called out to Sam.

"I'm in the lounge. Come on through."

Anika came straight over to her, wrapping her arms around her and pulling her close. Sam's skin on her face was hot and damp with tears, her eyes puffy and swollen. Finally, she stepped back, took Sam's clammy hands in her own and sat them both on the sofa.

"I feel for you, Sam, I really do. But let's stay positive. You said they have their coats, so I'm betting they are off playing someplace and will be home later. Didn't you ever go off when you were little and scare your parents half to death, like they're doing right now with you both?"

Sam nodded ever so slightly as she remembered. Anika smiled.

"And what made you go back home? Do you remember?"

Sam nodded again. "I got hungry. I'd missed dinner and it was going dark."

"There you are, then. They'll be famished soon enough and either make their way home or, if they've got lost, go and tell someone. You'll see I'm right." Anika beamed at Sam in the hope it would cheer her, help her think back to her own experience and how she'd got home that night. It made it all the more believable and was better than the alternative story.

"I'll make some more tea," Anika said, pointing to Sam's empty mug.

Sam tried to stand but her head had other ideas. Her vision swam and she sat straight back down. She closed her eyes for a moment while Anika busied herself in the kitchen. By the time the fresh tea was ready and the two mugs were on the coffee table, Sam was fast asleep.

Chapter Seventeen

THE ELDERLY WOMAN had been watching from her bedroom window. Two young girls were playing alone in the park and had been enjoying themselves for more than an hour. She'd thought it strange that they weren't in school, but in this neighbourhood it wasn't that unusual to see truant ones hanging about – though she had to concede they were generally older than the two she'd been watching. Still, they were having fun out in the open; no harm in that.

Mrs. Skeen had never had children of her own, never been lucky in that way, but she had always enjoyed the company of young ones where she could, helping as a teacher's assistant years back and with local playgroups until more recently. She so enjoyed their chatter, their young words of random wisdom and oblivious reasoning, their eager young minds so alive with wonder before reality set in. She always hoped their lives wouldn't turn out as hers had.

She checked the clock on the mantelpiece as she passed it on her way to get her coat and boots, but that really wasn't necessary. Instinctively, she knew it was time, time to bring them inside, time to make a call. She pulled on an old pair of knitted gloves, put her hood up against the cold wind and set off. It would take her a while to move the short distance, but that didn't matter; time was something she had plenty of.

Closing the back door behind her, she made her way down the side alley and out towards the park and the busy A57 that ran along it, right along the front of her house. A heavy-goods truck whooshed past and whipped the cold, damp air into her face. Miniscule droplets of moisture clung to her skin, making the fine hairs on her jaw look like cobwebs drenched in heavy morning dew. She waited on the pavement opposite the park entrance. And waited. Finally, the traffic cleared, and she ambled across towards the metal railings and the gate. How she was going to get back across the busy road was a different matter, but she figured the answer would come to her at the time. It usually did.

Each breath preceded her like small fog clouds in front of her face; her breathing was short and shallow. As she made her way towards the two little girls, she wondered absently what their education had been thus far on not talking to strangers. Her task could prove a little more difficult than she thought. Again, the answer would be clear soon enough.

Little voices giggling up ahead made her smile. Oh, so innocent. Oh, to be that tender young age again, with not a care in the world, no knowledge of what lay ahead of them. Oh, the changes she would have made to her own life — if only she'd been able... The giggles increased in volume as she neared them both and now the old woman could see their matching pink coats, their matching rosy cheeks, pink from the cold.

They stopped giggling when they saw her. Victoria, the eldest at seven, gently nudged Jasmine behind her, much to Jasmine's annoyance. The old woman noticed and smiled; one day protecting her sister in that manner might come in handy, she thought. Bending down to their level, she spoke.

"Having fun?" she enquired cheerily.

Victoria didn't say a word. Jasmine nodded in reply. Both wore serious expressions on their tiny faces. It was clear the 'Don't talk to strangers' message had been learned in their home. Wise indeed, thought Mrs. Skeen.

She pressed on. "I couldn't help noticing you were out here alone on such a cold day, and not at school. Are you on an adventure, by chance?"

She beamed at them both. The moisture clinging to her hairy chin made the dark hairs look lighter than they really were.

Victoria had never seen such a hairy chin, and fixated on it, trying not to blink.

"I won't bite you, you know. I'm not the bad wolf, my loves. You can tell me what you're up to. I'm guessing it's your secret?"

Jasmine nodded again and opened her mouth to speak, but Victoria dug her elbow into her ribs.

"Ouch!" Jasmine exclaimed.

Then Victoria spoke. "We're off school. Mummy isn't feeling very well, so we've left her sleeping." Still, she couldn't take her eyes off the woman's damp chin.

"Well, since you've been here a while now in the cold, who would like some warm blackcurrant and a biscuit or two? I'll be betting you're both hungry by now?"

Two little faces bobbed up and down as they nodded.

"I live just over there," Mrs. Skeen said, pointing to the house across the way. "Let's get you warmed up, and I'll see if there's a chocolate biscuit or two left, shall we? Then we can let your mummy know you're both okay."

Two blank faces stared at her, so she carried on. "I'll be betting when she wakes up and finds you gone, she'll be worried, and we don't want that, do we?"

The girls shook their heads gravely, taking in her every word. Mrs. Skeen reached out to take their hands now, enfolding one in each of her woolly paws. Hand in hand, the little group walked slowly out of the park gates and back towards the A57.

"So," said Mrs. Skeen brightly as they walked slowly along, "what are your names?"

"I'm Victoria, and this is Jasmine."

"What pretty names for pretty girls. Do you live around here?"

"Sort of. It's quite a walk away."

"Not to worry. Let's get across the road and have some juice, shall we?"

Both girls had started to relax a little and nodded excitedly. They'd missed breakfast and were hungry. The thought of something warming in their tums was appealing.

The three of them stood on the edge of the pavement waiting for the traffic to ease. Finally, there was a gap, and they made their way across and up the short distance to Mrs. Skeen's house. Steering them both down the side entry, she unlocked the door and led them both inside. The warmth of the house took the chill off them all as she led them through to the lounge and the welcoming open fire.

"You get yourselves warmed up and I'll get the juice ready," she said, and pottered off to the kitchen out back. She flicked the button on the kettle, poured cordial into three mugs and searched the biscuit barrel for six chocolate biscuits.

Then she made a phone call.

Chapter Eighteen

"It's got to be time for a break, hasn't it? I'm starved," moaned Ruth. "My stomach thinks my throat has been cut it's so long since it was last fed."

Amanda smiled across at Ruth. "You can when we've finished this wall. I'm almost out of paint in the tray anyway. Hold on until then?"

Ruth rolled her bottom lip over her top like a child, knowing it worked most times on Amanda. She'd get what she wanted almost immediately. Today though, Amanda wanted to get the walls finished at the very least. She had pale blue paint in her blonde fringe, which was sticking out from under her cap, and paint covered the top of that too.

"That won't work on me today, sweetheart. I'm on a mission to get this finished. I'm over it already – aren't you?"

"I'll be fine when I've been fed and watered – ready to go with gusto, I'm sure. I just need sustenance to carry on." Ruth wiped the back of her hand across her forehead to mimic fainting.

"You sound like a frail old woman, Mrs. McGregor-Lacey. If you stopped moaning and finished the wall, you'd get your sustenance quicker."

Ruth smiled broadly. "It sounds great, doesn't it? 'Mrs. McGregor-

Lacey.'" She enunciated each word, feeling each of them on her tongue, and beamed at Amanda. "What a fab day that was, wasn't it?"

Amanda watched Ruth savour the memory, paintbrush in hand, nowhere near the wall she was supposed to be doing the edges of. Ruth was someplace else.

"Okay, you win. Down tools," Amanda said reluctantly, though without any malice. "I'll put the kettle on. Or do you want coffee?"

Smiling, knowing she'd won, Ruth placed a sticky brush on the upturned paint tin lid and went to Amanda, arms open.

"Coffee, please, and a kiss. Then I'll have some of that banana cake you bought if there's any left."

The two women embraced, savouring for a moment the closeness of being a newly married couple.

"Feels good, doesn't it?" Ruth said softly.

"It certainly does." Amanda smiled back at her. "Okay, I'll get the coffee while you clean your hands. How on earth do you manage to get so much paint off the bristles and onto places you're not directing them? Is the wall not a big enough canvas for you?" She looked Ruth up and down. "I bet you were terrible at potato-stamp painting in preschool," she added as she headed downstairs.

Ruth smiled to herself and went to gaze out of the front bedroom window. The pale sky blue of the nearly finished walls almost matched the winter sky outside. The sun had only managed to climb a little way up and was hanging low over the rooftops. Wet washing blew on clotheslines in back gardens like bunting at a fete. An elderly couple sauntered up the road together and unclipped a front gate; Ruth heard it clank and rattle as it closed again. Probably visiting their grandchildren, thought Ruth. Would she and Amanda ever have children? she wondered, not for the first time.

Ruth was a career woman, running her own successful digital business, and her biological clock was rapidly approaching its use-by date. Amanda had already passed that point, though a pregnancy at her age wasn't impossible, just riskier – if they decided to go that way, that was. If not, there were plenty of other ways to have a family.

Ruth could hear the coffee machine chugging in the kitchen as she headed out the back door to the outside tap. Bits of blue sluiced onto the concrete as she rinsed her hands, though her fingernails looked like they'd need a scrubbing brush. She sensed Amanda nearby.

"Perhaps rubber gloves for you, eh? That's going to take some removing later," she said, watching over Ruth's bent body.

"Good job I've not got a hot date tonight, then," Ruth quipped. "Which reminds me, I'm thinking Wong's for takeaway later, then we can order and pick it up when it suits rather than go out to eat. Cooking is too much bother when the place is in uproar with decorating. Does that work for you?"

"I'm never one to turn down sweet-and-sour pork balls; you know that," Amanda said.

"And since we need to keep on painting, why don't we go have brunch tomorrow before we get started?" Ruth said. She cocked her head back and painted in the imaginary sky with her hands. "Crispy bacon, lightly scrambled eggs, thick toast and a couple of mugs of coffee. Mmm, bliss – my idea of heaven. What do you say?"

Looking bemused again, Amanda conceded. "Talking of bacon, Jack and I called in at a layby food van for a bacon sandwich and a cuppa a couple of days ago. And the oddest thing happened."

"Oh? What was that?" Ruth asked as she turned the tap off and dried her hands on her shirt-tail.

"It was tipping down, but the van was as busy as ever, and the men in front of us went back to their BMW with their order, sat for a moment or two as we watched, then threw their bacon sandwiches and drinks straight out of the window and drove off. They weren't speeding off in a mad hurry, but it was odd. Who throws bacon sandwiches away? And they were damn good too, if ours were anything to go by."

The two women went back indoors and sat down to coffee and banana cake.

"Well, not me, that's for sure," Ruth said, licking frosting from her fingers. "Did you do them for littering?" She took another big bite of cake. Crumbs dropped down the front of her paint-splattered shirt.

"No, I had better things to do with my time. Anyway, I was busy with my own sandwich. We both thought it was strange, though."

With a mouth full of the remaining cake, Ruth stood and grabbed her coffee, scattering crumbs on the floor.

"It is. But now, Sherlock, it's time to get the next and final wall done, so bring your coffee and let's get to it."

"Yes, master – or should I say 'Yes, Doctor Watson'?" Amanda kidded, and followed Ruth back upstairs for the final leg of decorating their bedroom. But despite their joking, the question still nagged at her. Why would someone, two people actually, throw perfectly good bacon sandwiches out the window – ever?

Chapter Nineteen

JACK WAS hard at work when Amanda put her face around his computer screen.

"Morning, sunshine," she greeted him brightly. Jack noticed a twinkle in her blue eyes.

"Morning, Lacey, or should I say McGregor-Lacey now?"

"Either is fine, but Lacey will do. You've called me that for so many years now. What are you up to?"

Jack peered closely at a list on his screen.

"I had a bit of a thought – a hunch, really." His forefinger scrolled down the screen like a pointer as he read, the words coming slowly as he searched.

"Oh? What about?"

"About the chaps who threw away their sandwiches at that food van the other day." He continued to scroll.

"I've not got that out of my mind either, funnily enough. Seems silly, eh?"

Jack looked away from his screen. He wore bright-pink reading glasses perched on the end of his nose.

Amanda smiled. "But not as silly as you wearing my spare reading glasses. Where are yours?"

"First, I'd have thought this early on in your newly wedded bliss you'd be thinking about other things at weekends than sandwiches flying from windows. Second, someone has swiped mine from my drawer and I can't see a damn thing close up without a pair."

Amanda ignored him. "So, back to my previous question: what are you up to?"

Jack sat back in his chair and slipped the glasses up on top of his head, Kardashian style. "Remember those ice cream vans that were selling cocaine to students outside the library on campus? I got to wondering if that food van was selling something a bit more lucrative than tea and sandwiches. Easy enough to hide a baggy inside a baggy, eh?"

"Well, it's not a new thing, is it? The drug wars back in the eighties in Glasgow were about ice cream vans and drug turf disputes, so I guess it's plausible. Could be anything, though, not just cocaine."

"My point exactly. Anything small enough to slip inside a sandwich bag along with a sandwich as disguise. And something not too obvious to insert, from the vendor's point of view, though they'd have to be extremely careful. Take us, for instance: two coppers. They wouldn't have known us from Jack."

Amanda smiled and rolled her eyes at his unintended pun.

"Yeah, yeah, very funny," he mock-growled at her. "You'll be reminding me of the Schitt family next." He started to recite what he could remember, using his fingers to get all of the names right. "Jack Schitt was married to Noe Schitt. They had several kids: Holie Schitt, Giva Schitt, Fulla Schitt, Bull Schitt, and the twins Deep Schitt and Dip Schitt..."

Amanda waved her arms in the air in defeat.

"Okay, stop!" she called before he went on any further. "And Noe went on to re-marry Ted Sherlock after a divorce and kept her double-barrelled surname, making her Noe Schitt-Sherlock. Yes, I and everyone else in here have heard that story, Jack."

"I know, but it cracks me up every time I hear it, so humour me sometimes, eh?"

"Funny, that's the second time I've heard Sherlock in the last forty-eight hours. Must be something in the water."

"Let's hope it's not Schitt." He grinned at her.

"Riiiiiiight." Amanda cleared her throat, refocusing. "So, again, what are you searching for?"

"I'm looking at recent and old cases, because if they had turf wars in Glasgow back then, they may well have turf wars down here too. These vans are mobile, remember? So, they might not be locals."

"Good thinking. So, what's the plan, then?"

"I don't really have one yet. We don't know if there's even been a crime committed."

Amanda looked at her watch. It was still early but what the hell. "Then do you fancy a drive out? I suggest we grab an early coffee from that layby van again and see what we can see for an hour. If nothing happens, we'll keep an eye out from a distance, get a couple of the others to pop in for sandwiches on occasion, that type of thing. It's only a hunch there's even anything going on at this point."

Jack stood and closed down his computer. They grabbed their coats, scarves, and bags, and headed out to the car park.

"I'll drive," Jack said, getting his keys out. He really hated being the passenger and much preferred to be in control. Driving also gave him the right to choose the music if they played any. And since he'd discovered music streaming without the need for CDs, the music world was his oyster. In reality, that meant he listened to even more of the old stuff, not the modern noise whose words he couldn't hear.

The car blipped open. He climbed into the driver's seat and Amanda got in beside him. They set out into a bright but cold winter's day. The sun's glare hit him straight in the eyes and he pulled his visor down.

"Shit, that's bright," he moaned, and pulled what he thought were his sunglasses down off his head. Amanda threw her head back and laughed as her pink reading glasses settled back on his nose.

"Very bloody funny. Very funny indeed. You were waiting for that, weren't you?" Jack growled and yanked the glasses off his face.

"Of course I was! I just wondered when you'd finally notice," she said, and carried on giggling until Jack finally saw the funny side of it too.

"I'll get you back for this, Amanda. You mark my words."

"No shit, Sherlock," Amanda roared, and the two of them howled together as they set off towards the layby.

64

Chapter Twenty

BY THE TIME they had pulled up at the food van, there was quite a queue, made more bearable by the tepid winter sunshine. The pale yellow ball in the sky gave off a feeble heat, like half a bar on an old electric heater at a grandmother's shins. No need for sunscreen today; there'd be more danger in a hot cup of tea. Jack approached the van and joined the back of the queue. Amanda stayed in the passenger seat surveying those parked up in the layby. Cars of all types were parked up – a few small vans, a motorcycle; nothing out of the ordinary. Trucks were not an option; the parking was too limited.

Amanda watched Jack watching the queue. A tall blonde woman, her head covered in 80s-style frizz to her shoulders, stood directly in front of him, making it difficult for him to see round. Amanda doubted she was the motorcycle rider; she'd never get her comb through her hair ever again. And she wasn't wearing leathers either, although the person in front of her was. This one was shorter in stature, with short dark hair and the typical V-shaped body of someone who spent time developing their upper chest; probably a male, Amanda thought. Then it was suit in front of suit in front of suit, all varying heights and widths, all playing with their phones. A total of seven people patiently waited their turn, and considering it wasn't really breakfast time or morning coffee time but somewhere in between, that struck Amanda as quite a lot. Maybe the food van was that good and these people were regulars. Yes, her bacon sandwich had been nice, but queue-worthy?

A suit up front took his bag and Styrofoam cup back to his car and got in. Amanda adjusted herself to see what he was doing, but he was too far away. But he didn't just drive off; he sat long enough to perhaps eat what was in the bag. Another suit made his way back to his Mercedes, slipped inside, and then immediately hit the road and sped off, at unnecessary speed Amanda thought. That left two more suits, the biker and Blondie as well as Jack. Another suit joined in behind Jack, a woman this time, in a dark trouser suit. She began texting while she waited. The two remaining suits were served quickly. Both clutched white bags and soon left the layby.

Finally, Jack was served and trotted back to the car with their order. He climbed into the car, and he and Amanda watched the layby activity as they slowly chewed on fresh bacon sandwiches and sipped their tea, in no particular rush.

"There was nothing to see waiting in the queue, and I didn't hear anything untoward either. The most I got was 'red sauce or brown.' And I couldn't see big notes being handed over either, so if they are selling something illegally, they're not taking payment at transaction time, and dealers don't do that. It's not good business sense – drugs on the never-never." He took another bite and red sauce dropped down his tie.

"Oh, sod it!" he exclaimed, and Amanda passed her napkin across, not wanting to wipe the sauce herself and smear it. Naturally, he managed to smear it himself and Amanda chuckled to herself, careful not to let him hear.

"Well, maybe payment is cashless now," she said. "Everything else we buy is going that way. Maybe the crims are going the same way – technology. You've heard of monthly subscription services for things like Netflix and what have you? Maybe these vans are doing the same thing, or maybe they have an app?"

"Eh?"

"Well, think about it. Why not? Open an account, pay some money in, then transfer it as or before you purchase." Jack looked sceptical and Amanda carried on, "I'm not saying that's what they're doing. I don't even know if that's possible – and again, we don't actually know if anything *is* going on. The queue could be because they sell great sandwiches and tea, which is no crime.

"I can think of plenty of places that I've bought bacon sandwiches from that *should* have been a crime they were so bad. I mean, who in their right mind cooks bacon so it's still pink? It's got to be well cooked, crispy even. Just don't give me pale pink, not ever."

Amanda nodded in agreement as she scrunched her bag up and wiped her mouth on a tissue from her bag. She gathered their rubbish and opened her door to get out. As she threw the waste paper into the bin, she noticed a couple of what looked like miniature empty sachets of salt sticking out from under a cup.

She pondered for a moment. "Now that's odd," she mumbled quietly to herself. "Who puts salt on bacon sandwiches?" She checked her surroundings, then, using her discarded tissue, she carefully pulled them out by their corners. She folded the tissue over them and slipped them into her pocket. Then, she gently pushed other debris so one side and saw a couple more. In fact, as she focused, she could see the edges of yet more little packets, identical to the ones in her pocket. She took another tissue from her bag, had another quick look round to see that no one was watching, plucked the rest of the packets out, then headed back to where Jack was waiting.

"You got something?" he enquired when she was safely in. He'd seen her lean into the bin and figured she wasn't still hungry.

"Let's see, shall we?"

Chapter Twenty-One

LUKE AND CLINTON had glumly gone their separate ways for the weekend. It had been a depleting day for them both. Nobody said getting a business off the ground was going to be easy, and Luke hadn't expected it to be a walk in the park either – more a walk through the Yorkshire Dales, he'd figured – but he *had* expected it to be less emotionally challenging. The constant rejection was tough to handle, and he felt the need to flake out a while and stop pretending that everything was going to be all right.

His granddad would have warned him that each finance rejection was fate telling him to leave well enough alone, that the banks had his best interests at heart when they said no, even if it didn't seem that way at the time.

'They have rules in place for your own protection," he'd have said. "Don't force it." Luke smiled as he imagined his grandfather giving him a stern talking-to, an arthritic forefinger pointing directly at Luke's chest, his cloudy eyes crinkled with distress. He'd loved his wise old granddad. The old man had been gone a few years now and there was no one left in Luke's life to fill his place.

Luke closed his eyes as he lay stretched out on his bed in the back room at his parents' place. He'd hoped to have moved out by now; a twenty-five-year-old shouldn't still be living at home, never mind paying room and board. He should be making his own way in the world, living in a nice little flat somewhere, with a girlfriend maybe, a steady job to go to every Monday morning. He had none of that. And now it looked like he'd be sleeping in the tiny room for a while longer.

"Get a job," his father had said. "Stop with the romantic notion of running a big company. Knuckle down and do some proper work."

His father's ideas of a proper job were something physical – and join the union while you're at it. Like he had. It certainly hadn't done him any harm, had it? Yeah, until miners weren't needed anymore, foundries were closed down and dock workers were taken over by steel containers and hoists. No thanks. In Luke's mind, running his own business wasn't a romantic notion: it was a very real opportunity and he wanted in. Owning a mobile food van and selling well-cooked, wholesome organic food was what he wanted to do, *knew* he could do, if only they could find the funds to get up and running. Then they'd franchise the idea and take it nationwide and beyond. They had everything lined up – suppliers, menu ideas, locations even – but without funds, there was no way of getting it started.

Hit.

The word nagged at him again. He sat up and swung his feet to the floor. There was no harm in doing the research, was there? He grabbed his laptop from the bedside cabinet and opened Google. His hand hesitated over the keyboard. Would the search term send a flag up somewhere? Would cookies then track him on his computer? There was only one way to find out. He typed in the search box.

Hit man for hire.

And pressed enter.

"No going back now. I hope I don't need to have an explanation ready for the cybercrime division when they come knocking."

To Luke's astonishment, Google returned more than three million results. So, like everyone else, he started at the top of the first page and looked at what was on offer. There were the usual Quora and Wikipedia pages, but about halfway down, a web address caught his attention. He read the small piece of text, his finger hovering over the keyboard as he wondered whether to click the actual link or not. Curiosity got the better of him and he hit it. Half of him expected an actual alarm to go off like a police siren; half of him thought, "It's just a website. Don't be so silly."

The website came to life, and a page with "Hit Man for Hire" emblazoned across it filled his screen. But a quick glance told him it wasn't a shop front; rather, it was an old news story about a company that had been hired to build a website for such services and had quickly been shut down. Luke took a couple of deep breaths in and relaxed a little, taking comfort in the fact that something so illegal wasn't as easily available as he'd first assumed. He hit the back button, went back to the search results and scrolled further down. The other results were stories about hits taking place on the dark web, websites that had sprung up there, guns for hire of all kinds and in all parts of the world. It seemed no matter what you wanted done – bones broken, beatings or a straightforward hit – it all could be found in a much darker place than Google.

Luke closed his laptop lid, leaving the Google search page open, and rested his head back against the wall in thought. The dark web – that's where he needed to do his research, find out more, maybe join a group or two and see what people were looking for and how they were getting their requirements filled. He had to admit, though, that the thought of doing a hit repulsed him: beatings to order sounded too personal, too brutal, and not something he'd be able to do even if he wanted to. He wasn't built that way, in mind or in body. Stabbing someone was in the same "too personal" box, as he knew from watching far too many movies. It was a close-up act of violence, and it took a certain kind of person to take a life that way. And again, he didn't have the physical build to overcome someone, never mind the mess factor.

But shooting someone? That could be a different matter. He'd often thought, when road rage had overtaken his senses, that he could pull a trigger as easy as changing gear, wipe slow-moving traffic out of the way in an instant, clear the way for himself to get through. Blow away someone who had stolen the last parking space or cut him off on the motorway. He'd feel nothing but the smooth trigger with his finger, squeezing it gently. Powerful, almost hypnotic even. Yes, he could easily do that under any of those circumstances.

It wouldn't be personal at all.

Chapter Twenty-Two

AFTER DINNER, which consisted of a simple bowl of tomato soup and several slices of buttered toast, Luke took a quick walk in the drizzly evening air to blow some metaphorical cobwebs off. His hair had since dried, and his now tight curls looked a lot like a brown poodle's coat though without the damp dog smell. Now he settled down to work in his room, laptop balancing on his thighs as he typed.

Expanding on his earlier realization that he could easily fire a gun at someone, it seemed the sensible (if that was the correct word) thing to do some more research. From the little he'd found out already on the regular surface web and trusty Google, prices ranged from around £5000 to £30,000, depending on the quality of the kill and what was required.

Quality? Sounds like big game hunting rather than a hit. Aren't all shootings equal?

If an experienced ex-Forces officer or similar was required, that was where the heftier price tag came in, whereas a dodgy backstreet pub dweller would do his best for a measly £5000 – balls over brains, he supposed. Luke figured that as an inexperienced but intelligent beginner, he'd sit someplace in the middle. He had the brains, he was clever, and he had common sense, something many people didn't have –

common sense wasn't that common. But did he have the balls? Time would tell if he got that far.

Luke began thinking out loud, a lifelong habit that had always helped him organize his thoughts.

"I'm going to need a gun, and some training on how to use it," he mumbled, "but which gun? I'm thinking with a silencer, so that means a pistol probably. Still too noisy, though. Maybe I'll still need to use a pillow. Either way, first job, see if I can get the right gun." He mentally filed the thought and went on to the next problem to solve – getting a customer.

"I'd be out of place in a seedy pub, so how will I get a client? And how much should I charge? Hmm, I'm thinking a nice round ten thousand, so I only have to do a couple maybe, and I don't want to price myself out of the market." He added those thoughts to the other already in his mental filing cabinet. There was so much to organize, so much to think about. On the surface so far, though, it all seemed rather simple: get a weapon, get a client, decide on the situation and squeeze. Ten grand, thank you very much. Please call again. The thought amused him: "Please call again, and tell your friends!" He laughed.

If he planned it out rigorously, nothing would go wrong. One thing he wasn't planning on, not yet anyway, was telling Clinton, not until he was sure of how it would all work. Luke hit the Tor browser icon on the Mac's dock and launched the dark web search page.

"Here goes. Let's see if I can pull this off."

Luke was no stranger to the dark web. He'd spent time there on and off over the years, mostly in chat rooms where he'd purchased a few odd small packets of hash. They'd arrive wrapped in plastic film, all folded up nicely and stuck to a fake gym invoice for cover. Not that he had any money to buy any at the moment, of course, but he knew his way around the place. He'd also seen more than his share of stuff he rather wished he hadn't clicked on during his travels. Still, seedy stuff existed everywhere, he knew, whether it was on an actual physical street corner or a virtual one.

But buying a weapon was a bit different than buying a gram of weed for personal use. He typed 'buy pistol and silencer' into the search box and hit enter. He then spent the next hour clicking links to various 'stores' and making notes of availability and pricing until he knew roughly what he was looking at cost-wise and what he'd get for his money. Some vendors were a little more security-conscious than others; some only accepted payment in Bitcoin. But all of them could offer a pistol with silencer with the serial number filed off for a fee, a fee he'd yet have to think about how he'd raise.

He sat back, staring at the screen and tapping his fingers in thought, and suddenly it came to him. Maybe he could get his client first and use the advance to purchase the necessary tools? That way, if there were no enquiries about his service, he wouldn't be out of pocket and left with an unregistered gun that probably came with a nasty history.

It sounded the bright thing to do. He searched on, this time with a different set of keywords, to see what the competition were up to and how they preferred to run things. Scrolling through the results, he chose one and clicked the link. A basic website filled his screen. The heading at the top made no bones about what their service was: a hit for hire. He scrolled to the contact page and hovered his mouse, debating whether to click or not. If he was going to set himself up in a similar fashion, he had to know how the competition allowed clients to make contact. Surely it wouldn't be by a regular email or text message; that would be way too stupid and easily traced.

"Here goes," he said out loud. "Let's see how this all works." He clicked the link, which took him through to a message board where he registered and asked his question. There was no request to confirm an email address, because that would take away the anonymous advantage of using the Tor browser. So it was all done via messages on a private board, he said to himself. Nobody knew who else was there, nor could they see them. On the one hand, if the cops were looking, you couldn't see them. But if other criminals were looking, you couldn't see them either – nobody could see anybody else. And that was why the dark net experience was so successful – it was virtually impossible for anyone, even the cleverest person, to monitor, unless they knew *exactly* where to look.

He typed, "Looking for a hit on my husband. South London area. How much and when?"

He stared at the words on the screen, his chest thumping with each heartbeat. Telling himself this was only research and not the real deal, he reconciled it in his head and clicked send. A whoosh of air left his chest. How long would a reply take? How much would it cost? What would the timeframe be? What other information would the outfit need from him? He felt panic start to rise.

"Holy hell! I'm not sure if I'm cut out for this," he muttered.

The reply was almost instant.

Chapter Twenty-Three

LUKE SAT on the bed and stared at the screen like it had morphed into something from a Jack Reacher movie. Did this shit really happen?

Yep, it did.

The words stared at him, begging to be answered. He knew there was a person on the other end of them expecting a response. Would they understand his nervousness and give him time to think? And, perhaps more to the point, was this what it would be like for his prospective customer when it came time to place an enquiry, talk about the needs, the finer details? Probably so.

He sat back in his chair again, considering. Should he be cagey or direct with his requirements? What was the etiquette, assuming there was one? He sat forward again and typed his reply: "Looking for price and availability. Suggest quick shot. What else do you need?" Send.

Wow, that felt funny, he thought. He waited. Had he been too direct? There was no mistaking what he was asking – but how you ask for a hit without actually saying the exact words? A pow-wow? A water pistol? A cap gun?

He needn't have worried. The reply came back quickly. He read it out loud to himself, slowly moving over the few words to make sure he understood the message.

"£15,000, half up front, half on completion. I'll tell you when and where later. What will the location be? Need a picture. Bitcoin or cash – you choose."

Luke couldn't believe that he was actually conversing with a killer on the other side of his screen, someone happy to take fifteen grand and snuff out a life to order.

Isn't that what you're thinking of doing, Luke?

He began to type his reply – all in the name of research, of course.

"Thanks. Need to figure that kind of money. I'll come back then." He pressed send and closed the site down before he said anything more. The person on the other side would put him down to being a tyre kicker, a time waster, which is exactly what he was to them while he researched. But he'd gained valuable knowledge from the brief encounter.

He wondered how the cash option would work; obviously they wouldn't be giving him account details for their local building society or high street bank – more likely a nearby rubbish bin and a brown paper bag. Perhaps he shouldn't have been so hasty in closing the page down. Clearly, he needed to find out the answer.

"One more," he said, as he re-entered the search term and chose another site. This one listed various other services, beatings and the like as well as straightforward hits. Luke got the impression the site operated out of eastern Europe, though he couldn't say why and had no way of finding out; it was just a sense. Maybe it was the way the text read; it had a sort of accent, if it was possible for the written word to have an accent.

He registered and composed another message, this time feeling a little calmer and more in control.

"Looking for a hit on husband. South London. How much and what do you need?" Send.

The cursor blinked while he waited for a reply. After five full minutes, he was about to close up and give up for the night when the answer landed.

"No problem. £12,000, half up front. Accident or shooting? How big is he?"

"Shooting probably. Rougher part of town. How do I get cash to you?" Send.

He waited, and this time the reply was quicker.

"Can be organized. Cash is OK, drop-off place TBC. Need photo and location. Rest on completion. Interested?"

Shit, he was pushy. He assumed it was a man. Pushy or weeding fakes out, one or the other. How should he respond? What else did he need to know? What would someone who really wanted their husband gone want to know?

"Sounds good. How long until complete? Don't want him to suffer either." Send.

Luke waited, willing the guy to respond quickly so he could get the hell out of the site. It gave him the heebie-jeebies. He needn't have worried; once again, the reply was almost instant. It seemed the person was keen for another quick payday.

"This week if needed. Quick and easy. Depends on you getting what I need."

Luke wanted to end the conversation – he had what he needed – but one more question needed answering.

"How do I contact you? Through here?"

"Yes. I'll send a mobile number on delivery for final payment."

Good to know. I'll need a burner phone or two, Luke mused. He had the surreal feeling that he was in a bad cop movie. He told them he'd be back and disconnected from the site. Closing the lid to his laptop, he took a couple of deep breaths and rolled the cricks from his neck. Feeling the need for some air, he gathered his jacket off a nearby chair and headed down the stairs and out the front door into the cold night. His breath was visible in short, misty bursts as he walked, the amber glow of street lamps lighting his way. The air was damp as usual, though thankfully it had stopped raining. He pulled his collar up against the cold and rammed his hands deeper into his pockets, head bent slightly as he walked. He spent the time sorting through what he'd learned so far. On the surface, it all seemed simple enough. But could he do it? Could he take someone's life when it came to it? Or was this whole thing too much of a wacky idea? Maybe he should forget it completely, he told himself uneasily. He'd fantasized about shooting someone in a road rage − hell, most people he knew fantasized about that, when it came to it − but sneaking up on someone who hadn't pissed him off directly and snuffing them out, well, that was different. That was cold-blooded murder.

But £12,000 in cash was awfully tempting. It was more than enough funds to get his business going. And if he did it two or three times . . . Luke quickened his pace as the pieces fell into place. The more he turned it over in his head, the easier it sounded. Now he just needed to talk to Clinton about it.

And get a weapon.

Chapter Twenty-Four

"I THOUGHT YOU WERE JOKING!" Clinton was incredulous. "You've got to be dreaming! Kill someone? For money? Are you out of your mind?"

Luke had cemented his plan in his head as he'd walked round to Clinton's place.

"I've worked most of it out, and it's pretty simple," he said calmly. He counted on his fingers as he spoke. "One, I know how much to charge. Two, I know how the contact is made. Three, I know how to build a basic website. Four, I can probably get a weapon on the web. And five, we only have to do a couple of hits. Where else are we going to get the money? Because we've worked too hard to chuck this dream away. This will give us the start we need. Think about it, Clinton."

"I don't need to think about it! It's nuts! And what if we get caught, eh? That's prison for the rest of our lives, or at least a good twenty years of it. And I don't fancy being someone's bitch, either. Trust you to be the one to come up with the harebrained idea." Clinton rubbed his face with his hands.

"And trust you to be the one that pooh-poohs it," Luke said crossly. "I don't see much coming from you in the way of money-earning ideas. You're supposed to be the accountant brain of the two of us. I'm the creative one, remember."

"Well, I can't say your idea isn't creative, now can I? It's about as creative as it gets, actually, so top marks for that," Clinton spat back. His face had gone beet red.

Luke sat back and waited for Clinton to cool down and catch his breath. It was a good job Clinton's parents were away on holiday; they surely would have heard every word.

For a few moments they sat in tense silence, eyeing each other uneasily. Clinton spoke first.

"I'll give it some thought," he said, "but that's all I'll do. I'll be right up front, though: I can't see me changing my opinion. It's way too risky *and* it's cold-blooded. I'm not sure I'm that desperate."

Luke stayed silent, let him have his airtime.

"Do you even know how to fire a gun, of any kind?" Clinton asked him.

"I've shot a rifle and a shotgun, but not a handgun or revolver, no. Daresay I could learn, though. There's got to be a gun club I can join somewhere, get some lessons."

"I wouldn't be so sure, actually," Clinton retorted. "This is England, remember, not the US. It might be a tad more difficult than you think. And then there is the small issue of actually purchasing a gun." Clinton picked up his phone and typed into his browser. "See?" He turned his screen towards Luke. "Since the Dunblane school shooting in 1996, all handguns are effectively banned from the ranges. Only rifles and muzzle-loading pistols are allowed." Turning the screen back to himself, he added, "I'm guessing those are the really old ones like they used to use in duels." He almost looked chuffed.

"There'll be a way to get some lessons," Luke insisted. "Once I've got something to practice with, mind. I haven't looked at the cost yet, or the availability. I need to research a little more."

"Like which one you actually need to start with. Calibre and whatnot − silencer, size, that sort of thing."

Luke smiled broadly at Clinton.

"What?"

"Listen to you. You were so freaked out a few minutes ago, yet here you are now, calmly chatting away about the best gun to get."

"Leave out the 'we', will you? I'm simply talking to you, having a conversation and nothing more. I've not agreed to anything yet. And I won't be either, I expect."

He went back to his phone and Luke watched him silently. If he was going to get fixed up with a weapon, it wasn't going to be with the help of Google; more likely a backstreet pub off a rough council estate tower. He looked down at his pretty-boy hands, hands that didn't get dirty that often. His mother used to say his hands were nicer than her own, and they probably were. In any rough pub those hands would give their game away; he'd stick out like a nun at a disco and probably get himself killed in the process if he tried. And there was still the issue of funds. No, he really had no choice: he'd have to buy the gun when he'd secured his first client with his first advance.

But he still had to make the enquiry.

Chapter Twenty-Five

MRS. STEWART HELD out a plastic box for Jack as he left his house for work.

"Here, a piece of iced lemon loaf for your mid-morning snack, and I've put a piece in for Amanda too. See she gets it, please." She nodded knowingly at Jack. They both knew that there was every chance Amanda would never see the extra piece, but Jack's waistline would. It had happened before.

"I only did that the once, as you well know, Mrs. S," he teased. "Though iced lemon is one of my very favourites, so I wouldn't like to guarantee its delivery to the rightful stomach."

Mrs. Stewart smiled as Jack set off towards his car, which was parked on the driveway. She raised a hand and waved him farewell, waiting for him to fully reverse and drive away before she shut the front door behind him.

Jack smiled as he drove off; he loved this little ritual of theirs. He blushed to admit it, but his life was so much nicer now with Mrs. S. in the picture. She was Jack's housekeeper, and she cleaned and cooked for him three times a week, usually in the mornings. Since his Janine had passed a few years back, he'd been muddling along on his own, and the habits he'd got into had needed intervention from Amanda and

Ruth. It wasn't that he hadn't been coping, mind; he'd simply become a little scruffy round the edges, and ate appallingly, and his health had started to suffer a little because of it.

Janine had done everything for him when she'd been alive, bless her, and so through no fault of his own he hadn't known how to do laundry properly, or cook a decent meal, or most of the important but mundane things that happened round a house in terms of cleaning and maintenance.

After he'd fallen ill and been laid up in hospital, Amanda and Ruth had installed Mrs. S. on a trial basis to help him out. He had balked at first, of course, but it had turned out to be the best gift the two women could have given him. He now had three wonderful women in his life.

Jack smiled to himself and looked across at the little plastic box on the passenger seat. No doubt about it: Mrs. S. made him feel better about himself – and made him look better too. His old work shirts with the fraying collars had vanished. Replacements had been bought and were laundered carefully for him.

He stopped for a red light and reached for his phone. He tapped the Spotify app, pressed on his Time Capsule, and Simon and Garfunkel's *Mrs. Robinson* filled the car. He listened to the words as he waited for the lights to change. "Heaven holds a place for those who pray...". Janine had prayed, and so had Jack when she'd been diagnosed with cancer.

"God bless you, Janine," he said huskily, and wondered what she was doing right at that moment. A toot from a car horn behind him brought him back to reality and he drove on as *Scarborough Fair* began to play.

Ten minutes later, he was parked up in the station car park and retrieving the little plastic box along with his old briefcase. Raj was parked up nearby and shouted his good morning as he too made his way towards the building. Jack liked Raj. He was young and polite, and had brains, though they didn't share the same interest in music. Not many had Jack's limited tastes – ELO, Rainbow and little else. They fell into step together. Raj nodded at the box.

"More homemade baking?"

"Keep your dabs off it or I'll know exactly where it's gone," Jack said, though he meant no malice. "One piece has Amanda's name on it and the other is all mine. Play your cards right, and I'll ask Mrs. S. to cut you a piece one of these days."

"I wish I had someone to bake for me. Shop-bought is nowhere near the same. How do I play my cards right, then? What do I have to do?"

Raj opened the glass double door and Jack slipped though. He followed.

"Put a rush on those packets from the bin if you can. I've a feeling they might be the key to something bigger."

"Oh?"

"Call it a feeling in my water, but I think we could be looking at something landing in our own backyard. Get some results for me today, and there's cake in it for you tomorrow."

Jack increased his speed and Raj fell behind.

"Done. Make it a big piece," he called after him, and made his way to his own office and desk, no doubt to make the phone call.

Amanda materialized from a doorway as Jack passed by. "Hey, slow down," she said, struggling to keep up. "What's the rush?"

"No rush, just want to get on," he said, and passed the box to her. She opened the lid as she walked.

"Oh! Mrs. S., I think I love you." She reached in and helped herself to a slice. She took a mouthful and savoured the taste before replacing the lid and catching Jack up again.

"That's supposed to be for later with your coffee, not right now," he said as he reached his desk and hung his jacket on the back of his chair.

"Can only eat it once, and I've saved some."

"Well, don't let Raj see you with it. He's after a piece. I've told him it's his tomorrow if he can work his magic and get those packet results today." He flung himself into the chair. Stale air escaped in a whoosh at the sudden impact. The chair groaned as he turned in it to face Amanda.

"Sounds like too much cake to me. Even your chair is complaining," she teased him.

"Funny, Lacey. You're just jealous."

"Probably, though I don't need the extra calories right now." She patted her stomach. "Married life brings a couple more glasses of wine here and there, though I'm not complaining."

Jack looked over her shoulder and got to his feet. She turned to see Raj striding towards them. From the look on his face, he wasn't bringing good news.

"Oxy and codeine. High strength," was all he said.

Jack's face fell. "Shit!"

Chapter Twenty-Six

"NO SURPRISES it's a shell company that runs the van."

Raj had been digging most of the morning while Amanda caught up on some massively overdue paperwork. She looked up from the report she was typing. Raj stood by the corner of her desk. Dressed smartly as usual, he looked handsome in a pale blue check shirt that contrasted nicely with his dark skin. Amanda often thought he should have been a GQ model rather than a copper and not because he wasn't good enough. No, Raj had a reputation for his diligence, but he also had a reputation for his good looks. She sat back in her chair.

"Hmm. It's never so easy, is it? Why can't the criminals we have to deal with be a bit more obvious? Make it a wee bit easier for us just for once."

"Sorry, not this time. A bit more digging on this one, I'm afraid. Good old-fashioned leg work. Though I did pick up something along the way, a name. Not sure if it'll lead anywhere but you never know."

"What's that?"

"Well, from what I can tell, there could be a link to the north – Manchester, actually. One of the names that popped up in the background was linked to a bust some years back, though nothing came of it. Might be worth chatting to your buddies up there to see if they know of anything like this on their patch. I'm guessing a similar system with the food vans. There's probably more of them up there than there are down here."

"Worth a chat. Give me the name."

Raj handed over a slip of paper and Amanda sat thoughtful for a moment. "Thanks Raj."

"Let me know, eh?" he said over his shoulder as he began walking back to his desk.

Manchester.

She knew a couple of the detectives in Manchester. She and Jack had worked on a case there together in the past. The infamous Sebastian Stevens had become a trophy for a different type of hunter, and the case had introduced her to DS Duncan Riley and DS Rick Black. The whole case had become a little too close for comfort when her friend Stephanie had become involved, though she herself had escaped unharmed. But both Rick and Duncan were competent detectives. In fact, Rick, who looked remarkably like Buddy Holly, was on a fast-track program to becoming a DI. He'd mused that he might find himself promoted to Croydon in the near future and become her direct boss. While she had no problem with him being younger than her, she'd wondered about his worldly-wise experience. Had he had enough to be a decent DI? 'Dopey' Dupin sprang to mind. His own youth hadn't done him too much harm, though his nickname wasn't particularly confidence-building or flattering.

Her stomach growled like an old dog. Perhaps another bacon sandwich from a mobile van? She called over to Jack, who was fiddling with a coffee capsule that was stuck in the chamber. He had a knife in his hand trying to pull it back up and out. Amanda shook her head in amazement. For a fine detective, he found basic things a challenge at times.

"I'll buy you one. It'll be quicker. Grab your jacket."

He didn't need asking twice and left the offending capsule in situ for someone else to wrestle with. He hadn't seen Dupin making his way in, mug in hand, but Amanda had. While Jack caught her up, she made her own quick exit out into the corridor, encouraging Jack to quicken his pace after her. He had the good sense not to yell at her to slow down. Perhaps he had seen Dupin on his tail after all.

When they were both out in the car park, Jack finally asked where they were going.

"Raj reckons this van might be linked to a set-up up north, around Manchester," Amanda told him. "It seems a company name that was thrown up with his search was linked to another drugs case last year up there, but nothing was proved. My guess is the two are connected. No smoke without fire, or in this case no pills without pain. I'm going back for another look, see who's working the counter. Might even mention I've a headache or something – you never know. Now we know there is probably something going on, we need to take a closer look and do a bit of fishing."

"You spoken to Manchester yet?

"No. Thought I would after this. Needed a bacon roll anyway." She turned and smiled at Jack, who was never one to turn bacon down. "Figured you'd like one too."

Amanda walked across to the van to place their order. Jack watched from the car, trying his best to take photos without being seen. As usual, there was a queue, and apart from an elderly couple, everyone else looked like regular business people. They all wore the same style of uniform, male or female: standard dark suit, pale shirt or blouse. The only thing that differed was age and shoe style. Amanda joined the back of the line and turned her ears up high in the hope of eavesdropping on a useful morsel. But nobody was talking, not to each other at any rate. The only conversation she heard was when an order was placed and the server asked about sauce colour.

"Yes, love?" the server enquired, taking her away from her thoughts. The man was dressed in chef whites with a matching cap. "What can I get you?"

"Well, if you could deal with my stonking headache, that would be handy." She smiled up at him sweetly. The man looked unsure how to respond to her request. Amanda took the opportunity to study his face as he processed what she'd said. His eyes darted rapidly to his sidekick further inside the van.

Amanda pressed on, this time in a hushed tone. "I don't suppose you have any painkillers, do you? And I'll have two bacon rolls wrapped separately as well." That perfectly innocent smile again. Did his face register what she meant or was she mistaken? Hopeful, but maybe mistaken. Finally, he spoke.

"Sorry, love, I don't have anything," he said, and turned to make up the two rolls, though not before she caught his glance again to his partner at his side. When the two bags were ready, she paid her money and turned to walk back to the car where Jack sat watching the proceedings. As she climbed in, she noticed him staring at a young man approaching the car. With a start, she realized he had been behind her in line. Amanda rolled her window down for him. He looked to both sides and then leaned closer to speak.

"If you have a bad headache," he started, "You'll need to ask for something a little more specific, like special sauce. That's all they need to hear. Too many pigs about; have to be careful."

Amanda slowly nodded her understanding.

"Thanks. Good to know. What about payment?" She took a bite of her sandwich, carrying on with the pantomime.

"Get the app," he said briskly and walked away. They watched as he got into his own car and drove out of the layby.

Jack raised an eyebrow at Amanda. "Well, if prostitutes have apps now, I guess it's only natural progression drug dealers do too. Special sauce, eh?"

Amanda, with a mouthful of food, could only nod in amazement.

Chapter Twenty-Seven

Back at the station, Jack and Amanda made a bee-line for their desks.

"I'll get straight on to GMP, see what they know. You get on to cyber. Or is it drug squad? Could be either." Without waiting for a response, she dialled Rick Black's number. He picked up on the third ring.

"DS Black here."

"Rick, hello, it's DS Amanda Lacey from South Croydon. Remember me?"

"Of course I do, Amanda. Not an easy lady to forget. Or case, for that matter." There was laughter in his voice and she couldn't help but smile a little at the phone. "That sounds ominous. What did I do to be so memorable?"

"Kicked butt, if I remember rightly. Another madwoman behind bars. How are you, anyway, and what can I do for you?"

"I'm great, thanks. Got married recently and I'm back busy at work as usual, which is why I'm ringing you."

"Congratulations, Amanda. Now what can I help you with?"

"I thought I'd ask and see what your local drug dealers are up to currently, but not your old-school crack gangs. I'm talking the newer breed, the opiate pushers, oxy and the like. What's happening on that front near you?"

"Well, I can tell you there is definitely a market and a distribution. Drug squad could tell you more. Can you be more specific?"

"Just following a hunch, though we did find some little empty packets in a public rubbish bin that tested positive for high-strength oxy and codeine. I'm thinking a food van nearby might be involved. Orders are placed with a bacon roll, transactions paid for possibly via an app rather than cash. Know of anything like that on your patch?" Amanda could hear a clicking on the other end of the receiver. She imagined his pen tapping his desk, a habit she remembered he had. It stopped as he began to speak again.

"What makes you think of Manchester. Something linking it back up here?"

"Yes, two things, actually. You're not far from the Irish Sea – not that we have any reason to think that's how it's getting in, but it's convenient. We also traced a company, though rather tenuously, back to a name from your area. Not directly of course, but his name came up from a previous case that, as usual for him, went nowhere."

"Oh? Who's that?"

"Wilfred Day."

Rick let out a long whistling breath through his teeth and stayed silent for a moment.

"Are you still there, Rick?"

"Yeah, just thinking. He's like damn Teflon that one. Nothing sticks to him. Slips around like a fried egg in a greasy pan." Amanda smiled at the analogy. Why did detectives have such vivid imaginations when it came to descriptions? Jack was just the same.

"What's he like?"

"You mean other than slippery?"

"Yes, what's he like generally? Hard man, local mob, what?"

"He's one of the most politely spoken, well-dressed blond-haired blue-eyed thirty-something men you could ever meet. To look at him you'd say he came from money, probably a finance background or similar, complete with diamond-patterned sweater, chinos, and nicely polished brogues. Your typical hard man stereotype he's not. Far from it."

"So why has he never been pinged?"

"You mean apart from probably buying off everyone that he can? The juries he's been in front of love him. He comes across as sweet-natured, funny, articulate, and they lap it up. Lap *him* up."

"And that's not the real him." It wasn't a question, more a statement.

"Correct. He might be baby faced and smartly dressed, but behind those blue eyes of his is a ferocious brain working overtime. Kneecapping and grunt work is not his style, but he's clever, all right, and employs other clever people, of the technically clever type. Hackers and the like, those that can infiltrate bank accounts and data and hit the competition in their pockets rather than their balls. Less mess, less evidence, and probably gets results a lot quicker.

"Sounds like a saint. And he operates in opiates in the main or something else?"

"He's like all the rest in that respect, running women and booze, but yes, drugs are his forte. I've not known him to deal with heroin and the like. Not for some time, actually. Maybe they've split the turf into substances instead of geographical area. Opiates attract a more discerning clientele than Skank and heroin. I wouldn't be surprised if he was bringing in fentanyl too."

"That's a worry, then. It's really hard to tell heroin and fentanyl apart. They're almost identical to look at."

"Tell me about it. We have the deaths to prove it. It's the quantity that causes the deaths. A lethal dose of heroin could be thirty milligrams, but with fentanyl, you're only talking three milligrams to overdose and kill someone −barely enough to cover the bottom of a test tube. Mistakes get made, I know. I've cleaned up the bodies."

"Christ, let's hope he's not responsible for distributing that." Amanda fell thoughtful for a moment, pondering her next question. "So, do you know how his distribution works, how he's selling it?"

"Typically, he's had women mainly, that I know of − your stereotype 'soccer moms' looking to earn some money while they mind the kids all day." Amanda could almost see him making speech quotes in the air with his fingers. He went on, "I daresay they are probably customers too. Getting high is the fashionable thing to do with their bored glamorous buddies. But I'm only talking oxy and codeine now, not fentanyl. And he's had a few students working for him too, looking to earn beer money without doing much. Easy money until they get caught."

"How about food vans, perhaps?" Amanda wasn't sure what she wanted the answer to be.

"Not heard anything, but that doesn't mean no. Ice cream vans and food vans have been used in the past for both booze and drugs distribution, but it did get cleaned up. So, have you got something going on down your way?"

"Not sure yet. Just those empty packets testing positive. If the vans are dealing, it could be a lucrative outlet for someone, and if others get wind of it, it could get a whole lot busier around here."

"I'm afraid so. Well, thanks for letting me know what's happening. Hey, keep in touch eh?" The pen was clicking again in the background.

"I will, and thanks for the info. Say hello to Duncan for me."

"Will do." Then he was gone.

Jack was hovering like a spaceship.

"That was interesting, what I could hear of it. What next, Boss?"

Jack never called her Boss – unless he was feeling stumped and was hoping she had the next move.

"No idea."

Chapter Twenty-Eight

DUNCAN DROVE SLOWLY past the park. The traffic behind him on the busy road was impatient; drivers gesticulated rudely as they cruised past in the adjacent lane, wondering who was being such a slow-moving dick. If they had known he was a police officer looking for missing children, they might have been a tad more forgiving, but everyone these days only cared for themselves. As it was, they were all in a hurry to get from A to B and he was in the way, holding them up from something pressing – like morning takeaway coffee.

Another horn blared. He ignored it. Up ahead, he could see the main gates to the park and indicated to pull over. The clicking was almost hypnotic. A light drizzle was falling again, clinging to everything it touched. On a day like today, the park would be empty, dogs 'in need' having to make do with a quick in and out on a nearby grass verge or in their backyard. Duncan didn't care about the dampness as he entered the park and paced down the main path. Finding his girls was more important. Up ahead he could see a uniformed officer who had joined in the search and he sped his pace up to a slow jog to catch him up. As he got closer, he called out to the officer.

"Any luck?" He knew the answer – someone would have called him – but still he was hopeful.

"Sorry, nothing yet," the officer said. His badge said PC Daniels. Duncan knew he would be wanting to say something more reassuring but couldn't. Adding your own comments like 'I'm sure they will be fine,' or 'I promise we'll get them back,' was something police officers avoided at all costs. It always came back to haunt you if, in the end, things didn't turn out to be fine. Daniels gave Duncan a sympathetic look. His radio chirped, neatly breaking the awkward pause.

A scratchy voice said something he couldn't catch.

"Repeat that please, over," Daniels said.

"Call from a woman on Hyde Road. She has two young girls. Can you attend?"

"What number?"

He and Duncan ran together back towards the gate as the reply came back. When they reached Duncan's car, he yelled at Daniels to get in. Duncan threw the car into reverse and hurtled out onto the busy main road towards the number they'd been given – and hopefully his two children.

The house was only a couple of minutes from where they had been, overlooking the park.

"There, on the steps!" Daniels yelled, pointing to an elderly woman on the front steps, and Duncan did a U-turn to get across. Angry motorists blared their horns but he ignored them, pulled up on the pavement directly outside and leapt from the car. He ploughed up the front steps two at a time, almost knocking the woman flying, Daniels on his heels.

"Are they okay? Are they hurt?" he asked as he pushed past her. There in front of the fire, eating biscuits and drinking warm cordial, were his two little girls, faces still pink from the cold morning air.

"Daddy, Daddy!" they squealed delightedly and leapt to their feet. Both girls flung their arms around his neck and he squeezed them tightly, then held them at arm's length, swallowing back tears.

"We got a bit far away. Have you come to take us home?" Victoria asked. Duncan took both their small hands in his big ones and squeezed affectionately.

"I have, my darlings. But first, tell me what you've been up to." He smiled encouragingly so they wouldn't think they were in trouble, which they weren't. But he wanted to know the story. The old woman stepped forward.

"Perhaps I should tell you," she suggested. "Won't you sit down?"

The other officer, who was standing to one side, took his notebook. Duncan sat on the old sofa with Victoria and Jasmine each on a knee. He gave them another joint hug and Jasmine giggled. For some reason, the woman looked familiar, though he couldn't place her.

"I saw them from my window upstairs," the woman said. "Playing in the park they were. It was cold, so I went over. There was no one with them. So I said I'd make warm juice if they'd like some. And they did. And then I called the police. I figured they shouldn't be out on their own." Her voice croaked with age and something more, something like emotion perhaps.

PC Daniels put his arm around her and gently guided her to sit in the big chair by the fire. The crochet blanket on the back of it told him the chair was hers. Then she began to weep softly. A siren could be heard in the near distance, then car doors banging outside, so Daniels went out to the front door where more uniforms were arriving. Duncan could hear voices. One of them was Rochelle.

He turned to his two girls. "I'm just glad you're both all right. But we need to go home now, so say thank you to the lovely lady for the juice." He forced a bright smile onto his face.

"Thank you for the juice," they both said dutifully, but the old woman had her head in her hands and was crying gently. Rochelle walked in at that moment and took the situation in. Duncan guessed that Daniels had briefly filled her in. She nodded at Duncan, indicating that he was to leave and she'd look after the woman and take some further notes. Together, he and his girls left the warm comfort of the lounge and headed out to his car. The cold, wet air suddenly didn't seem so wet on his skin as he opened the rear door, helped them both in and fastened their seatbelts.

Even though he was happy to have them both back safely, he knew that he now had to deal with Sam.

Chapter Twenty-Nine

DRIVING the short distance home with the girls safely strapped into their seats behind him, Duncan' thoughts tossed around his head like a tumble drier. Relief had flooded his system when he'd seen his daughters' pink little faces, that his babies were indeed safe and well after their adventure, that nothing sinister had happened to them. He knew full well that, with two children still missing and a predator out there, that his situation could have turned into something devastatingly heart-wrenching. He gave silent thanks as he drove, raising his eyes for a moment to the sky as he did so.

Now he had to decide what to do about Sam, though: be thankful or be angry? The only thing he felt right at this moment was thankful, but he knew when he saw her face his emotions would flash over to anger at her incompetence, her laziness, her sloppiness. To have allowed such a thing to happen in the first place was inconceivable. She had one job, and one job only while she was unemployed – to look after the children and the house – and it seemed she couldn't even manage that. Honestly, lying in bed and oversleeping until 9 a.m.? What had possessed her to do such a thing, on a school day particularly? She wasn't ill, so why? *Why?*

It was true their relationship hadn't been good in some time.

They'd both changed over the last year or so. He had been working some difficult cases and staying away late, and then Sam had lost her job and been staying around the house most of the day. She'd appeared to enjoy the time initially, but things had gradually tumbled into disarray, and look where they were now. Yes, he still cared for her, but did he feel anything more towards her? he wondered. Did he still fancy her, find her attractive? He knew the answer was no. They hadn't been close in many months; neither of them had wanted to make the move, and neither wanted to risk the rejection.

As he turned into Clumber Road, Sam was stood out on the front path, still dressed in her pyjamas. Her friend Anika was by her side, arm draped around Sam's shoulders for support, he assumed. Sam rushed forward as he pulled up, arms wide, wailing loudly. Victoria was already opening her door.

"Thank God you're both safe! Where have you been?" Sam buried her face into Victoria's hair and, as Jasmine came around the car, grabbed her too and pulled them both close. Noisy, gulping sobs came from her mouth.

At last Sam stood, and Duncan ushered the small group back inside towards privacy. He turned to Anika.

"Thanks for taking care of her," he said, and she nodded her understanding.

No longer needed, Anika called to Sam that she'd call later and left, though whether Sam heard her or not, who could tell? She didn't respond. Once Anika had left, Duncan closed the door behind them and headed into the lounge where Sam was now taking the girls' coats off. Her face was red from crying, her eyes swollen; she looked terrible. Duncan stood for a moment and didn't say a thing; he just looked at her. When had she last washed her hair? he wondered. That was old dirt and grease, meaning Sam had missed more than just today's shower. And why wasn't she dressed? Had she gone back to bed after she'd called him? Surely not.

She looked up at him and caught his eye, gave him a weak smile that he tried hard to return. Tears were starting to well in her eyes again, threatening to spill over. He stepped over to her and pulled her in close for a hug. Her face was hot against his cheek as she sobbed again, her shoulders shaking as she cried. Automatically he brushed her head with his hand to soothe her as she tried to tell him that she was sorry. He'd loved Sam once, even if he wasn't sure he did now. They had a history, a family together, but as he held her close waiting for the tears to stop, the ball of disappointment sat heavy in his gut. Finally, she pulled away a little.

"Here," he said, handing her his handkerchief. He caught the strong smell of old sweat and tried not to wrinkle his nose. Instead, he stepped away and began to turn towards the kitchen – away from her.

"I'll make some tea. Why don't you go and have a shower, get dressed and we can talk? I'm not going back to the station just yet."

Sam's face morphed into a mask of hatred so suddenly that he stepped back.

"You're going back to work!? Really? What a wanker!" she screamed.

Duncan stood stock still, aghast. Her face was a deep purple, her lips drawn back in a snarl. Sam looked nothing the woman he'd married.

She carried on, filling Duncan's surprised silence. "Have you no time for your own children, Duncan? Because perhaps if you did, they wouldn't have gone walkabout this morning, now, would they!" Sam picked up a mug from the coffee table and threw it across the room. Brown liquid splashed up the wallpaper as shards of china dropped to the carpet. Duncan watched, mesmerized, as cold tea ran in rivulets towards the floor. He couldn't quite believe his eyes or his ears.

Sam was blaming him for the girls' disappearance.

He finally found his voice.

"I don't fucking believe you're putting the blame on me! You were the one looking after them. You were the one that lay in bed oversleeping. You were the one with the responsibility of keeping them safe! You, Sam, you! You have one job! *One job!* And you can't even manage that," he screamed at her. He could feel that his face was almost as red as hers.

But Sam was in the mood for a fight and wasn't about to back down. With crazy in her eyes, she screamed back at him. "They're not always my fucking responsibility. They're yours too, though you'd never know – you're never fucking here!"

Duncan opened his mouth to respond and was horrified to hear the sound of a child crying. *Oh God.* Victoria and Jasmine were still in the room. His heart in his mouth, Duncan went over to them and bent down, clasping them both in his arms. Out of the corner of his eye, he saw Sam looking on.

"I'm sorry for arguing," he said, ashamed. "You aren't meant to hear us shouting. That's wrong of us." As calmly as he could, Duncan suggested they both go upstairs and play for a while until their mummy and daddy had finished talking. And as a special treat for being good girls, they could choose what they ate for dinner later. He and Sam watched as the girls left the room, and then Duncan turned back to Sam. At least the girls had taken the wind out of her sails for the time being; she no longer resembled something possessed.

"I work Sam, to feed this family. That's my job. Your job is to look after this family while I'm not around. When you get a job, that role is split between the both of us, with probably some outside help like other families manage. But since you don't have a job, you're it. Can I make it any plainer? Do you get that?"

"Oh, I get it, all right. I'm at fault again," she said snidely.

"In this instance, yes, you are. While you were lying in bed, they," he pointed up towards the girls' bedrooms, "they managed to get out and walk to the park. With a suspected child abductor running loose, I might add. So yes, it was your fault. What were you thinking?"

"Fuck off," Sam shot back as she turned and headed up the stairs. Duncan heard the slamming of their bedroom door above and rolled his tired eyes at the ceiling. He flopped into a nearby chair to think. This wasn't how it was meant to be. Something had to change. *Sam* had to change. When she'd calmed down, he'd talk to her again and spell out their future together.

If they had one.

Chapter Thirty

IT WAS over an hour later when Sam finally made it back down the stairs, though she still hadn't cleaned herself up. In her absence, Duncan had picked up the smashed mug and wiped the wall down, and generally tidied the room up while the girls quietly watched cartoons on TV. The depressing rain had finally stopped and a weak sunshine was trying its best to warm the front room. At least it was brightening, if not heating. Duncan stayed put on the sofa. His shoulders sagged wearily with the weight of the day. He waited for her to speak.

"I thought you'd have gone by now, back to work." She sauntered over to the vacant chair and slumped down on it, gathering her feet up beneath her, not really looking his way. He could see her face was still red and blotchy from the tears, but he had stopped feeling sorry for her. He let her comment go without rebuff.

"You were sleeping, I assumed, so I couldn't leave them." His voice was steady and even, with no amplification. Just the facts.

"Well, I'm up now, so why don't you go? I'm sure you've plenty to be doing."

Duncan watched her as she pretended to be watching cartoons, looking anywhere rather than at him. "I'll perhaps go in later. But now you're up, I want to talk to you properly, without either of us shouting."

"Oh? You think we can manage that, do you?"

The sarcasm wasn't lost on Duncan, but he ignored it. When she saw he wasn't going to rise to her malice, she visibly lowered her shoulders. Duncan turned to the girls. "Why don't you play upstairs for a while? Then we can go for pizza if you like."

"Yeah!" they cheered, then stood and headed to their rooms. Duncan shouted after them, "I'll call you when it's time to go, okay?"

"Okay, Dad," they replied. Like two peas in a pod, two coffee beans in a jar. He smiled, despite himself. When they were finally out of earshot, Duncan leaned forward on the sofa, head lowered, hands hanging in front of him. He'd spent some time, while Sam had been upstairs, thinking through what he wanted to say, and the best way to say it. Now, his practiced words had gone astray, and he searched his head for some clear space. It was full of missing children it seemed, though not his two anymore.

"Sam," he began. "We can't go on like this. Today has been a disaster, a worrying, emotionally draining disaster. We both know that, and I'm not about to point the finger at you again. Let's put it down to a bad experience, and one we'd both rather forget, I'm sure." He looked up at her from under his brows. She was listening. He carried on. "But things have to change, and soon. Things between us haven't been that great for some time now, since you lost your job probably, and I feel for you, really I do."

Sam scoffed, "Oh, great. Thanks very much. Here we go again."

"But that's when things changed, Sam, like it or not. And I'm not prepared to go on as we have been. Either you clean your act up and sort yourself out, or I'm out of here. I mean it, Sam." He was looking straight at her now, wondering what effect his words would have on her. There was no easy way to say he really wanted to leave, didn't like what she'd become, so he'd stuck with the basics – for now.

But true to form, that was more than enough to set her off again.

"I don't fucking believe it! You're threatening to leave me and the kids because I lost my job? Are you that fucking mean?"

"That's not what I said and you know it. I said things hadn't been good since then but yes, if things don't change, yes, I'm considering leaving."

He watched as she leapt up from her spot and paced over to the window, then turned and faced him full on. Her eyes flamed with rage and spittle flew from her lips. So much venom, so much anger; she really did look like a woman possessed. Again.

"Well, if you're that unhappy, why don't you fuck off now, eh? You're never around much anyway, so you may as well leave us. I'm sure one of the girls at work would let you stay on her sofa." She paused and gave him an evil smile. "Or her bed. I'm sure Rochelle wouldn't kick you out in a hurry."

Duncan felt himself grow pale. Sure, he found Rochelle attractive; most men did. But he'd never done anything behind Sam's back, ever. His family was precious to him and he'd scowled at other colleagues for playing away from home. It wasn't right.

"Ah, come on, you know there's never been anything going on there, or with anyone from work, or anyone else, full stop, actually." He was starting to lose his cool, aware his voice was escalating in pitch and volume again. He didn't want the girls to overhear his words but he wanted to respond, needed to.

"And you know that deep down. Sam, this is about us. You've got to clean your act up, get some help from someone, get your life back. All I see every time I come home is you in your nightclothes. You don't look like you've even had a shower for a couple of days, and your anger has skyrocketed. Whatever I say, you fly into a rage so quickly, it's frightening. What the hell has got in to you?" He took a breath and then carried on, momentum pushing him to complete what he had to say. "If things haven't changed in one month's time, I'm leaving. That gives you time to sort yourself out and at least be applying for a new job. After that, if there's no change, I'm taking the girls with me and we're leaving." Duncan bowed his head.

Barely audible, Sam confirmed, "One month. Then you're taking the girls."

"Yes. And I'm deadly serious. We will leave."

Wordlessly, Sam turned on her heel and ran back upstairs to the bedroom. Duncan heard the door slam once again and hung his head in despair. He had hoped it wouldn't come to this.

Chapter Thirty-One

SAM WAS angry and upset all at the same time. In the privacy of the bedroom, she alternated between pacing with clenched fists and a screwed-up, furious face and sobbing in desperation, tears streaming down her cheeks. She was drained. Drained of energy and drained of feeling, though not for her children. Tired of pacing, Sam lay on the bed and buried her face in the pillow where she screamed out her frustration in short bursts, safe in the knowledge no one could hear her.

When the tears finally stopped, she stayed face down, eyes closed, waiting for the world to go away. What she wouldn't do for some help right now, a little something to knock her out, something to numb her, if only for a couple of hours, but she had nothing left. The side pocket of her handbag was empty again. If she hadn't taken her last six that morning, she'd have had something to take the edge off now, but they were gone. She couldn't leave the house, she knew, so there was no way to get what she desperately needed, not yet anyway. No, she'd have to wait and slip out later when he'd gone to work. Maybe Anika would keep an eye on the girls for ten while she went. Yes, that's what she'd do – drive out later tonight.

Safe in the knowledge she'd get some relief later, she turned over and stared up at the ceiling in the growing dusk. Winter days were so short; sometimes the sun never reached full brightness before fading away again in the late afternoon. Soon, the street lamps would come on again, giving her unlit room an eerie yellow-orange glow. In her head, she went over what Duncan had said. How could he have been so mean, show so little understanding of what she was going through? And now he'd given her an ultimatum – get sorted or he was leaving and taking Victoria and Jasmine with him. That was the part that stung the most: the thought of losing the girls, not having them by her side each day, not taking them to school and picking them up again, not going for burgers with them. It would be soul-destroying.

No, she needed to figure this out – get a job and get back into Duncan's good books, show him she could change, that he could love her, be attracted to her again, that they'd both be all right, that they could be a proper functioning family again. And soon. Sam sat up on the bed with new energy, a new motivation, swung her legs over the edge and headed towards the bedroom door. She opened it quietly and stood listening for voices or movement, unsure how long she'd been lying on the bed. Maybe Duncan and the girls had gone out for pizza without her. Was she all alone?

She tiptoed across the landing towards the bathroom. Victoria's door was wide open, the room empty, as was Jasmine's. Maybe they were all downstairs. In the bathroom, she wiped her blotchy face and stood for a moment gazing at the woman who stared back from the mirror. Her mousy hair was greasy and lank, as Duncan had so eloquently pointed out earlier, her nightclothes faded and worn – she looked hideous. And she stank.

She padded out of the bathroom and quietly headed downstairs, hoping none of the boards would creak, holding her breath until she got to the bottom. There were no lights under doors, no flickering blue light of a TV screen, no sounds of any kind. She put her ear to the lounge door and heard nothing. She turned the handle and peered inside.

The room was indeed empty – they had all gone out. She was alone.

Sam let out a deep breath. "Thank fuck for that," she said to the empty room, as she turned a lamp on in the corner. The clock on the wall said it was coming up to 4:30. It would be dark in a few minutes.

She leaned towards the window to see if Duncan's car was parked out the front or on the drive – both spaces were empty.

But had he just gone for pizza? Or had he packed a few things while she'd slept? Had she slept? With the sudden realization he could have already left, she flew from the lounge and back upstairs. She ran into Jasmine's room and flung open the wardrobe. Frantically, she assessed the contents: backpack and shoes still there, clothing still there. She bolted into Victoria's room; everything was still there, too. She let out another deep breath. Nothing was missing. They hadn't gone for good. This time.

Her heart was still pounding. She realized she had been as terrified, just now, as she had been earlier that morning when the girls had gone missing. No, this wouldn't do at all. This was a feeling she never wanted to have again, one to be avoided at all costs. With a new feeling of determination, she headed back to the bathroom and a much-needed shower. If she was going to change the status quo at home, she needed to start right now. Nobody, not anybody, was going to take her children away from her. Not ever.

As steam filled the room and Sam stood under the hot water, another option came to her. A slight smile played on her mouth as it developed into something resembling a plan. Slowly she carried on soaping herself, replacing her sour smell with lemon zest, her idea filling her with fresh new hope. Her mother had always said there was more than one way to skin a cat, and Sam had just realized what that other way would be.

Get rid of Duncan.

Chapter Thirty-Two

DUNCAN and the girls were nearly home. They'd gone out for pizza together and then stopped off for ice cream. Victoria and Jasmine were side by side in their booster seats in the back seat. Patting her stomach, Victoria exclaimed, "I'm stuffed, Daddy. Do you think I'll be sick?"

Laughing lightly, Duncan replied, "I hope not, because that would mean a waste of pizza and a messy car."

Jasmine piped up, "And stinky too. You'd be stinky."

Both girls began giggling, and Duncan joined in, shaking his head and thoroughly enjoying himself. As he turned into Clumber Road, he realized he hadn't had so much fun in a while.

"We should do this more often, just the three of us. What do you say?"

A chorus of "Yeah!" filled the car as he pulled into the driveway and parked up. The girls leapt out of the vehicle and dashed to the front door. It opened, and Duncan saw Sam standing there. She was showered and dressed, he noted with surprise. Perhaps their conversation earlier had had an effect. He watched as she bent to give the girls a kiss on the cheek each as they passed through and stood to one side as Duncan approached.

"They look happy," she said to him. "What did you do for dinner?"

"Pizza and ice cream − every kid's dream." He wasn't frosty as he replied, but he wasn't exactly warm either. "They might be on a sugar high for an hour or so but I figured today hadn't been like any other and they deserved a treat."

He carried on through to the lounge, gathering the girls' coats to put back in the cupboard. The girls were fizzing with giggly energy; Jasmine was bouncing up and down on the sofa. Duncan hadn't the heart to tell her to slow down so he ignored it.

"I'll go and run you a bubble bath, then you can read for a while before sleep, okay?" he told them, to a chorus of groans. "I think you've had enough fun for one day, and reading is good for you, remember? It makes the brain bigger, so you get to be cleverer than the other kids at school."

How many lies did parents tell their children while they were growing up, he mused? Father Christmas and the Easter Bunny were two straight off, never mind carrots making you see in the dark and crusts making curls in your hair. What hogwash. The biggest lie that Duncan had found out while growing up was there really wasn't a tooth fairy either, having caught his dad putting money under his pillow in exchange for a tooth. He'd worked hard on dislodging it fully in anticipation of seeing what the tooth fairy looked like and hadn't been expecting his dad that night. From then on, he'd questioned all of the major events a child looked forward to, his inquisitive mind demanding to know the real answers, and as his parents couldn't come up with proof that any of these mythical beings did exist, that had been the end of that.

He herded the girls up the stairs and went into the bathroom to start running their bath. He focused on adding bubble gum-scented bubbles to the bath water and stared into them as they formed on the surface, steam rising and clinging to the window. By the time bath time had finished, the glass would be running rivers of moisture down onto the tiled sill like fresh tears pooling. Maybe the room could sense the emotion in the house. He swished the water round; the temperature was just right. Standing at the bathroom door, he called them both.

"Bath is ready − Victoria, Jasmine!"

As they trotted in and began to undress, he left the room to gather their nightclothes and give them some privacy. He let them bathe in peace, leaving the door open so he could hear them from the bedroom next door. When they were dried and dressed, he'd go back in.

He sat on the end of the bed and listened to their girl talk. They were seemingly unaware he was close by.

"Do you think Mummy is all right?" Jasmine asked.

"I think so. Grownups cry sometimes. I know Kate's mum cries all the time – she told me."

"Why?"

"Tummy ache sometimes, I think. Grownups get tummy ache too."

"Oh."

Duncan couldn't help smiling at their naivety; they had so much yet to learn about life and growing up. He heard Sam climbing the stairs and he watched her as she put her head around the door and chatted briefly with them. To his surprise, she came and sat down next to him on the bed.

"Are you feeling a bit better?" he asked.

Without turning she replied that she was, that she had taken a shower and felt better, that she was sorry for yelling.

Duncan nodded mutely. After a couple of minutes of silence, he said, "I'm going into work for a couple of hours shortly. Will you be okay?"

"I'll be fine. We'll be fine. I'll probably be asleep when you get back. It's been a draining day."

"Yes, yes it has," he agreed.

The girls came out of the bathroom, struggling into their nighties. Behind them, water gurgled noisily down the plughole.

"Right," he told Sam. "I'll say goodnight to them, and I'll be off."

When Sam heard the front door close behind him, she went back down the stairs to find her phone and dialled Anika's number.

"Would you mind coming over for an hour? Only I need to pop out and Duncan is at work. The girls are both tucked up asleep."

Anika asked if she was all right.

"Yes, yes, I'm fine. I just need to nip to the all-night chemist." She waited for Anika's response.

"Great. See you soon."

Sam knew that her youth, her swollen eyes and her haggard look meant the night chemist probably wouldn't question handing over a packet of strong codeine-filled painkillers.

That was what she was banking on, anyway. But first she'd have to find a chemist who didn't recognize her as a recent visitor.

Chapter Thirty-Three

DUNCAN LEFT the house feeling a little brighter himself. He was pleased that Sam had had a shower and got dressed, even though it was nearly time to go back to bed. It was a start, though; he hoped his words had hit home.

The streets were dark save for the amber-yellow haze of the street-lights, and on a cold damp evening, there weren't too many people out, on foot or otherwise. He was in the station car park and parked up in only a handful of minutes. He scanned the other vehicles to see who else was working and noticed Rochelle's black Triumph motorbike sat in the corner. It always made him smile; she was the perfect type of woman to ride such a thing – hot, fast and not to be messed with. He pushed the thought away quickly. He needed to keep a clear head.

The corridor into the building was quiet as he headed to the squad room and his desk. Rochelle saw him arrive and sauntered over, her head cocked questioningly to one side.

"What are you doing here? We didn't expect you in tonight."

"I had to get out the house. And the girls are fine after their adventure so I thought I'd come in for a couple of hours. There are still a couple of children out there needing our help." He gave a weak smile and Rochelle picked up on his vibe.

"I'm just headed to the canteen. Want a cuppa?"

"Why not? Then you can fill me in where you're up to."

"And you can fill me in on why the long face," she said knowingly.

Duncan lowered his head slightly. "That obvious, eh?"

"I'm a detective too, remember?"

"So you are. But save the interrogation, all right? I've had enough for one day."

"We'll see," she said as they made their way towards the canteen. No matter the time, there was always the smell of coffee brewing or lingering food smells, sometimes good and sometimes, well, not so. Tonight, the odour of curry lingered in the air and Duncan remembered he hadn't eaten. While the girls had stuffed themselves silly, he'd had no appetite; the stresses of their disappearance and then rowing with Sam had seen to that. But now his stomach was catching up with him.

"Have you eaten?" he asked Rochelle. "That curry smells good."

"I had some earlier, but you go ahead. It wasn't bad, actually." She placed their order – a plate of chicken curry for Duncan, a mug of tea for herself. The cashier looked bored stiff, waiting for her shift to be up so she could go home. They made their way to a deserted table in the middle of the functional dining-cum-relaxation room and Duncan sat down heavily on a plastic chair. A 'whoosh' escaped his lungs involuntarily.

"So, what happened at home? You look like shit."

Duncan smiled. Rochelle was never one to mince words. "You're too kind. Just feeling pretty deflated and a little wrung out. The girls are safe and well..." Duncan let the sentence hang in the air.

"Go on," Rochelle probed. "I can sense there's more."

"Sam and I are most certainly not."

"How so? What happened this time?"

"I told her it was her fault they had gone. It was on her lookout and she dropped the ball completely."

"Ouch. That wouldn't have gone down well, I'm assuming." Her tea arrived and she wrapped her hands around the mug like it was a comfort blanket and took a sip while the cashier informed Duncan his curry was en route. He watched the bored woman saunter back to the kitchen to await his plate for delivery. Absentmindedly, he wondered about her life for a moment or two, what she had to go home to. Did she have someone? Not everyone did. He was aware Rochelle had stopped chatting.

"Sorry. I was miles away. What did you say?"

Raising her voice slightly, she said, "I said I assume that didn't go down well, you saying it was her fault and all."

"No. We rowed, and I threw her an ultimatum." The cashier returned and placed his curry in front of him. He picked up a fork and dug in, scooping rice and tikka masala up in one motion. "Mmm, not bad," he said. He scooped up more with the side of his fork and ate.

"This is like pulling teeth," groaned Rochelle. "What was the ultimatum? Have I got to guess?"

"Sorry, mate. I'm just really hungry. It's been a long day. But to answer your question, I told her if she didn't sort herself out and at least apply for a job or two, I was out and I'd take the girls with me."

He took another forkful and Rochelle watched him as he chewed, waiting for him to swallow and go on. When he didn't, she said, "I'm guessing that didn't go down well either. No wonder you're feeling rough. Have you left her on speaking terms this evening or is it the sofa for you tonight?"

"Well, we're speaking, and when I got back with the girls after pizza, at least she'd had a shower, so my words must have had some effect." He cleared the last forkful of curry into his mouth and Rochelle watched and waited for him to carry on.

"We'll see," he said at last. "I hope she does sort herself out." He put his fork down and wiped his mouth on a serviette. "But I'm serious. I will leave with the girls. I can't trust her. This isn't the first time things have gone haywire since she was made redundant. It's like she's lost her grip on life, and I can't deal with it." Rochelle nodded and he carried on. "I have to know the girls are safe at all times and I don't think that's too much to ask. There's already two children missing. I don't want there to be any more."

"I agree with you there."

There was nothing more to say, really. They stood, ready to get back to work. Duncan realized he was feeling more invigorated for both the chat and a decent meal.

Chapter Thirty-Four

THANK THE LORD FOR ANIKA, Sam thought as she searched for her bag and slipped some shoes on. Since the two lived close by, it would only take her friend a minute or two to get to the house and then Sam could get on with finding a chemist that didn't know her. If she'd had the cash, it would be easier and probably quicker to go to the house for a pill and a cup of pretend tea, but she'd only got £10 in her purse and not a lot in the housekeeping account to draw another lot out. She knew Duncan watched the account and though he'd never asked her to explain every penny, she felt like she should be as inconspicuous as possible so as not to raise his suspicions.

Car headlights came around the corner and she pulled the curtains closed and made her way to the door. As Anika pulled up, Sam scurried over to the car and waited for the engine to stop and her friend to get out.

"Thanks so much, Anika. I owe you one! I'll only be a few minutes, promise," she said gaily as she turned and trotted to her own car. She pressed the fob to unlock it and jumped in quickly before Anika could ask any further questions. She reversed out onto the road and waved airily to Anika, who was now stood in the open doorway. Sam watched in her rear-view mirror as the front door closed. With luck, the girls would be none the wiser that their mother wasn't home.

Again.

Sam drove to the nearest chemist and parked up outside. Through the window she could see a handful of people waiting in line for their prescriptions and contemplated trying her luck. If the pharmacist was busy, he might not give her the third degree about what she needed the tablets for or recognize her from her custom last week. And the previous week. The "terrible period pains" and "bad head" excuses could only work for so long, and she knew she'd likely be getting a sideways glance this time at the very least.

As she watched, a customer came out; that left three others still inside. Undoing her seatbelt, she took a deep breath. She figured she might as well try, because the next chemist was a bit of a drive away and she really didn't want to be out too long. After all, she'd promised Anika she'd only be a few minutes. The cool night air wrapped itself around her as she made her way inside the shop and joined the end of the queue. The pharmacist gave her a cursory glance but nothing more. Had he recognized her fleetingly? Or was she imagining it? Sam kept her head lowered as she shuffled forward to wait her turn to be served, wishing she'd brought a cap to disguise or change her appearance slightly. Was she being paranoid now? As the person in front of her, an elderly woman with a walking stick, turned and made her way slowly towards the door, Sam stepped forward. Her turn now. She did her best to look ill, and frankly this time it wasn't hard: her mouth had gone dry, and the words felt like bricks in her mouth.

"A. . . A. . . A packet of Paramol, please," she stammered. Sam tried for a little eye contact, hoping it would make her look less suspicious, but she knew the pharmacist would ask the question regardless.

"Can I ask what you'll be using them for?"

"Dental pain. I have really bad toothache," she said, and rubbed her lower jaw convincingly.

"Have you used them before?" he enquired, sounding like he was on autopilot. To her relief, he wasn't paying her much attention, simply asking the question to satisfy his professional obligations but too busy to really care about a truthful answer.

"Yes, occasionally." She smiled, but he was looking at his computer screen.

"Seven pounds, please," he said, and she handed over the £10 note. The drugs were almost hers.

"And three pounds change."

She watched as he put the black packet into a paper bag, then reached out as he handed it across the counter and gently took the bag from him, resisting the urge to snatch it, get a handful of tablets inside of her and feel the blessed drug circling around her system as quickly as possible. With the package in her hands, she thanked him and walked back outside as calmly as she could. Another transaction completed successfully.

A small shop was still open just along from the chemist and she went inside to purchase a bottle of water to swallow them down with, then went back to her car. Once inside, she relaxed a little. All would be well with the world in just a few short minutes. Sam opened the bag, then tore open the box and slipped out the blister of tablets. She popped out six tablets and threw them all to the back of her throat, then took a couple of long drags on the bottle of water. The placebo effect was instantaneous: just knowing she had the pills in her stomach made her feel instantly better, and when they did actually kick in, she'd be back home in the comfort of her lounge to feel the full effect.

But there was one task to do before she got home – get rid of the evidence. If Duncan saw the number of packets she was disposing of each week, he'd know something was up. She quickly slipped the rest of the tablets out of their blisters and put them all into the side pocket of her bag, a place Duncan never went. They'd be quite safe there. She put the car in gear and headed home, stopping briefly outside the chip shop to throw the packaging in a bin. She'd smiled at her ingenuity. Maybe being the wife of a detective had its uses after all: she had learned to cover her tracks seamlessly.

With her mission complete, she pulled up on the driveway and went inside the house to thank Anika for covering.

"No problem," Anika said. "Glad I could help. Did you get what you needed?"

"Yes, thanks. Jasmine has a bit of a cough, poor mite. See you tomorrow for coffee maybe?"

Anika was already putting her coat back on and Sam watched as she grabbed her bag and headed for the door.

"Yes. I'll call you tomorrow. I've a few errands to run, so I'm not sure when."

"Okay, see you tomorrow. Drive safely," she said, but Anika was already half way down the path to the curb. Her friend lifted a hand and waved and a moment later was gone. Closing the front door, Sam leaned against it and rested her head back, her eyes closed, and took a couple of long, deep breaths. The pills were starting to take effect.

Just what she needed.

Chapter Thirty-Five

SAM AWOKE sometime during the night in their bed. Duncan was sleeping quietly beside her. She hadn't heard him come home or slip in beside her, but then not much would have wakened her after six tablets. Her mouth was parched and she rolled her tongue around the inside trying to lubricate it, but she knew she needed water. The bedside clock glowed three a.m. and a handful of minutes. The dull sensation of a headache made her wince as she pushed the bedclothes back and silently headed to the bathroom. The house was in darkness save for the eerie glow of the streetlamps; it was just enough light to mark her way without needing to turn another light on. She sat and took a pee, then rinsed her hands in the basin, then filled them like a cup and drank the cold water down, repeating the process to quench her thirst. Her head buzzed. How could that be when she had taken painkillers? she wondered. Shouldn't they dull her pain rather than give her more?

Drying her hands, she padded quietly out into the hall and looked in each of the girls' bedrooms. Both were fast asleep, not a care in the world. Had they been aware of the commotion they'd caused earlier on that morning, when no one knew where they'd gone? Her head vibrated again, and she closed her eyes for a moment to let the stab of pain pass. What with the amount of upset, her continual tears and Duncan's harsh words, was there any wonder her head hurt? She loved both her girls with all her being, and the thought of someone taking them away from her was unbearable, something she couldn't fully imagine and never wanted to experience.

She went back into Victoria's room and lightly kissed her forehead, then gently brushed a couple of stray strands of hair away from the sleeping girl's eyes. Then she tiptoed back into Jasmine's room and did the same.

"Love you both," she murmured into Jasmine's hair, then crept quietly back to her own room. Duncan was still fast asleep as she lay down and pulled the covers up to her chin, staring straight up at the ceiling.

Throb, throb, throb.

She massaged her temple and closed her eyes, willing the pain to go away, but she knew it wouldn't, not yet. Her thoughts went back to Duncan's words, his threat to take the girls – *her* girls – away and leave her behind to fend for herself. How could he be so heartless, so damn mean? She turned her head towards him as he lay there asleep and dared herself to open her eyes again and watch him. Peeling one eye open then the other, she focused on his face, a few inches from her own, so close she could feel his breath on her face. His breath smelled of garlic and she wrinkled her nose in disgust, but carried on watching him, taking in every wrinkle, every pore that she could see in the dim light and etching it in her mind.

What would life be like without him in it? Would it be so terrible? Could she survive without him, without his income? It would be tough, sure, but Duncan worked for CID, meaning if anything happened to him, she and the girls would receive his salary and his pension.

The downside, of course, was that the police looked after their own when something happened. If one of them was murdered, for instance, the whole station and probably beyond would be thrown onto the case, leaving no rocks unturned, as the cliché went. Yes, that's exactly what would happen, she knew. They knew all the tricks, and Samantha knew none. But as she lay there thinking, mulling things over in her mind and listening to his steady breathing, Sam realized there was another way.

If she didn't know the tricks to work with, she'd find someone else who had.

The kitchen was cold but that didn't bother her as she filled a glass at the sink and looked out into the darkness. It made her wonder about death, and what it would feel like. Was there really a bright light that beckoned the dying to come towards it? Was there an afterlife, a heaven, some sort of reunion with the Divine? Or was there nothing at all, just a big black hole that everyone fell into, without feeling anything, without knowing anything, like turning a switch off?

Sam glanced at her glass of water she was still holding and remembered why she was in the cold kitchen at gone three in the morning in the first place.

Another tablet.

And some research.

Chapter Thirty-Six

IT WAS NEARLY five thirty in the morning when she looked up from her computer screen as someone entered the kitchen. Duncan stood in the doorway, blurry-eyed but quite awake, a confused look on his face. She answered his unspoken question.

"Couldn't sleep and didn't want to disturb you so I came down here."

Duncan rubbed his fleecy cotton-clad arms against the cold.

"You must be frozen," he said. "The heating is only just coming on. How long have you been up?" Duncan entered the room fully and headed over to flick the kettle on.

"Sometime around three, I think, then I kind of lost track of time until you just walked in. I didn't realize I'd been sat here so long," She smiled at him as she stood and closed her laptop lid, then busied herself getting mugs from the cupboard and teabags from the canister nearby.

"Shall I put you some toast in or would you like some eggs for a change?" She smiled sweetly at Duncan, who wore a look of mild surprise on his face.

"Er, yes. Eggs would be great for a change. Thanks."

"Well, go and get your robe before you freeze and I'll make them for you. Scrambled or poached?"

"Scrambled, please," Duncan said, and, still looking at her strangely, left the room to grab his robe. Sam heard him pad slowly back up the stairs, probably wondering if he was still asleep and dreaming at her transformation.

By the time he returned, the kitchen smelled of hot toast and a mug of tea was set on the table, his place set with cutlery. He took a sip, though he didn't say a word.

"Eggs will only be a minute," she informed him, her voice almost sing-song, as she stirred them. In her head, she was being the perfect wife, and it wouldn't do her any harm to do so – while he was still here. It was almost enjoyable, but only almost. "Here we go," she gushed as she scooped eggs onto the waiting buttered toast and set the plate down in front of him. She wanted to scream 'Voila! I hope you choke!' but venting inside her head would have to do for now. Before leaving him to eat, she gave him a quick peck on the cheek – which did actually make Duncan almost choke on the mouthful he was chewing. Then, with another unusual gust of energy, Sam informed him she was heading for the shower while he ate, before he needed the bathroom himself, and made her own way back upstairs.

Once in the bathroom, with the door firmly closed behind her, she let out a billowing breath as if she'd spent the day in a labour camp rather than simply making eggs on toast. She turned on the shower and stepped under the warm jets, letting the water run over her head and shoulders. She ran her mind back over what she'd decided during her early morning kitchen research. The main thing was she couldn't do the actual act herself: she wasn't that kind of woman and certainly wasn't a killer. No, that task was for someone else – a professional. She'd run through the various options open to her and hadn't found one she could get away with all by herself. If she shot him, someone might hear, and besides, how would she remove his body on her own? If she poisoned him, how would she make it seem natural or an accident? And again, there was the question of what to do with his body. Suffocation? No, she wasn't strong enough – and again, the body issue. Ditto for drowning or hanging or beating him to death. So as Sam combed conditioner through her hair she mulled the options left to her: make it look like an accident or make it look like a disgruntled villain had taken his revenge and shot him. Ultimately, it needed to look like he'd been killed in the line of duty in order for his salary and pension to continue.

Clean and dried, Sam blew her hair dry and applied a little light make-up before getting dressed in jeans and a nice blouse and going back downstairs. Now that her decision had been made, she needed to make sure he stuck around, and the way to do that was to make him think his words had had the desired effect on her. She smiled at just how far from the truth that was...

Duncan was finishing the last of his mug of tea when she re-entered the room. He did a cartoon-style double-take as he looked up and saw her.

"That startling, eh?" she asked with another pleasant smile.

"No. I mean yes," he stammered. "Oh, I don't know what I mean but it's good to see you so bright-eyed and bushy-tailed for a change. I was beginning to worry about you."

"Well, there's no need, I'm perfectly fine. And you're right: I need to clean up my act, get a job again – give me something to do. Then we can get a cleaner to help around here, and maybe some help with the girls for after school. What do you think?"

"I think that sounds perfect," he said encouragingly. He smiled at her as he stood to put his dirty dishes in the dishwasher. "Well, I need to get a move on and go shower. Let's talk more tonight when I get home."

He headed upstairs and after a few moments, she could hear his faint whistling as he got ready for work. It wasn't a tune she recognized, but that didn't matter. It was good to hear him being happy.

Was she being rash with her decision? Should she try and sort her life out with him in more conventional ways? The hateful, blame-filled words he'd thrown at her only the day before surged back into her head now and filled her with resentment almost immediately: if someone could say it, she told herself, deep down they meant it. No, there was no going back: she was going to carry out her plan.

There was no way she was going to allow him to leave her and take the children with him.

Chapter Thirty-Seven

SHE HAD A FULL, though, paradoxically, empty day ahead of her. The front door was finally closed. Duncan and the girls were gone for the day and that meant Sam had a large expanse of time all to herself. The quietness of the house seemed to be more pronounced today for some reason, though in reality, today was no different than any other day. The only thing to have changed was her being up, showered and dressed rather than still bumming about in her nightwear watching TV until lunchtime or beyond.

She flicked the kettle on to boil and sat down at the kitchen table with her laptop and the basic instructions she'd found out about accessing the dark web. While the kettle came to the boil, a text pinged on her phone, making her jump. It was Anika, following up about meeting for coffee today.

Coffee at Macs later? Say eleven?

Sam tapped out her reply, that she'd see her there, and looked at the digital clock on the cooker. It gave her nearly two full hours to do some research before she had to leave. She made herself a hot mug of tea and got to work.

It was all new territory for Sam. She did not really understand the difference between the dark web and the regular web, but she had learned last night she needed to use a different browser than the one she used normally, to keep her safe and to keep her whereabouts secret. If she was going surfing in an ocean filled with sharks and other sea life she wasn't accustomed to, she was going to need more protection than her swimsuit.

"Okay, here goes. Let's hope I don't get bitten or catch a virus or something," she said, and hit the button to download the Tor browser software. Sam watched the download timer tick over until the icon told her it was complete. All that was left was to install it and she was ready to go. A few keystrokes later and she was in.

To her puzzlement, the search engine page looked like a basic one from back in the 90s. Figuring the page worked exactly the same as the regular web, she put her search term in the box and hit enter – then sat back for a moment and waited. And waited some more. It seemed to her that the ancient-looking page resorted back to dial-up speed. Had she known a little more about what was happening behind the scenes, however, she'd have understood that her hidden ID was bouncing across servers all over the world before finally settling and bringing up what she wanted – that's what took time.

At last, a list of hits popped up, and from there, it was simply a case of scrolling through and clicking the links. There was a smorgasbord of places to look, and when she finally came back up for air and stretched, it was almost time to go and meet Anika.

"Shit, that went quick," she exclaimed, and closed her laptop down. She carried it upstairs and slid it under her pillow, though she couldn't have said exactly why. Duncan knew she had a laptop – that wasn't a problem – but after what she'd been looking at, it felt like the right thing to do.

Ten minutes later she was pulling into the car park and headed over for coffee with Anika. Her friend beamed at her when she entered the café.

"Wow, you look great! And happier, too. What happened?" Anika squeezed her friend affectionately and they both sat down. "I'll get you a coffee. Latte?"

. . .

Sam nodded her approval and Anika went to place their order. While she waited for Anika to return, she glanced around the café and realized she was smiling a little, smiling because she felt better, lighter; a stress had gone.

Anika noticed it too.

"Well, I have to say, it's good to see you looking so well," she said as she sat back down. "And that blouse looks really cool on you!"

"Thanks. I feel a whole lot better now. Things are clearer in my mind and I know what I have to do."

Did she ever.

"Well, like I say, I'm pleased for you. And changing the subject, how is Jasmine this morning?"

Sam was perplexed. "Jasmine?"

"Yes. You needed cough medicine for her last night, remember?"

"Yes, sorry. Seems so long ago, and yes, she's fine. Gone to school as normal." Big smile.

Their mugs of coffee arrived and they sat in silence for a moment enjoying their beverages. Friends could do that; space didn't always have to be filled with conversation. A baby started crying across the café and a young mother attempted to soothe it, rubbing its back over her shoulder. A couple of people turned to watch, their expressions a mixture of 'How gorgeous' and 'Oh dear, must be wind.'

"Do you remember when yours were that age?" she asked Anika. "Such a beautiful time, when they are totally dependent on you for life. They grow up so quickly, and it's hard to believe in another ten years, mine will be off to university or jobs. Yours too."

"I know," Anika replied. "Time goes so fast. It's important to savour as much as we can, eh?"

The conversation brought Sam back round to her big decision – keeping the girls with her at all costs and ridding her life of the man she no longer wanted in it.

"I've got a question for you, Anika, kind of a trivia question, actually," Sam said, smiling brightly. "I saw the question online somewhere and it was fun reading the answers so I thought I'd see what yours would be."

"Okay, fire away. What is it?"

"First, think of the dodgiest person you know. Don't tell me who it is." She gave her friend a few seconds to think. When Anika signalled she had someone in mind, she carried on. "Now, what would be the dodgiest thing they could get for you? I mean like a stolen TV or something. What do you think they could get if you asked them?"

"Oh, that's easy. The person I'm thinking of could probably get you just about anything you wanted. He's as dodgy as they come."

"And how do you know such a dodgy person?"

"I don't know him, really. He's a former work colleague of Steve's but he sees him down The Feathers sometimes. I've met him. He's really seedy."

"So, you mean he could get cocaine or hard porn or a gun, for instance?" Sam added a bit of incredulousness to her question for effect.

"Definitely. Nothing would surprise me about what he could get his hands on. Why? Are you looking for something kinkier to watch?" Anika gave an exaggerated Benny Hill wink, and both women burst out laughing, so much so that heads turned their way.

"That's too funny, Anika! No, no extra kink required. Well, not for me anyway, though I couldn't speak for Duncan," she said, and they both laughed out loud again, causing more heads to turn. "I guess we should quiet down, judging by the looks we're getting."

"What does Mr. Seedy look like?" she went on. "Something stereotypical from a movie, skinny and twitchy maybe? Nasty bleached blond hair and dark roots?"

Anika nodded rapidly through her restrained laughter. "You've got it – that's him! And Mr. Seedy is called Sid, poor sod. Who calls their kid Sidney these days?" and off they both giggled again. When they'd finally stopped laughing, Anika asked, "Fancy another?"

Sam checked her watch, "No, thanks. I should be going. I've a few errands to run myself." She stood ready to leave. Anika joined her and they left the café together. They exchanged a hug as they reached their cars.

"Ah, that was fun," Anika said to her friend. "Glad you're feeling better."

"I am, yes. See you soon, eh?" said Sam, and blew her a best mate kiss as she climbed behind the wheel.

Sam waved at Anika through her window as she drove past, but her mind was in overdrive, scheming, planning a visit to The Feathers to see Seedy Sid.

Just in case.

Chapter Thirty-Eight

"WHAT ARE you two love-birds up to tonight? Or shouldn't I ask?"

Jack wore his best cheeky grin and Amanda whacked him affectionately with the back of her hand as they left the building heading towards the car park.

"Oy, careful! Not so hard." Jack winced, rubbing his arm as though he'd been stabbed.

"Barely touched you, and for your information, we're finishing decorating the bedroom. In fact, we're almost done. We seem to have been in turmoil for weeks now and I'm over it already. And it's only the first room." Amanda sighed. "And I still have to hold down a full-time job."

"That's why I don't bother. Nothing wrong with the paper that's still on my bedroom walls. Well, nothing that a bit of glue on some of the corners wouldn't fix. But it's not bad enough to be replaced."

Amanda turned to stare at him in disbelief. She'd only been in his bedroom once, and that was while he'd been in hospital and needed a few personal things picked up. If there had been time to decorate while he'd been away she'd have got someone in to bring the room into the twenty-first century. But when it came down to it, it was his place, not hers.

"I think it feels worse than it is because everything from our room is scattered around the house temporarily, so there's things in the living room that really don't belong there. And we've still got some of my stuff in boxes looking for a home. Perhaps we should have bought a bigger place between us instead of me moving into Ruth's."

They had reached Amanda's car and she opened the driver's door, resting her arm on the top of it while she spoke. She ran her fingers through her short blonde hair in an effort to restyle it before she arrived home.

"You'll get there. It will get done. Always does." Jack tipped his imaginary hat and said goodnight, walked the few steps to his own car and climbed in. Amanda watched him while she stood, then gave him a wave before getting inside her own and turning the engine on. She might be bored of decorating and the mess it created, but at least she'd be going home to someone tonight, and every night hereafter. Jack would be going home to an empty house. The realization sometimes made her sad, but Jack didn't seem to care much. He was used to it. Janine had been gone some years, but at least he had a part-time housekeeper now in Mrs. Stewart, so his fridge probably had more choice in it than hers and Ruth's did on any given day.

She headed out of the car park, destination home. Would Ruth be there yet? It was still quite early for a change, so that was unlikely. Amanda planned a bath if the house was empty. A long, soapy bath, with a glass of red on the side. She could almost taste the full body of a glass of Merlot, feel the warm water soothe her stressed body.

She was right – when she got home, the house was indeed empty, so Amanda headed straight up to the bathroom and turned the taps on, adding fragrant lavender bubbles as the water cascaded into the tub. For a moment, she watched the white suds form, watched them grow in volume like a meringue, and was almost tempted to scoop some onto her finger and see if it tasted as sweet. Walking to their bedroom, she stripped out of her work suit and grabbed her sweats to put on after her soak. Then, wearing only her underwear, she went back downstairs in search of a bottle of full-bodied red. Ruth had built a wine storage area out of pieces of terracotta drainpipe stacked on top of each other and then glued together; each hole fit a bottle perfectly.

It looked simple, stylish and a whole lot hippy at the same time, and had been the talking point of many a dinner guest. Grabbing a stemmed glass and a random bottle, she made her way back to her waiting bubbles, hoping they hadn't spilled over the top in her absence.

In a few moments, she lay up to her chin in lavender foam, breathing in the steam, smiling to herself and relaxing as the feeling of wine on an empty stomach took hold. Amanda closed her eyes and enjoyed the peace in the house, the time alone to drift for a while. Her body felt like it was floating, the warmth and the wine making her sleepy, and absentmindedly she wondered if this was what it felt like to someone who took drugs – that feeling of being out of one's body, away from reality. With her eyes still closed, and floating safely in her bathtub, she tried to imagine never waking up, not resurfacing ever again and drifting off to another world on a chemical-induced pleasure craft. How sad it would be for those left behind to find only the soulless shell of their loved one's body floating in a cold bath.

The water was cooling now, bringing her back to the real world. She lay still for a moment longer, savouring the last whiffs of lavender. She hadn't heard the door close downstairs, hadn't heard feet on the stairs, hadn't heard someone enter the room.

"Hello, darling."

Amanda screamed and shot up from the depths of the water, bubbles and wine sloshing over the side as she opened her eyes and tried to focus.

Ruth burst out laughing at the mess and her wife's extreme reaction to her intrusion.

"Having fun in there, were you?"

Chapter Thirty-Nine

AMANDA SAT BACK and stretched like a cat, then groaned deeply and yawned. She caught Raj's eye as she returned to her normal posture and blushed.

"Late night?" he enquired, lifting an eyebrow. Everyone in the station knew she had recently got married and while they hadn't said much to her face, she was aware of sniggers and crude jokes behind her back. It no longer bothered her, and she let them have their fun at her expense knowing it would die down soon enough. Her skin was the required thickness to work in the Metropolitan Police and not much bothered her anymore.

"Nothing exciting to report. We're just finishing up decorating. We've done one room and I don't want to do any more."

"Can't you get someone in and do it?"

"We said we'd have a go ourselves. We thought it would be fun. Truth is, it's hard graft and both our day jobs are hectic. It's not like I can hide in the back room and do some filing for a rest."

"You could do some of my paperwork if you want." He grinned at her cheekily.

She knew he was joking; she had more than enough of her own, judging by the pile of folders balancing on her own desk. "I'll pass, thanks. I need to do a bit more research."

"Drugs?"

"Yep, fascinating stuff, actually. I mean, we all know about cocaine and heroin and the synthetics, but prescription drugs are getting to be more and more of a problem every day, and they're so easy to come by."

Raj came closer to her desk, obviously interested in what she was talking about. "My brother had a car accident a while back," he said. "Broke his leg, smashed a rib or two, and they gave him some pretty strong painkillers to help him through. I can't remember what they were now, but they did the trick. Anyway, they used to make him happy, happier than normal, and I wondered then if he was getting hooked on them, if he liked the feeling they gave him."

"Is he still taking them, do you know?"

"I've often wondered, and officially he's not, but sometimes when we're out having a pint or at a match, he seems different – euphoric and upbeat, but to another level. I guess he could be taking them recreationally, but maybe not all the time."

"Have you asked him?"

"No. I think I'm afraid of the answer, if he'd even tell his big brother the detective. And what if he did say yes? What would I do or say then?"

"Hmm. I know what you mean, but he is your brother and if he is addicted or taking them recreationally, he may need help. He can't live like that forever. He's risking getting ill, or worse, as you know."

They lowered their voices as several more of their colleagues drifted into the room. They were deep in their own conversations and not paying Amanda and Raj any attention, but still, Amanda was aware of flapping ears.

"Look, best wrap this up, but it's worth a heart-to-heart with him, isn't it? Voice your concern as his brother and see what he says. Just don't go in accusingly and piss him off. Be the support he may be looking for."

They both looked up as their boss, DI Dopey Dupin, entered the room and headed their way.

"Morning sir," they said almost at the same time. Raj started to move away, figuring it was Amanda he was after.

"Yes, morning," Dupin said, though he was obviously distracted. He turned his full attention to Amanda.

"I hear on the bongo drums you've been making enquiries at Manchester about Wilfred Day. What's that all about?" Dopey had a habit of looking stressed even when he probably wasn't, but the twitch in his left eye said he was wound up about something. It was one of his 'tells.' He'd never make a decent poker player.

"His name came up rather tenuously connected to a prescription drug thing I'm looking into."

"And? Is that it?"

"Yes, sir, that's about it. DS Black filled me in on what he knew of him, which was not much more than a slippery modern mob wannabe who has impeccable manners and dresses smartly. May I ask what's up, sir?"

"Just keep me posted, that's all," he said, and left as quickly as he'd entered.

Amanda watched him go. He'd never been the most talkative person in the station and was not an easy person to warm to, but he was her boss and she respected that. To many, it was still a quandary how he'd ever made the DI promotion; some speculated he must have intel on someone higher up, but others couldn't see him being smart enough to blackmail his way. It was kind of sad he lacked the respect of the team he led, she thought, not for the first time.

She sat back down at her desk and looked at the web page she'd been reading about opioid addiction in other countries. The US had a massive problem with pharmacy break-ins, prescription books nicked and youngsters getting into the game as dealers to fulfil demand. Many were nicking their parents' pills, swapping them out for something that looked the same and then selling on the potent stuff at a profit. Prescription pills were deemed a little more upmarket than typical street drugs, and housewives, sports stars and everybody in between was regularly looking for their endorphin fix or dopamine surge. And like any addiction, the more a person consumed, the bigger the craving. While it wasn't quite as bad in little old Blighty, opioids were already on the street and readily available.

She sat back in her chair, feeling deflated. Or was she just feeling sluggish? Looking at the clock on her screen, she realized it was time for coffee so she headed to the coffee machine, the one that always caused Jack so much consternation. As she waited for her cup to fill, she was deep in thought. Caffeine was no different than other drugs in a craving and uplifting context. So why wasn't caffeine banned and thrown in with other stimulants? A triple espresso would shoot her into oblivion, yet could it feel the same as a hit from something outlawed? It was a sobering thought.

Amanda took her fix back to her desk and carried on with research.

Chapter Forty

DUNCAN HAD DRIVEN to work that morning in a mixed mood of thankfulness and utmost surprise at finding Sam up sipping tea in the kitchen. But what had doubly surprised him was she'd then showered and made him breakfast, all with a smile on her face. Maybe he hadn't been too hard on her after all; maybe she'd turned a corner and was starting to sort herself out. He certainly hoped so. A red light up ahead slowed him to a stop and he absentmindedly looked across to the car that had pulled alongside him at the traffic lights. There was no mistaking whose car it was, though the windows were tinted so dark there was no way of confirming who was driving. A top-of-the-range custom-coloured metallic tan Bentley – there was only one person with a car like that.

Wilfred Day.

The driver was probably looking straight at him, but there was no way he could tell for sure. So Duncan smiled like an idiot anyway and wiggled his fingers in a casual wave just to be the friendly cop he was – and annoy the hell out of whoever was at the wheel. The passenger window of the Bentley rolled down smoothly, and the driver leaned across the empty seat in an effort to talk to Duncan.

It was the man himself.

"Pleasant morning, isn't it? A slight nip in the air, but at least the rain has gone." Wilfred Day smiled broadly. His face wasn't so much handsome as striking. His jaw was strong, his eyes as blue as could be, and he had a perfect set of teeth that were currently being displayed in all their chemically whitened glory. Maybe *GQ* had finished their photo shoot with him early.

"Morning, Wilfred. What gets you up so early on a school day? Or are you just going home?"

"Early bird and all. Early bird." He flashed a smile again and revved his engine, yelling "Have a fantastic day!" as the lights changed and he drove off. Duncan watched as Wilfred accelerated out in front of him. A car tooted behind him so Duncan pulled away too. Day's rear lights were already pinpricks of red in the distance.

"And the second mouse gets the cheese, my friend. Second mouse," he mumbled. "Fantastic day," with its play on his surname, was something the man said to amuse himself, and it always grated on Duncan. The fact that Wilfred Day had managed to stay out of jail stuck in the craw of the GMP in general, and many had taken him on in an attempt to be the local hero in law enforcement, but the egg continued to slip around the fry pan.

"One day, Day. It won't be so fantastic, then. Well, not for you at any rate," he mumbled. Duncan had fantasized about what he'd say to the man when the law finally caught up with him and he was sent down, because he did believe it was only a matter of time. As his mental scenario went, he'd walk up to him in the courtroom before he was led away and tell him 'The day is done.' It was so poetic, so eloquent in its simplicity. All Duncan needed now was the occasion. The right day.

He turned into Grindlow Street; the station was just in front of him. The area was still quiet, with only a handful of people out walking dogs. Rochelle's bike wasn't parked in its usual corner, but Rick's BMW was in his usual spot. Duncan pulled into a space himself, then headed indoors. Rick was talking to a uniform in the doorway.

"Hello, early bird." Rick gave him a friendly slap on his back as he spoke.

"Morning, Rick. You're extra exuberant this morning, aren't you?"

"Oh, just good to see you back, and glad your little family is all safe and sound, too. A bit of a stressful day, I'd imagine."

"You could say that, yeah."

They both headed into the building and towards the canteen. Coffee first. Always. They placed their orders and then grabbed a seat to wait.

"I popped back last night when the girls had gone to bed, caught up with Rochelle. Still no news on the two missing children, I hear. That's not good."

Two mugs of steaming coffee arrived and they each sipped in silence for a moment or two. Children who went missing were rarely found alive so many hours after their disappearance. It was one of the hardest things for officers to deal with, one of the worst parts of the job. They both knew that some point, probably soon, their task would turn from rescue recovery, and the grief of informing next of kin. A hateful task, but one that had to be done nonetheless.

"No, absolutely it's not, but with such a lack of leads to go on, I'm doubtful we'll bring them home anytime soon. Though I'm praying for the opposite, just like you are." Changing the subject, Rick asked, "Are you still out tactical training next week, or has that been postponed?"

"No. As far as I'm aware, it's still on. I'm actually looking forward to seeing the fake town they've built. From what I've seen the riot set-up is pretty realistic, and the rent-a-mobs are pretty realistic too. Why do you ask?"

"Remember DS Amanda Lacey from Croydon?"

The blonde one, yes. She put away that woman who collected human hunting trophies. Quite a tough cookie, I remember. Why?"

"I spoke to her yesterday while you were out. Seems they might have a prescription opioid issue developing. She found evidence, little packets that tested for codeine and oxy, by a mobile food truck down there, and guess whose name came up with a bit of a dig?"

"Tell me."

"Wilfred Day. Loosely on a company trace, but still, here he is popping up yet again."

"I saw him on the drive in, all bright and breezy," said Duncan. "The guy will get his day, and I'll get my day to say told you so. One day." He smiled at his own weak joke. "Poetic, don't you think? I can't wait to deliver it to the arrogant git."

"Well, if Lacey has something going on down there, you never know your luck – Day might slip up. So, my point is this: why don't you pop in while you're passing on your way down to training? It might be worth an hour's detour; buy her dinner or something." Duncan thought for a moment. If Day was moving his operation south into new unchartered territory, he might indeed slip up somehow. And either he or Lacey could be the one to catch him if he fell.

"I'll give her a buzz now."

Chapter Forty-One

JACK WAS LOOKING EXPECTANTLY at the coffee machine once again,
and Amanda was trying not to notice and smirk. It wasn't that he
hadn't had the practice; he'd had plenty, but for some reason unknown
to humanity, he struggled with the concept of water, capsule and milk.
And the relevant buttons. One day, he'd grasp it, she was sure, but until
that distant day, it was invariably quicker and less painful all round to
make him a mug when she made her own. Shaking her head, she
quietly made her way across and picked up a clean mug.

"Great idea, Jack. I think I'll have another."

With a thankful sideways glance, he allowed her in, pretending to
be gallant with a wave of his hand for her to go first. She took the hint
and the machine fizzed and spluttered into life, dark liquid filling
her mug.

"What can I make you, Jack?" She held out her hand for his mug
while hers finished brewing.

"I'll have a trim macchiato with sprinkles, please," he teased.

"Coffee with milk coming right up."

He had the same every day, every time.

"Just had a call from Manchester, from DS Duncan Riley," she said
as Jack's coffee brewed. "He's coming down our way for tactical train-

ing, so he said he'd drop in. He's quite clued up on Wilfred Day by all accounts, so I said we'd take him out for dinner, a curry or something. You up for that? He seemed a decent sort. And it would be good to pick his brains on what's happening up his way."

"Always up for a curry, you know me. Or Chinese. I don't mind. It's a shame Wong's don't have seating. We could treat him to crispy pork balls. Or we could take it back to your place?"

"Probably not while the house is in decorating turmoil. I'll organize a table some place. He won't be in a flash hotel, so he'll welcome the dinner date rather than a garage sandwich in his room, I should imagine."

"How much is there to know about Wilfred Day – any idea?" Jack asked as they headed back to their desks. Jack's was a mass of manila files and paperwork, with barely enough space to put his mug down freely. Amanda's, in contrast, was exactly the opposite. They say opposites attract, and that's why they worked together so well. He was the milk for her cereal; she was the mug for his coffee – metaphorically speaking. His seat groaned again as he sat, letting it swivel slightly to one side and back again as he sipped from his mug. He looked deep in thought, miles away.

"Duncan is very familiar with him by all accounts," Amanda said. "Day sounds like a special sort of character from what I know of him already, a real charmer. Seems he's a new breed of gangster, a new generation, less thug and more brains and a good technological fit for twenty-first-century crime. Like we talked about, even prostitutes have moved more online now, away from the drafty doorways, so it follows that pimps and drug lords have done the same. I wouldn't be surprised if half the prozzies are GPS tracked by their pimps now, maybe even timed. Check the customer in and check them back out again, like some sort of productivity tool almost. If they're holed up in a flat, say, how many paying customers could you get through in one night if they don't have to stand on street corners and the client comes to them in their room? That could be big money for some – pimps and solos."

"You reckon there is such a thing?" Jack asked. "Is nothing exempt from the clock? Not even getting your leg over?"

"It's business. No matter what the service, it's a business and time is money. And technology comes to us all eventually, Jack, even you."

"Having a dig, are we, Lacey? I didn't do too bad when I was ailing in hospital and you wanted me to delve into the dark web. I found what we were looking for, didn't I?" Jack mock-buffed his nails, looking chuffed with himself. His nails were looking neater, Amanda noticed, since Mrs. Stewart had taken him under her wing.

"I'll give you that one, and I'll be sure and hit you up when we need more dark web research done. You'll be the man," she said with gusto and a smile. "If only we could get you to master the coffee machine..."

"Cheeky − watch it," admonished Jack. "Well, with that in mind, maybe I should take another snoop around, do a bit more on prescription meds and see how they are being traded, see where I end up. I've still got that old laptop Ruth gave me, too." He looked thoughtful as he added, "In fact, that's a great idea, Jack. I'll do it later." He slapped himself on the back and swung his seat round to face his desk, conversation over.

"Good plan, Jack,' Amanda said. "Meanwhile, while you're playing Inspector Clouseau with a piece of apple pie on your side table and Bake Off on the TV, remember me hard at it decorating, will you? I know which I'd rather be doing." Amanda groaned inwardly at the thought of physical hard work after a day of mentally tough work. She wasn't meant for physical work; her body didn't appreciate it. A slice of pie and the TV sounded more than appealing. "Right, then. I'll book us a table at Chat House. Will that do for you?" But Jack was engrossed in something on his screen so Amanda carried on talking to herself, her words falling on distracted ears. "Yes, okay, Amanda, you do that. Seven p.m. work for you?" she mocked. Since she was having both sides of the conversation, she turned her head to the other side to await the reply. "Perfect, Jack. Got to love a good Jalfrezi." She turned her head again in reply. "That you do."

Amanda picked up the phone and booked them a table. Seven o'clock it was, then.

Chapter Forty-Two

IT COULDN'T BE that hard to do, could it?

Luke had built web pages before, but he'd never had to host them on a secret server – a server on the dark web. From his quick search, he'd found there were plenty of tutorials, YouTube videos even, informing newbies how easy it was to host a page anonymously. It didn't seem to be much more than using hidden ports and directories. While Luke wasn't a tech whizz in this space, he knew enough to put together what he needed without having to ask for help. Asking someone for help would set alarm bells off.

He got to work creating, making the simple site look businesslike without being sinister, and three hours later he was ready to launch their temporary business venture into what felt like outer space, the big black unknown, another world. His finger hovered over the return key. When he pressed it, the site would be launched and there would be no turning back. Once it was out there, they were in business.

He pulled his finger away from the key without pressing it and sat back in the chair, thinking. Really? Was he really willing to kill for a few thousand pounds? Would he really be able to snuff out someone's life because he'd been paid for the task? Who the hell was he?

A hired assassin, that's who.

But he knew flipping burgers or scrubbing floors was not going to get them where they wanted to be. No, he couldn't see another way. Luke pressed return and waited for a confirmation message on his screen. When it eventually came, he sat and stared at it. He'd actually done it. His stall was set up and ready to go. Now it was a case of waiting and finding the next item on the list for the plan to take shape – the weapon. He texted Clinton, just one line to tell him they were now live. Then he closed his laptop and headed for the bathroom to mull over what he'd done in a hot bath. It was the next best thing to going down the pub with no money in his pocket.

The soak had in fact been fruitful. While he'd lain there steaming and thinking, his old friend Tommy had popped into his head. He'd been at school with Luke, but he'd lived on the other side of the tracks in North Kensington, a rougher part of town and nowhere near the Kensington that was famously fashionable. Trendy, suburban, movie-worthy Notting Hill, where Luke currently lived with his parents, was the meat in the town sandwich, slap bang in the middle. North Kensington was mainly mid- to high-rise blocks of estate flats where the tough kids at school lived, a place he'd only ever been once before, and a place he hadn't had the desire to go back to, either. His father had joked that the dogs went out in twos for safety, it had been that bad. No, his friends were not the same crowd, apart from Tommy, that was. Luke had grown up in greenery, among three-story houses, each with a reasonable car out front and white-collar parents inside, though his own parents had fought to keep up appearances. They'd struggled at times to give him the education and life they wanted for him, and while he appreciated it now, as a young, independent man, he'd no clue. Until that day that Tommy had taken him to his home on the Lancaster estate.

Tommy had been a bit of an oddball friend, and Luke had been drawn to him even though he was so different from all his other mates. He had a real mischief about him, though he rarely got in any real trouble because his cheeky personality found him a way out. It seemed everyone liked Tommy. With blue NHS-issued plastic glasses, he was the butt of many jokes, but he brushed them off like the cat hair on his T-shirt. He had a toughness about him that wasn't sharp like the thugs that lived by him. He'd meant no harm to anyone, but loved the attention his personality afforded him.

Looking back now, Luke realized Tommy was probably starved of guidance and attention and could well have morphed into a rich life of poor crime without support. Their paths had separated when Tommy's mother had died suddenly and he was sent away to live with an aunt up north; his father was already in prison. Whatever had happened to Tommy after that Luke had no idea. Neither boy had been big on writing letters, and there were no mobile phones back then. Luke wondered if Tommy was in prison himself now, like father like son, or if he was thriving somewhere, with a family of his own maybe, successful in a business of his own.

He thought back to a pub they had tried to get into; North Pole it had been called back then. They'd both sneaked in pretending to be part of a group of four men that had entered at the same time, hiding behind them in a vain attempt to gain their first taste of beer. They'd been rumbled almost immediately but one of the men, the youngest, Luke remembered, had bought them a half pint between them, admiring the two lads for their ingenuity and guffawing that it wouldn't hurt to try it. In a place such as the Pole, the landlord had turned a blind eye; two boys sipping half a pint between them in the corner were no big deal compared to the other activities that went on in the place. The police busted the dingy premises on a regular basis; fighting with broken bottles was the norm and whatever substance a desperate man desired was available in the toilets. Other desperate people took part in even more desperate acts in those same toilets.

Blind eyes indeed, Luke thought. Nobody had known anything about anything.

Luke wondered about Tommy. There was always Facebook to find him.

As for the pub? There was one way to find out.

Chapter Forty-Three

IT WAS cold and clear as Luke stepped outside. Pulling his collar up high and his hat down low, he rammed his gloved hands into his coat pockets and set off towards the bus stop, destination North Kensington and the Pole. It all seemed a bit surreal, knowing what he was trying to accomplish on his own with no experience in the line of work he'd volunteered himself for. It could all go terribly wrong, sure, but if he thought it through, planned it meticulously and practiced privately, he was educated and smart enough to pull it off. Criminals got caught because they didn't plan enough or were a bit thick, he reasoned. That's why they were criminals – it was their fall-back career. The successful ones were the men and women at the top, the drug lords, the modern-day gangsters, high-rolling madams. They played a different game, a game of strategy like inflated Monopoly, with huge stakes and obscene amounts of money.

Luke had read about some of the greatest criminal minds of the past; the best of them had been educated, clever and meticulous planners. And some had had values too. The infamous Ted Bundy, for instance. During his killing spree, where he had savagely mutilated and killed over thirty women including his wife, he had admitted he would never steal an uninsured car because he didn't think it was right. He'd happily kill his wife rather than divorce her, but he drew the line at taking an uninsured car because that wasn't fair. Go figure.

But prisons were full of the ones who had been caught, which to Luke's mind meant they were either stupid or hadn't given enough time and attention to the details. They had probably left evidence and clues like a trail of breadcrumbs for the police to follow.

But not Luke. He had no intention of being caught. He was the educated, creative one, and Clinton was educated and meticulous, so between them, they'd come up with the perfect plan.

After the toasty warmth of the night bus, the air outside felt like it couldn't get any colder. Yet it surely would. The worst of winter was yet to come and even though London rarely got snow, it got bitterly cold, the wind chill making the mercury plummet. Luke rubbed his hands together as he walked through deserted streets, head down against the freezing night air, focusing on keeping his feet out of the random dog shit that littered the cracked pavement. He'd not been down these streets in years, not since Tommy had left; there'd been no need.

Most of the low-rise flat blocks had cracks of light peeking out from behind curtains, a signal someone was home, but some were still in darkness. Many others were boarded up with graffiti-covered plywood. Some of the plywood sheets had been wrenched away at a corner as someone or other attempted to break in, use the empty space as a squat, for a quick lay maybe, or somewhere peaceful to get a fix and lie low for a while. It was a dark, murky, mostly uninhabited world, left to fend for itself, unchecked, unregulated and rampant with crime.

Tommy had lived further up the street, on the tenth floor of a tower block with his mum. Luke had been there only the once and had tried not to stare at how little they had, at the decrepit state of what they did have. But Tommy's mum had been a proud woman, and Luke smiled, remembering the big old blanket that had sat in pride of place on their sofa. She'd crocheted it herself, making the coloured wool squares out of wool from old unravelled jumpers or from skeins bought for a few pence at the market. How long it would have taken he'd no idea, but that blanket had covered every inch of the battered old sofa underneath. How sad it had been when she'd died and Tommy had to go.

As Luke approached the pub at the end of the street, he wondered once again about what Tommy would be doing now. He felt out of place and nervous in this part of town, yet Tommy had thrived here because he'd known nothing else. Luke hoped his aunt's place had been a step up.

The pub's entrance door opened while he was still a few steps away and a drunk made his way out, words slurring. Luke stepped aside as he passed and watched as he made it to the corner of the building before retching his liquid evening meal back up and depositing it on the concrete. A trickle ran from the splattered mess and Luke watched it roll away to the curb, feeling a little queasy inside himself. The man staggered off, wiping his mouth on his sleeve, going back the way Luke had come, back towards the darkness, the darkened homes of the derelict.

Reaching out a shaking hand, Luke opened the pub door and stepped inside.

Chapter Forty-Four

It hadn't changed all that much in nearly fifteen years. Cheap Formica tabletops, faded once-salmon-coloured velour upholstery on the chairs and foam-covered built-in seating that ran around one half of the dim room. A long wooden bar stretched almost the length of the left side. The mirror above it reflected a roomful of wary eyes on the intruder. Luke heard the lowering of conversation as he approached the bar. A huge man in a cut-off denim jacket, with arms like Popeye and wearing dark aviator shades, slowly made his way toward him. Inside, Luke's heart failed a beat and he swallowed involuntarily. Summoning courage from deep in his boots, Luke ordered half a bitter; it seemed the right thing to do. The man wordlessly grabbed a glass and slowly made his way back to a pump, lifted a brass tap. Luke watched it fill, a creamy head of about an inch forming on top of the deep brown liquid. It gave him somewhere to put his eyes; he dared not look up at the long mirror, where he knew he'd see so many eyes looking back at him.

Another man moved and stood next to him, too close, intimidatingly close, then another stood on his other side. Their body odour caught in his throat. The barman delivered his drink, and Luke handed over a note to pay, hoping it was enough, not really expecting to see any change. Luke was the only person who had spoken so far, though conversation in the room had resumed. With a shaky hand, he tried not to slop beer over the rim of his glass as he made his way, unaccompanied, to a vacant corner and sat down. So far so good, he thought uneasily, although it didn't quite feel good; it felt terrifying.

He sipped his beer and tried not to catch anyone's eye as he forced himself to look a little more relaxed than he felt. Whatever went on in the pub, the eyes he was purposefully avoiding would suddenly become blind, he knew – and stay that way. He glanced at the floor. The carpet underfoot had once been a deep pile, but over the years it had worn in places, almost to the thread backing in spots in front of the bar. In other spots, like up against the covered seating, it had plenty of years left in it. It probably had plenty of beer in it, too, and maybe even blood.

When he did eventually chance a glance up from the floor, nobody was looking his way. Everyone had gone back to their own business, back to more important matters. And as Luke relaxed a little, he thought about the business he'd come to this particular dive for – a weapon contact. He sipped and wondered how he might do that now he was here. What was he expecting? To see a dodgy bloke hanging his shingle out, a sign saying 'Guns for Sale'? He found some change in his pocket and nervously walked back towards the bar and waited. A packet of crisps would give him something to do while he sat. He hoped nobody would spit in his drink while his back was turned. Popeye could well be glaring at him from behind his aviators; Luke couldn't be sure. Popeye's sour-smelling breath greeted him on his arrival.

"Salt and vinegar crisps, please, mate."

Again wordlessly, Popeye reached into a brown cardboard box on the floor, one that had had the front cut out, and retrieved a packet. No need for shelf space when the box itself would do. He tossed the bag roughly onto the bar, and Luke handed over change for payment. Popeye checked the amount and tossed the whole lot into the till drawer, a drawer that didn't close. Nothing was rung through the till, Luke realized. Nothing went through the books in this place. Once again, he felt eyes all over him and headed back to his seat to consume his packet of crisps. His beer looked untampered-with; there was nothing floating on the top that looked out of the ordinary. He took a long mouthful and lifted his eyes again, his glance connecting instantly with that of a man of a similar age over to his right. He was wearing grubby jeans and a hoody, like Luke himself, so he decided to start with him. If he was going to make some headway here, if this evening's investigative journey was to be fruitful, he might as well make a start.

The chosen man didn't look away, and neither did Luke. When the man eventually did turn away, Luke carried on looking in his direction as he finished his bag of crisps. He hoped it was a wise move and not a killer move. Suddenly, without warning, the chosen man slammed his drink down and strode over to Luke so quickly that Luke spilled beer down his front with fright. All other conversation in the pub ceased as every eye in the place focused, laser-like, on Luke. *Shit,* he thought. *Here goes.*

"Got a fucking problem? Cos if you haven't, you're gonna get one shortly!" The man's face was screwed up like a discarded coke can, his eyes raging, his breath vile. Spittle flew as he leaned in and shouted into Luke's face; a wet blob landed on his cheek. Luke desperately wanted to wipe it off and tried not to grimace in disgust for fear of upsetting the man further. A fight was the last thing he wanted, and he had a feeling it would be the pub crowd against him. What had given him the crazy notion he'd be safe in such a place? Even dressed in jeans and a hoody, his oldest coat over the top, he still looked as out of place as a Chelsea supporter in the West Ham end of the stadium. And just as dangerous. Should he reply, he wondered, as if in a dream, and if so, with what?

"No problem, no. Just taking in the scenery." As soon as he heard how it sounded to his own ears, Luke knew he'd said the wrong thing. He did his best to recover before he got punched. Or worse. Quickly, he added, "I mean, taking in the ambience of the place. A fine pub you have here." He did his best to deliver a nervous smile and it must have worked because the man pulled back a little. Then he spoke, rather than shouting, for which Luke was grateful.

"What ya doing in here? I can see you're not from round here. You a pig or something?"

"Far from it, actually. And you're right, I'm not from here. But I am looking for something specific."

"Not a pig, eh? Then what are you?"

Conversation in the rest of the pub resumed as it became apparent that nothing further was on the tables, no fight imminent. Luke tried to breathe normally again as he spoke to the pock-marked face looming over him. At least the guy was out of his face now.

"Call me a customer. Like I said, I'm after something."

"Yeah? What, like a kebab or something?" the man said, unsmiling.

Luke lowered his voice as he said, "A piece, actually. Know anyone that can do that?"

"I know plenty, but what makes you think you can get one through this place? It's a reputable business," Pock-Marks said, waving his arms around the bar. He smiled at his own observation, showing caramel-coloured teeth that had probably never seen a dentist. Luke suspected the man didn't get too many kisses with a mouth like that.

"Figured I'd ask." Luke was feeling more confident with each sentence they shared. Taking a breath, he invited the man to sit. "Can I get you a refill?" Pock-Marks looked puzzled, and Luke gamely carried on. "Lager, is it?" Sometimes confidence was the best way to take control, particularly if you didn't feel it. The man nodded and Luke stood to go and buy his refill. He hoped his legs would hold out as he walked; he didn't dare to look back towards his seat and the man in case it ignited him again.

"You're brave. Or stupid," the barman said as he filled a pint glass with lager. Wordlessly, Luke handed over the cash and went back to his table. One thing he had learned was that most people appreciated the act of 'breaking bread' together before settling down to business, although tonight Luke's version of 'bread' came in a pint pot. He set it down in front of the man and let him take a sip before speaking.

"So, can you help me, then?"

"Tell me what you're after."

Chapter Forty-Five

IT WAS a night for seedy pubs.

Sam had asked Anika to sit for a couple of hours, which she'd gladly agreed to for two reasons: first, Sam had Sky TV, and second, as she'd had a bit of a bust-up with her boyfriend, she'd welcomed the change of scenery as well as the opportunity to drink the best part of a bottle of wine while she watched the girls.

"Take your time," she'd said as Sam had left her sleeping children with a woman who'd soon be passed out, fast asleep in front of the TV. She'd never been able to hold her drink. Sam would throw a blanket over her later when she returned; no sense in her driving home drunk.

Sam closed the front door behind her and set out into a freezing cold Manchester night towards The Feathers. As her little car chugged gamely down Clumber Road, she wiped the misty inside of her windscreen with a gloved hand to see where she was going. The windscreen heater would kick in shortly, but for now, the back of her hand would suffice.

The streets were quiet. More sensible folks were inside with their central heating on full, no doubt curled up with hot tea, the biscuit barrel and *Coronation Street*, but not Sam. With her toasty Ugg boots on her feet and wrapped in a thick, fleecy jacket complete with fake fur hood trim, all she wanted was to get this done and then get back home and relax a little. She thought of the pills she'd swallowed just before she'd left, a little something to spur her on, take the edge off being nervous. They'd probably kick in about the time she arrived to find her target.

While she had a clear description of Sid from Anika, she still couldn't quite visualize him. Hopefully she'd know him when she saw him. She reached into her bag on the passenger's seat and pulled out a bottle of vodka, setting it between her thighs as she unscrewed the top off with her left hand, the right on the steering wheel. At the first available chance, when she knew she could toss her head back and swig, she did. She then tossed her head back again and rapidly guzzled down a couple more mouthfuls. Clear liquid leaked out of the corner of her mouth, spilling onto her jeans, making her look down for a split second. A car horn blared as she started to cross the central line, and Sam yanked the steering wheel back to the left and the relative safety of her own lane.

"Fuck!" she said, wiping her mouth and brushing uselessly at the liquid that had now soaked into her jeans. She made a vain attempt to screw the lid back on, then gave up and slotted the bottle into the drinks holder in the driver's door; she'd secure it later when she got to the pub.

The pub.

Up ahead, the dour building came into view. There was not much in the way of inviting lighting, but then a pub with a reputation such as this one had, probably didn't exactly go looking for new business. The whole place was overdue something, though not a refurbishment – more a demolition, Sam thought. She parked in the dark empty street slightly down from the front door and sat for a moment, car doors locked. The vodka had found the pills from earlier; a glow was starting inside her stomach like a hot potato keeping her warm on the inside. She capped the bottle securely now and slid it under her seat, not wanting to leave it on display and not wanting to take it with her. She'd be glad of another swig when this was all over and done.

The strong odour of cigarettes, old beer and piss from the gents' toilets hit her full on as she stepped inside, and she did her utmost not to wrinkle her nose. Without making eye contact or looking round at all, she headed straight for the bar and ordered a bottle of lager from the woman on the other side. She was pushing sixty and was buxom with bright red box-dyed hair.

"Coming right up," she said cheerfully, and Sam watched as her leopard print dress rode up far too much as she bent to the fridge behind her.

Pass the mint sauce, Sam thought cattily. She tried not to look at the woman's legs; they were thick, with knobbly veins running up them like the M1 motorway. She needed support hosiery, badly.

The woman set down Sam's beer and Sam passed her a £5 note, then turned her back to the bar and risked a furtive, sweeping look to see who was in. And if anyone was watching her. The sound of balls clacking together in the distance pricked her ears up.

"Your change, love," the bartender said, and Sam heard the coins settle on the wooden bar beside her elbow. Absentmindedly, she scooped them up with one hand and slipped them into her coat pocket, then moved from the main bar room towards where the sound of clanking balls had come from, a room out back.

It wasn't hard to spot the man she was looking for. He fitted Anika's description down to a T. The dark roots had grown out to about four inches. He was still nervous-looking, and his jeans hung off narrow hips, exposing grey boxer shorts. He wore an old T-shirt with Begbie from *Trainspotting* on the front, layered over another grubby long-sleeved tee. Sid lined up with his cue and sank the black ball in one swift movement, then gave himself a little cheer. The youth he'd been playing left his cue on the table and headed for the toilets, shoulders slumped in defeat. Sid picked up the £10 note, his winnings, and pocketed it. Sam watched, taking it all in.

It was time for her to make her move.

Chapter Forty-Six

THE FIRST THING Sam did when she got back to her car was pull the vodka bottle up from under her seat and take another couple of large gulps. Her mouth had dried up, even after the bottle of lager. In a few moments, she felt the vodka start to ease her tension and regulate her breathing again, though doing it was doing nothing for her shaking hands. The man, Sid, had scared her a little, though since she was nearly twice his size in terms of body fat, she doubted he'd have hurt her. Although of course that didn't rule out a hidden knife up his sleeve or a knuckle-duster in his pocket. But she'd made contact, and that was all she'd intended to do.

For now.

There had been no point in making him suspicious and spelling out what she wanted at this stage of the game, so she'd simply bought him a pint and they'd played a little pool. She'd spent the time watching him, sussing him out as he eventually lost the game. Pool was one thing Sam was extremely skilled at. She'd let him keep his bet; there was no point antagonizing him. She wanted him to be glad to see her when it came time for her to return and make her purchase.

Sam smiled and took another swig of vodka. Yes, he'd been rough looking and she wouldn't trust him as far as she could arm-wrestle him, but he had actually turned out to be a decent pool opponent and not bad company for the evening, although she was well aware that she wouldn't want to meet his nasty side.

Time to get back to her girls.

As she'd suspected, Anika was spark out on the sofa, the empty wine bottle on its side on the carpet and a drained wine glass alongside it. A half-eaten pizza slice lay on a plate on the coffee table; the morning's mail lay unopened next to it. In the kitchen, the pizza box lay on the work surface, the lid open, three full slices untouched. Why Anika had bought such a big one if she hadn't been that hungry Sam had no idea, but Anika's loss was her gain. She took a slice, biting the now soggy crust covered with cold melted cheese. Pizza was one of the few take-away meals that tasted good cold as well as hot, and Sam stood staring out of the window again, munching absentmindedly as she pondered. A rapid movement caught her eye − a cat probably, darting through the back garden. She blinked and it was gone as quickly as it had come.

Just passing through.

Like life itself, she thought glumly − all of us are given just a short space of time as we pass through on the way to someplace else. Where, nobody quite knows. She helped herself to a second slice of pizza while she thought about the big decision she'd made. Would Duncan feel anything when the time came? She didn't want him to suffer, but she did want him out of her life. And the girls'. And she did want the insurance money and widow's pension, so really, there was no other way to get exactly what she wanted.

The great outdoors was still and calm. The temperature had plummeted as she'd driven home; her neighbours were all tucked behind thick curtains, too busy staring at their televisions to notice her departure or return on such a night. There was no one to tell Duncan she'd been out, and since Anika was passed out on the sofa, she'd have no clue what time she'd finally got home.

Sam quietly made her way up the stairs and checked on the girls. She dragged the quilt off the bed in the back room and went back downstairs, where she gently covered Anika over as she lay on the sofa.

She stirred a little but didn't say a word or open her eyes. Sam collected the unopened mail and leaned over Anika for a moment.

"Thanks for your help," she said softly, and turned the lamp out, plunging the room into darkness. Closing the living room door on her friend, she made her way up to bed then sent a quick text to Duncan warning him Anika was on the sofa asleep. She didn't want him barging in, turning the lights on and scaring her to death when he came home later.

How many more nights? she wondered. How many more did he have? She slipped into her pyjamas and sat up in bed for a while, her body still full of pills and vodka though the adrenaline rush had since faded. Soon she'd crash – she always did – but until that point came, she wanted to run her developing plan back through her head once again, trying to iron out the kinks.

Like where was she going to get the cash from?

She remembered the unopened mail that was waiting on the chest of drawers. She padded over. There were three envelopes in total, and she collected them and took them back to bed, where she ripped them open in turn. Electric bill, magazine subscription reminder and bank statement. Didn't anyone write letters anymore? Wouldn't that be a nice change from junk mail and bills?

But as an idea crept into her head through a disused back door, she smiled to herself at the simplicity of it.

She could forge his signature and get a bank loan.

And the sweetest part?

He'd never know anything about it – he wouldn't be around to find out.

Chapter Forty-Seven

THE ALARM BLARED like a ship's horn and Sam woke with a jolt. Duncan lay next to her. He stirred as she reached over, hit the snooze button and settled back down.

"What time is it?" he said groggily.

"A little after seven. Want a cuppa bringing?" Sam was doing her best to be the perfect wife.

"That would be lovely. Thanks."

She watched as he rolled onto his side, facing her, his hair mussed up, eyes barely open.

"What time did you get home? I didn't hear you come in."

"A little after midnight. We'd had a solid lead on the child abductor in the afternoon and the team went in last night. Nabbed the pervert but we're still uncertain where the two children are. He's not talking."

Sam slipped out of bed as the alarm blared again and switched it off, grabbing her robe at the same time.

"Well, it's good news you have him. He'll talk at some stage, won't he?"

"I'd like to beat the shit out of him to get him to talk, but you can't do that these days. Bloody politically correct crap. If politicians worked with what we saw day in, day out, they'd damn well change their minds." He rubbed his eyes wearily.

"I'll go and get your cuppa and give the girls a nudge. You stay put and rest." She bent over and kissed the side of his head gently before she left the room.

When Sam returned ten minutes later, she was carrying a tray with two mugs of tea and a plate of hot toast for them both. Duncan was sat up in bed, still bleary-eyed. She noticed the softness of his upper body, the paleness of it. He'd used to be so fit, so strong, when they'd first got together, but age and lack of time and energy had changed all that. And she was no different, she knew. Two children did the same to a woman's body, though at least she had an excuse.

"Thought I'd have breakfast in bed with you," she said with a smile. She passed him a mug then slipped back in under the covers. "The girls are eating cereal downstairs. They'll probably come and say hi in a minute or two. Toast?" She offered him the plate and he took a slice. She set the plate on the quilt in front of them both. "We've not had a picnic in bed since before the girls were born, I don't think," she said, almost reminiscing.

"I meant to ask, why is Anika on the sofa?" He took another bite, greasy butter making his lips glisten.

"She came over last night, drank too much and fell asleep. They'd had another row, so she needed to drown her sorrows. Then I covered her over. She was still asleep when I went through." Changing direction, she enquired, "What's your plan for today, then. Back in to work?"

"Yes. I'll have this and grab a shower. We've left him to stew in a cell overnight. His lawyer will be back in later this morning, I expect. Maybe then he'll come to his senses. Good timing, really."

"Oh? Why's that?"

"Well, because I've got that tactical training course. I wasn't sure if I'd be able to go, but now he's safely in the nick, it shouldn't be a problem."

"I'd forgotten about that. When is it?" Sam felt a prick of alarm in her gut.

"Day after tomorrow. Just one night away then back home. I could do with the rest here, really."

He munched quietly as an idea percolated in Sam's head. Could this be the opportune time? Could she organize herself and get her plan actioned this week? There was a lot to do.

"So, I'd better get a move on, get back in to work," he said, flinging the covers back. He held the edge of a piece of toast in his mouth. Sam watched as he pushed the remainder in, chewing, and left the bedroom. The sound of the shower running, then the girls' feet running up the stairs, brought her thoughts back to the practicalities of the day ahead.

With Duncan's revelation that he would be away in two night's time, she knew this had to be her window of opportunity. While he was away in another town all on his own, she'd be out of the frame for sure, sat snug at home in front of the TV with the girls, alibi sorted. Perhaps she'd invite Anika to stay over too. Yes – that would be the perfect alibi.

Anika was stirring as Sam entered the room. The girls were up and clattering around upstairs now, making too much noise for even the deepest sleeper to ignore. Anika clutched her sore head and groaned.

"Morning," Sam said brightly. "Tea? And maybe a Paracetamol too?"

"Ouch. Yes, and yes, please."

Sam took the recent revelation by the horns and sounded Anika out.

"Listen, Duncan is away for the night day after tomorrow. Why don't we have a sleepover? A movie, takeaway, a couple of drinks – it'll be fun. And if you don't fall asleep on the couch, there's a proper bed in the spare room. What do you say?" Sam fixed another bright smile on her face.

Anika frowned, no doubt feeling sick as a dog.

"Oh, go on!" Sam enthused. "Two girls, all night, no men? Sounds like fun!"

It did the trick. Anika smiled weakly and nodded. "But make me limit my wine, would you? My head feels like a thousand ants in work boots are stomping the inside of my skull for fun."

"Ah, the ant punishment." Sam smiled knowingly. "I'll get your

Paracetamol," she said, and went back through to the kitchen. While she busied herself making tea and finding painkillers, inside her head was a riot of activity. A mental checklist was forming, and her first task was already checked off the list. Would it be stupid to write things out, put a list on physical paper? It would make it much easier. No, her head would have to do.

Duncan put his head through the door.

"Right, I'm off. I'll see you later."

"Before you go, what time are you heading to your course, and where is it again?"

"It's in Kent but I'll be overnight Croydon. I'm meeting up with a couple from Croydon station for a curry then tactical the following day. Why?"

"Oh, just taking an interest in your plans." That sweet smile again. She was getting convincing at it. She planted a light kiss on his cheek and casually turned back to what she'd been doing.

"Right, then. I'll see you later," Duncan said. "Not sure what time."

"Okay. Enjoy your day," Sam said over her shoulder.

The front door closed and it was Anika's turn to put her head through the door.

"You two sound like you're getting on well."

Sam turned to her friend with the same smile she'd been delivering to Duncan over the last couple of days. She was working hard at laying the emotional groundwork.

"We are now, thankfully. I think we've turned a corner. I see big changes ahead."

Don't I just.

Chapter Forty-Eight

AT LAST, the house was empty and Sam could think. Planning to get rid of your husband in the next couple of days was not without its drawbacks; there was much to be accomplished to get every detail right. Could she do it another day? Of course she could – but she didn't want to. The stronger Sam of old had returned, pushing the recent Sam-the-pathetic off her metaphorical cliff, never to return. Her decision to carry out this plan had ignited her inner pilot light, filled her belly with fire again, and the freedom she'd garner at the end of it all – not to mention the money – excited every fibre of her being.

Her mental list had grown in size, but now, as she headed in through the main entrance of the bank, she was about to chalk a line through another item.

The money.

With the clock ticking down the hours, she had only been able to guess at the amount of cash she'd need for her plan. *How much does it cost to kill your husband?* But since Duncan wouldn't be around to question the transaction, she had decided to err on the side of caution and organize more than she thought she'd need.

"Good morning. I'd like to take a loan out, if I may," she informed the teller behind the screen, slipping her bank card under the glass partition. "I need to do the paperwork if I can, then get my husband to sign later today if that's okay. He's working late."

The teller smiled her understanding.

"Certainly. How much are you looking for?" Sam noticed the woman's engagement ring twinkling as it caught the light; there was no wedding band visible yet. "What a stunning ring," she said pleasantly. "Have you set the date yet?"

The woman blushed and smiled. "It's a bit soon yet. We only got engaged at the weekend. It is lovely though, isn't it?" She looked down at the ring and blushed again.

"Oh, congratulations!" Sam carried on, hoping she wasn't overdoing things.

The teller eventually came back to the business at hand. "How much would you like to borrow? I see you already have a preapproved amount noted on your account of up to twenty thousand pounds, which means I can confirm that to you today without any further paperwork. Over that amount, though, and I will have to get approval." The ring twinkled again.

"It's lucky I only need twenty thousand, then." Sam laughed lightly. "Save on the paperwork."

"Great. I'll do that for you now, then. It won't take me a minute or two."

Sam watched the pretty ring as it flew across the keyboard, creating a loan for £20,000. If the teller knew what she was *actually* authorizing with the loan, Sam mused, she probably wouldn't be so friendly or efficient.

Sam smiled to herself. Her plan was going better than expected now that one of her biggest obstacles was almost completed. Luckily, she and Duncan had always had a joint account rather than opting for a housekeeping account and both contributing amounts into that. It worked for other couples, but Sam and Duncan had never seen any point in it. When she'd been working, they'd saved a little each month, putting it towards a holiday or renovations or a new car, but those savings had dwindled a little since they'd been living on one wage.

The teller was speaking. Sam had missed the question.

"Which account would you like the money to be available from, Mrs. Riley?"

"The savings account, please." Sam watched the flying diamond again as the teller pressed a key to confirm the transfer. Smiling, she announced that the money was in their account.

All £20,000 of it.

It couldn't have been easier.

Sam left the bank with a spring in her step, destination unknown for the time being. A coffee shop sign up ahead caught her attention, and she slipped inside to quietly celebrate on her own.

In a few more days she'd be spending a good deal more time on her own.

"Cappuccino and a donut please," she ordered, and took a seat in a corner spot by the window to think some more. There was still so much to organize. It was quiet inside the coffee shop, though the take-away window was nonstop. Sam was glad she didn't have to rush off to the office or be at someone else's beck and call any more. Would she need to go back to that when this was all over? Get a job? The insurance money wouldn't last forever, she knew, and she'd probably have to move house. Clumber Road was okay, handy for Duncan's work, but there was the whole country to consider now, and far nicer places to settle down and start afresh.

And the funds to do it with.

The girls were young enough not to mind the move, thankfully. They were both a long way from exams that mattered and the upheaval of lifelong friendships. They could get a house with a field, get a pony or some chickens, have a puppy maybe; the girls would love that. Her coffee and donut arrived, and she tucked in, still musing about what she might do herself eventually. Buy a café business, maybe? Plenty of people had that dream – settle on the Cornish coast, open a little place with checkered tablecloths and serve scones with homemade jam. . .

Sam watched the barista diligently work through the orders in front of her, her hands frantically switching from adding coffee to the press or milk to the steam tap. It looked hot, hard work. Sam imagined spending hours with steam rising into her face, queues in front of her until lunchtime and beyond, when it would start up again for a couple more hours.

"We'll see," she mumbled, and turned away to watch the world outside the window while she ate her good fortune reward. Raspberry jam dripped onto her lap and she glanced down in annoyance, then gave a start. It looked like blood.

Duncan's blood.

And it didn't bother her.

Chapter Forty-Nine

SHE PRESSED her finger thoughtfully into the blob of deep red jam on her jeans, surprised at her lack of emotion. It was dark enough to be blood but thicker, and she spread out to the sides a little as she played with it.

She imagined now that it was Duncan's blood, that she'd somehow found him after the fact, had sat with him a moment or two before calling it in, reporting a death – not that she'd be in the vicinity if her plan went through, of course. But what if it did happen in their home? Would she find him lying in a pool of his own blood on the kitchen floor? What then? Would she play with a blob of blood between her thumb and forefinger like she was playing now with the sticky raspberry jam? Maybe. Or maybe she'd be crying, regretting what she'd been responsible for, or maybe she'd be whooping, dancing gaily around his prostrate body. Or maybe she'd have no emotion at all. That seemed the most likely scenario, because each time she'd thought, really thought, about what she was organizing, she had felt nothing at all about the task ahead. Maybe she could do the job herself and save the cash? No, the forensics team would be on her in a flash. Never mind the problem of an alibi: if she did the deed itself, she couldn't be out with Anika at the same time.

No, clearly it needed to be done by someone else other than her.

But two days seemed so ... soon. Perhaps she should choose another date, further in the distance.

Or did it? Perhaps she should take the opportunity in front of her after all: Duncan would be out of town, and she'd be at home with Anika – with a firm alibi right there. Fate had surely dealt her a gift, a timeframe in which she could act –so she should do just that.

She sipped her coffee and finished her donut, thoughts drifting. She remembered that night not long ago when the girls had been returned safe and sound, the look of disgust, of distrust even, that had been etched on Duncan's face, his accusation that she was unfit to take care of them, and his threat to take the girls and leave her behind.

And nobody was going to take them away from her, not now, not ever.

If her husband could say such venomous words to her face, it could only mean one thing: he didn't love her anymore. Well, Sam wasn't so sure she loved him either, so they were quits in that respect – not that she'd tell him, of course. Especially now. No, she was on her quest to be the perfect wife for the rest of their time together, happy in the knowledge that life for her and the girls was about to become quite different.

Back home, Sam stood gazing out of the lounge window, the white net curtains shielding her from the outside world, from nosey neighbours behind curtains of their own. She moved away from the windows and flipped the bird to whoever might be watching her now. She wouldn't miss the street, nor the town. The Cornish coast with all its seaside splendour would be far nicer, far more scintillating and a damn sight more welcoming than this dreary Manchester suburb. A place over-looking the sea, somewhere she could call home, make a new life for them all, would do her the world of good.

And there would be no need for any more pills; she was sure of that. Emptying the last four from the inside pocket of her bag, she tossed them to the back of her throat followed by a gulp of almost-cold tea. She winced as the capsules cascaded down into her stomach.

Taking several deep breaths, Sam worked on clearing the anxiety in her chest and got to work on her laptop with her next quest: how to access the dark web. While Seedy Sid was still an option, organizing something with him in person was a huge risk to undertake, and one she might not need to take at all if there was a safer way. From her understanding, the dark web was a way of staying anonymous. She could arrange her transaction and get the job done, and no one would know she was involved.

It took her several hours to get the results she wanted, and it was almost time to collect the girls from school when she came up for air. Gaining access to the space had been easy enough, it seemed, though she'd take a longer look at things later when the girls were doing their homework upstairs. But for now, she had a good understanding of how things worked.

She knew that what she wanted to do was . . . doable.

Maybe she could get her tablets from the dark web, too, she thought, get them posted rather than relying on chemists' shift rotations or finding a place further away from home that didn't know her. Her 'tea lady' was expensive and inconvenient, too, and not exactly local, but for the odd days when she needed a stronger jump-start or a sleepy peaceful day she had her uses. Or was buying her pills online too risky? She supposed she could use a private box rather than her home address for deliveries, but even that was traceable. Nonetheless it was worth looking into when the main business was taken care of. There had to be ways to safely receive goods.

Gathering her bag, she left the house to go the long way round to school, towards the shopping mall that had a supermarket with a resident chemist, one that she hadn't been to for a couple of weeks.

Those were getting harder and harder to find, it seemed.

Chapter Fifty

"Come on, girls. Time to brush your teeth and get ready for bed."

A whiney chorus of 'Oh, Mummmm' filled the lounge as two young faces turned to their mother, trying for sympathy. It wasn't working, not tonight.

"You stayed up last night, remember? I left you reading in bed, if you recall, rather than lights out. You'll be getting bags under your eyes like I have if you have another late one, and trust me, you don't want that." Sam was helping the girls pick toys up and put them back in the cupboard as was the rule at night – all toys had to be put away.

"Come on, quickly now. If you get upstairs and ready for bed in the next five minutes, you can read for ten more." There was a sudden flurry of activity as two skinny little bodies raced up the stairs together in an attempt to get ready within the allotted time. Two sets of soft brown curls bounced out of view and Sam stood at the bottom making sure no one tripped in the stampede to be first. They were a joy to call her own. The sound of the little girls chattering while they were supposed to be brushing their teeth made her smile as she picked out odd toothpaste-frothy words from her spot downstairs. They were going to a friend's birthday party at the weekend and both had new dresses for the occasion. Victoria wanted to know what Jasmine was doing with her hair – up or down.

At their age?

"Pigtails!" Jasmine had yelled, and Sam could imagine white specks of toothpaste splattering the mirror. Nothing a wipe with the towel later wouldn't fix. Her heart missed for a moment as she realized they might be fatherless by then. Would they still want to go? Would it be appropriate, even? She waited until her daughters were finished in the bathroom, then climbed the stairs and popped her head around each bedroom doorway and peered in. Victoria was ready, a book in her hands, lips moving slightly as she read the words to herself to help make sense of some of the longer ones. She looked pretty in her pink nightie, her teddy tucked in at her side. Next, Sam checked in on Jasmine, who wasn't quite ready. She was still picking a book to read from the bookcase behind the door, a little finger resting on her lip as she pondered her choices.

"Need a hand choosing?"

"I'm okay, thanks, Mum. But why don't you tell me a story instead?" Two bright, twinkling eyes looked up at her and Sam caved in.

"Come on, then. Jump into bed. I'll tell you a short one because I've lots to do tonight, all right?"

"All right." Jasmine slid under the covers and Sam pulled the blanket up to her chin. She sat on the edge of the bed and recited one of Jasmine's favourite stories, about how all the cats and dogs nearby crept into the forest late at night. Of how they'd each tell stories and light a bonfire to sleep next to for warmth in winter. Then they'd all awaken at dawn and wander back home so nobody would know they had even been out. Oh, the stories they would tell one another – the same stories that Sam recited to her own children as she watched them slowly drift off to sleep, eyelids fluttering as they fought to stay awake, in the warmth of their cosy beds. As Jasmine drifted off now, Sam kissed her forehead gently and turned off the bedside lamp. The light from the hallway was enough for her to see her way out.

"One more minute, Victoria, then lights out please," she called as she pulled Jasmine's door almost closed. Victoria nodded that she understood.

Back downstairs, Sam poured herself a glass of red wine, set her laptop on the sofa beside her and turned the TV on for a bit of background noise and comfort.

Comfort? You'd better get used to being on your own.

Clicking the anonymous browser icon, she resumed her search for someone to kill her husband – preferably while he was away in Croydon. She found the whole dark web thing fascinating and had been careful not to let her natural inquisitiveness get the better of her and click a link to something she might regret later. The headlines and the post titles urged the viewer to click and read, or in many cases observe, and even though she was anonymous, she knew full well that you can't un-see something you'd rather not have seen in the first place.

But it wasn't all weird stuff. Yes, there were links to encourage you away someplace else, but most of the stuff on offer wasn't much different than the hits from an old-fashioned search page from way back.

She typed a term for what she wanted and hit enter. Then she waited, sipping her red, for results to come home.

"Wow, so many to choose from," she mumbled as the screen began to fill. There was clearly a market for knocking people off. Her finger hesitated over her mouse pad as the cursor blinked, waiting for her decision. She made her selection, then sat back and took another sip of wine.

When the page had fully loaded, she read the brief description of what was on offer. Beside it was a link to get in touch and discuss requirements. She took a deep breath. Then another. The cursor flashed tantalizingly but Sam didn't click it. Instead, she reverted back to the search results and read a couple more descriptions before choosing one more and clicking through. As the last page, she read what services were on offer but this page had a somewhat different feel to it than the one previous. It seemed, well, less matter-of-fact and more "Let's solve a problem." There was something she liked about the way the words flowed; it felt a little more harmonious.

And it was that harmonious feel that caused Samantha Riley to make her decision. Funny that it was important at all, she thought as she clicked the link.

Her husband's killer had been selected.

176

Chapter Fifty-One

SINCE DUNCAN HAD CALLED to say don't wait up, again, Sam had snuggled up on the sofa under a fleecy blanket all on her own. Again.

It was like being single half the time.

Not much will change there, then.

She kicked the throw off her legs and poured another glass of red, grabbing the remote control before resuming her comfortable position. She rested her head back on a cushion, feeling a little drowsy, the wine and pills mixing as they shouldn't. A calmness blended with a slight numbness embraced her whole being and she slid further down the sofa before selecting a program she'd recorded a few days ago. After her recent research and actually making contact with a *professional hit man*, she wanted something that would simply wash over her and didn't require much brainpower. The food program would do the trick. Sam clicked select and the music started, followed by the deep voice of a male presenter that she'd seen on a show before but couldn't place where. No matter; it wasn't important.

She settled in for the program to finish the job that had been started by the substances she'd consumed. Not five minutes in and her eyes were fluttering a little, as if she was going to go to sleep, and drowsily she wondered if perhaps bed was in order. An early night, a nice deep sleep always did you good. But as the presenter chattered on, something stirred inside her mind and began to pull her back to the moment. Sam reared bolt upright on the sofa like a corpse coming back to life on an old Frankenstein movie, and did her best to focus. Suddenly alert to what he was talking about, she asked herself if she'd misheard him in her drowsy state. But no, the presenter's words were mountain-stream clear and the meaning just as cold. She turned up the volume. No, there was no doubt about the topic of this particular food program.

Naturally occurring poisonous foods.

Tossing the throw aside, she swung her legs down to the floor and listened intently. The segment was on the dangers of green potatoes and their potentially lethal ingredient – solanine.

"I thought that was an old wives' tale," she said to herself.

Apparently, it wasn't. She sat there thoughtful, drinking in the information, knowing she could use it somewhere in her plan. Fate had once again shown her something she could use in the demise of her husband, though when and where she'd add in later. Her mind snapped into gear, turning over the possibilities, as she took in the extent of what solanine could do. Yes, large quantities of it could be fatal, but it was no longer that common in modern-day potatoes you bought from the supermarket. Not unless you purposely grew such potatoes, like the Incas had done thousands of years ago, but even then, they had had a process for degrading the solanine before they ate them.

As the program went on, Sam knew she could incorporate the idea somehow: it was a natural substance and the notion of using it too good to be missed. But Duncan would have to consume more than his fair share of potatoes, even supposing she could find enough green ones to do the deed with, never mind convincing him to eat them. But distilling it and using it to immobilize him – well, that was another matter. Diarrhea, vomiting, drowsiness, mental confusion, shortness of breath and weak and rapid pulse were all symptoms that'd slow him down considerably, and the poison would likely never get picked up, because why would anyone be looking?

The more she thought about it, the more it made sense: Duncan was a big man, and strong too, so if someone broke into his room, he'd certainly be able to put up a fight and defend himself, even against a surprise attack in the dead of night. But if he had been slowed down beforehand by mental confusion and gastro problems, it would make the assassin's job much easier.

Sam's face broke into a sick smile as she stood listening to the rest of the show. Solanine looked to be the answer, but how to get it?

She shut off the television and fetched her laptop.

By the time she heard a key turn in the front door, it was nearly eleven o'clock. She closed her laptop and smiled winningly.

"Hi, darling. You look bushed. Can I get you something to eat or drink?" she asked cheerily.

A delighted but tired Duncan replied, "I'd love a proper mug of tea and a sandwich if you can be bothered. I'm done in."

Sam watched as he all but collapsed onto the sofa, resting his head back and closing his eyes for a moment. "No bother. Stay where you are. I'll bring it in," she said with a smile and a spring in her step as off she went through to the kitchen, looking for all the world like a loving wife attending to her exhausted husband's needs.

Tomorrow, a trip to the garden centre was in order. A bag of green seed potatoes with plenty of eyes should do the trick.

Chapter Fifty-Two

LUKE WAS sick of the sight of his small, functional room at his parents' place, but beggars really couldn't be choosers. At least it was cheap, and, with no money to speak of and no income prospects on the horizon, he knew he'd be staying put for a while longer.

Currently, he was nursing a mug of coffee at a corner table about a mile away. As a precaution, he had begun to vary the locations he accessed his new business website. Being over-cautious was better than the other way around and getting busted unnecessarily, he figured. While the site was anonymous, he knew there was always going to be a way to trace it eventually, if the tracer knew who they were searching for.

As he sipped, there was a ping, signalling that he had a new message. He sat forward, hardly believing his eyes.

That was quick...

Keeping his face as neutral as possible, he hovered the cursor over the message, willing himself to be calm. Taking a deep breath, he clicked it. The message filled his small screen and even though he was tucked in a corner unable to be overlooked, he still did a sweep of the café before he read it in its entirety. It was short.

Looking for a removal. Quickly. Window of opportunity has come up Thursday evening in Croydon. Interested?

Holy shit. Thursday evening was only a few short hours away. Suddenly all of his and Clinton's planning over the last couple of weeks seemed like children's daydreams. Stuff was getting real, and fast. *Thursday.* Was there even time to get things organized? He stared at the message as thoughts catapulted themselves through his head like a circus act on steroids.

Well, this was what all those plans had been leading up to, wasn't it? So what was he waiting for?

"They're simply a prospect, a number, a business transaction," he told himself. His hand cupped the mouse; the cursor wriggled over the reply icon. By thinking of this ... this *thing* he proposed to do as just another business deal, could he take the humanity out of it and get on with satisfying his first customer?

For £12,000, he could try.

Remembering his own tentative first enquiry, he decided to keep his reply brief and noncommittal. He began to type:

Not much time but can be done. £12K. Half now; half on completion. Need photo and whereabouts to get rolling. Stand by.

He hit send and sat back in his chair. How long it would be before the prospect came back with further information and funds he'd no idea, though he hoped it would be today. To his surprise, his nervous energy had changed to excitement, anticipation even.

It's new business, remember? A prospect.

He rubbed his hands down the front of his jeans to dry his sweaty palms and rolled his shoulders back to remove the tension. If he was going to fulfil his first order, there were a few things to do, namely purchase a weapon with the first instalment of money.

Money. How was he going to set up the exchange of funds? Mentally he smacked himself in the forehead. He'd assumed a car park rubbish bin would suffice, but what if his client wasn't in Manchester? What was he going to do then?

Steady on, Luke, he told himself. What did he usually do when he had to find a location he'd never visited before? Google Earth. Yes. After the prospect revealed their location, Luke could zoom in and find the perfect spot nearby. Even the smallest of towns had supermarkets, and most of those had a rubbish bin by the entrance.

Okay, that was step one. As for picking up the funds, after midnight, no one else would be rifling through the bin and make off with his fee, would they? But there'd be cameras present, recording, and he wasn't going to risk losing £6000 that easily.

So scratch that. What about Bitcoin? But he had no clue how that even worked and how he his prospect could use it anonymously. Besides, there was not enough time to learn.

Shit, shit, shit.

Right, then. Back to the drawing board. He needed to learn how to do cyber-currency transactions, and he needed to learn it quickly.

Chapter Fifty-Three

ANOTHER LATE NIGHT, another early start. Duncan, gulping down a sausage and egg McMuffin and a coffee in the McDonalds car park, looked like he'd been a couple of rounds with Tyson his eyes were so puffy, but the end was in sight for the case, it seemed. For that he was grateful. And the sun was promising to make an appearance later. After a string of wet, grey days, some orange in the sky, no matter how low, would be a welcome mood-changer. And speaking of moods changing, what was with Sam and her dramatic transformation lately? It was welcome, of course, but it made him uneasy.

A starling hopped by his car looking for scraps for breakfast, found a stray French fry, and tucked in. The activity alerted another bird close by who swooped down to stake its claim on the same find. Feeling sorry for the first bird getting moved on, Duncan lowered his window and tossed a piece of bread its way. Wasting no time, the starling picked the whole piece up and moved further to one side to eat it in peace. Duncan smiled as he started on his hash brown, his first good deed for the day already in the bag. His phone buzzed. Sam.

"Morning, early bird," he said, thinking of the starling.

"Morning, hard-working husband. Just wondered if you're in for dinner tonight and what time you're leaving for your course tomorrow?" Sam enquired.

Duncan again thought about the change in her mood, then answered, "I should be home by six and as for tomorrow, I'll leave home just after lunch. I'm meeting up for dinner while I'm down there so I'll crack on with some reports in my room if I've time beforehand. Only way to get some peace. Why do you ask?"

"Thought I'd make something nice for dinner since you'll be away. Might even bake you some brownies to take with you."

"No need to do anything special on my account. Though your brownies are the best." It had been a while since Sam had last baked brownies, and the thought of the fudgy centre, the way it stayed fudgy, made Duncan drool slightly. "On second thoughts, brownies would definitely be welcome if you can be bothered." As soon as he'd said 'bothered' he regretted it and hoped she didn't take offence. He scrunched his face up in anticipation. But if Sam had noticed the word she didn't show it, and when she spoke again, his face resumed its normal expression.

"Great – I'll make a batch," she replied cheerily. "I've got to go out shopping later anyway so I'll get the chocolate. Need anything?"

"No, I'm all good, thanks. I'll see you later, then."

"Okay. Bye!" Her sing-song voice hung in the car. Duncan scrunched his empty packaging into one bag and left the car to deposit it in the nearby rubbish bin. On the way, he grabbed a paper cup up that had missed its destination and put it with the rest of the rubbish. Good deed number two. His thoughts turned again to Sam and her change of attitude. It was like old times, and Duncan had an overwhelming desire to believe things had got better.

Perhaps he'd get her a little gift or some flowers, just because. He filed the thought away for later. Back in the car, he headed for the station and pulled in to his second car parking space of the morning. Rochelle's Triumph bike slid into the space next to his and Rochelle, clad head to toe in black leather, nodded her greeting through his side window. He watched as she turned the bike off, swung her leg over the seat, and removed her helmet. At six feet tall, she was a vision many men couldn't ignore – no matter how hard they tried.

Her long blonde hair fell to her shoulders like a sexy slow-motion chocolate advert, and Duncan felt himself groan inside involuntarily. Rochelle smiled as their eyes connected in a work colleague kind of way. Shame on Duncan's part. He opened his door and got out, pulling his coat collar up against the cold morning. In the distance a bit of orange was breaking the skyline in amongst the grey buildings. He felt brighter than he had done in weeks despite his exhausted state.

"Morning, Duncan. You look like shit."

"Cheers, Rochelle. I don't have the benefit of make-up to cover up my bags – I suspect you've already expertly buried your own," he said coyly.

"Perks of being a woman," she replied with a wink. "Makes up for PMS and the other crap we have to put up with."

As they walked together towards the building, Duncan said, "Well, at least you girls don't have to shave every day."

"And neither do you, actually, but we girls shave more often than you'd think, so that's your argument gone to crap. In fact, we wax, which really isn't pleasant."

She had a point. A vision of long, slim, smooth, silky legs flashed across Duncan's vision – and they weren't Sam's.

Oblivious, Rochelle carried on. "And talking about who has the better deal, how's Sam doing these days. Any improvement?"

They were inside the building now, headed robotically for the canteen and a coffee.

"Funny you should ask. Since my ultimatum, she's done a full three-hundred-and-sixty-degree turn, and she almost seems like Sam from old. She's up and dressed in the mornings now, and she even made my breakfast a couple of mornings ago. And earlier today, she rang me to see if I wanted her to bake some brownies."

Rochelle raised her eyebrows in surprise. "Well, that's great news! Looks like your chat worked. I'm pleased for you, for you both, because separating would have been a bitch, let me tell you. Stressful doesn't even begin to describe it, and with two little ones to argue over …"

Her words trailed into nothing and Duncan could only nod his head. But Rochelle had more to say. "Of course, there could be another explanation for her complete turnaround."

"Oh?"

"Come on, Duncan. What's the most common and obvious giveaway clue when someone is murdered and we question the spouse's friends and colleagues?"

Duncan looked at her in puzzlement.

"Think, Duncan. You were on the same profiling course as me last year. What is the most obvious thing the spouse does before they strike? What's the classic giveaway?"

She waited. Then it hit him.

Pre-offence behaviour − when a spouse has a sudden and unexplained change in behaviour towards their partner. It was textbook stuff. A significant change in a partner's behaviour can mean the partner may have already begun to plan for a change in the status quo.

Rochelle looked at him, levelly.

"You seriously think she is planning to off me?" he said incredulously.

Rochelle gave him a questioning look but said no more.

Chapter Fifty-Four

It was Sam's turn to stare at a message.

Not much time but can be done. £12K. Half now; half on completion. Need photo and whereabouts to get rolling. Stand by.

This was what she wanted, wasn't it? Her husband out of the picture, leaving the girls and her on their own with money in the bank? Wasn't she sick of his continual late nights and his endless moaning about her not being up to his expectations? She'd tried to keep things together when she'd lost her job, but it was a struggle. She had found the constant rejection from possible employers hard to deal with, even though she was overqualified for many of the roles she'd applied for. But she'd found a way to cope; the painkillers had taken the edge off her anxiety, relaxing her, letting her sleep. It had been her oversleeping that day that had been the catalyst for the sorry situation she now found herself in.

The message was still waiting for an answer. The money wasn't a problem, nor was getting a photo. Nor, it seemed, was the time frame – tomorrow night. So why was she hesitating? Because once she hit reply and did what the message asked, there'd be no turning back. Hit men couldn't be turned off once the switch had been flicked. It was a one-way decision and only Sam could make it. Was she ready?

No messy divorce to worry about . . . money in the bank . . . Cornish coast . .
.

She'd only spoken to Duncan a matter of minutes ago, asked him if he'd be in for dinner and about the time of his departure tomorrow – and so casually too. Sam longed for a piece of paper to write down the pros and cons. If the hit did go through, she knew the police would immediately suspect and question her. She knew they had all sorts of ways of finding proof, most of which she was unaware of. Had it been the other way around – Duncan getting rid of her – he'd have a much better chance of getting away with it. He'd not only know the processes and procedures the crime scene officers would use, but he'd be nice and close to the case to monitor what was happening, whom they suspected. He'd be able to destroy or tamper with evidence, something Sam wouldn't be able to do. Absentmindedly, she wondered how many officers over the years had committed such a crime – and got away with it.

But thoughts like these were not going to help. All she could do was limit the evidence, set the emotional groundwork and spread a few crumbs of her own to keep suspicion away from her door.

Still the message went unanswered. Was that a sign in itself, that she didn't really want him dead? Wouldn't she have clicked it by now if she felt sure? What the hell was she supposed to do? Pressure was building, her nerves rattling in their sheaths, and she gulped down a deep breath like a hiccup. Anxiety tightened in her chest; her breath came in shallow gulps as she fought to calm herself and breathe normally again. She felt beads of sweat on her forehead and wiped them away with the back of her hand.

A tablet or two would fix it.

Collecting her bag from the banister end where it was hanging, she slipped her hand into the side pocket and felt for the pills she knew would be waiting in there. She clutched two and slid them out. Would two be enough? Sighing, she reached in for two more. Staring at them, stark white and smooth against the palm of her fleshy hand, she hated them. Hated them for what they stood for, hated having to take them, hated that, without them, she would be crushed by the feelings that hurt her so much. Sighing again, she swallowed the lot of them down and headed to the kitchen for a glass of water to speed things along.

The sun was not far above the horizon in the distance, the promise of a brighter day to come, and she remembered the girls still upstairs, tucked up snug in their own beds. It was time to get them ready for school. Perhaps she'd walk with them this morning. The fresh air and sunshine would do them all good.

The girls. The pills. The two most prominent things in her life at that moment. One a blessing, the other a curse. She climbed the stairs to wake her daughters.

She went into Victoria's room first, planted a kiss on her cheek.

"Time to get up, darling," she cooed as Victoria opened her eyes. "It's a lovely day. I thought I'd walk you both to school this morning. We could stop at the shop and get you a little butterfly cake each if you'd like?"

Victoria smiled sleepily and nodded her approval before pushing the covers back and slowly climbing out. Sam watched as her eldest daughter made her way sleepily to the bathroom, then went into Jasmine's room. Her heart swelled as Jasmine followed her big sister into the bathroom and the girls began their morning chatter. They were the most precious things in her world.

Bar nothing else.

She went back downstairs to make breakfast and wait for the girls to appear. As she put the kettle on, she made her final decision.

She opened her laptop and clicked reply.

She attached a recent picture of Duncan, along with the address of where he'd be staying that night. She typed:

Money OK, picture and address included. What next? Send.

The deed was done. The ball was rolling. The status quo was about to change.

What happened from here on in was out of her hands.

Chapter Fifty-Five

AFTER SHE DROPPED the girls off at school, she went into a café and logged into her laptop again. As she'd suspected, there was a message waiting for her. If the other café customers knew what she was up to, sat in the corner organizing what she was organizing, would anyone try and stop her? Would she herself stop Anika if she was planning on doing the same thing to her partner?

But Anika wasn't married to Duncan, and Anika wasn't a disappointment to her partner, unlike Sam was. If Duncan was flippant enough to tell her he was out of there if she didn't change, then he could have what was coming to him.

The message was simple and included two links.

Time and place noted. Please transfer funds by following instructions in link. Message when half has been transferred.

Sam clicked the first link and was a little surprised it wasn't a regular banking transaction. But then she thought about for a moment and almost laughed aloud at herself. Who in their right mind would order a hit and transfer funds through a regular banking entity along with their account name? While that would have been simple, as would putting hard cash in a carrier bag and dropping it into a nearby rubbish bin, it was neither secure nor practical.

She scanned the link he'd sent her – she'd assumed he was a 'he' – and read the basic instructions on opening a crypto currency account. It looked straightforward enough on the surface. Well, there was no time like the present. She needed to get this underway now, and opening an account and transferring the first instalment correctly was step one in getting the job completed.

A few minutes later, she looked up from her screen with satisfaction. The first part was almost complete. She clicked the second link – how to buy currency and then transfer it to pay for the deal. Again, it was straightforward enough and it wasn't long before she was ready to hit send. With everything lined up ready, this was the final part in sending the boulder careering towards Duncan. And it could never be undone. Looking away from her screen for a moment, Sam gazed out of the café window at the people outside going about their own business. What was going on in their lives right now, today? she wondered. Did they ever feel like obliterating someone from their lives? A boss, maybe? An abusive partner, a boring partner, or a parent, even? Perhaps a child that was causing distress or annoyance? Was anybody safe from the ideals of someone they knew?

She looked at each person in turn as they moved past the window and tried to image what the imaginary thought bubbles coming out of them would say. Who would be making a shopping list, working on a presentation, figuring out an apology, or contemplating suicide? Everyone had their own set of problems that varied in importance, and what was important to one wouldn't necessarily be important to another. Like when people moaned about having a bad day – one person's version of a bad day would be totally different to the next person's; a surgeon losing a patient topped finding out that your child has crayoned the hall wall. But whatever went on in a person's own particular world, well, that was the most important thing, Sam knew, no matter how trivial it might seem to others. What would someone read from her thought bubble? she wondered. An involuntary shiver brought her back to the present, and the blinking transfer button. There was no point in delaying it any longer.

She hit the button.

A confirmation popped up to tell her the funds were now on their way, and Sam gulped nervously.

Tomorrow night, her girls would no longer have a father.

But she'd be single, in control of the girls' future and comfortably well off for the rest of her life. It was a small price to pay for such luxury, and reconciling it in her head that way, she instantly felt better. The Cornish coast could be a great new place to settle her little family into a new routine and a new life.

She drained the last of her coffee, closed her laptop and headed out. There were still a couple of things to take care of before tomorrow night, but the main part was complete. Well, at least the first half of the money had gone. Idly, Sam wondered if she'd ever use her crypto wallet again when this was all over.

I'm not planning on buying more pills.

Back outside in the bright, cool, sunny morning, all felt well in the world. A smile crept slowly across her face, and she realized that for the first time in a long while she felt good about things, about the future, albeit without the man she'd once promised to love and obey, in sickness and in health. What a load of old cobblers that had turned out to be. As she passed a fashion chain store, she heard Fleetwood Mac over the sound system, suggesting folks go their own way. Her smile grew wider until, by the time she'd sung along to a few lyrics, she was laughing out loud as she walked. Oh, the irony. Going her own way was exactly what she intended to do, and from the day after tomorrow, when everything had been completed and she was expertly playing the grieving widow, she'd be most certainly going her own way.

Next stop: the garden centre and the greenest seed potatoes she could find.

Chapter Fifty-Six

EASY ENOUGH SO FAR. The equivalent of £6000 was in his crypto account now, with another six to come in the next 24 hours. So far so good. There was enough to pay for a firearm with and time enough to finalize the loose ends of his plan, making a tidy profit in the process. It was turning out to be a good idea.

His first hit was tomorrow night and he planned to drive down and back again in one go. He'd leave the car in a side street nearby, walk to the victim's hotel, whip in, do the job, and then head home. He and Clinton would share the driving; it would be early morning when they made their way back and he didn't want to risk falling asleep at the wheel.

He'd yet to tell Clinton about his precise role in all this, but since Luke had been the initiator of the project, it was only fair on Clinton that Luke himself would do the actual deed.

The thought terrified him.

He took out the scrap of paper that Caramel Teeth Man in the pub had given him. There was a mobile number on it. No names; just a number to contact and organize a drop-off, cash of course. Luke found this funny somehow. Perhaps he should educate the man on the finer points of using a crypto currency. It really was quick and simple, and less risky than a rubbish bin deposit in a park somewhere. And besides, being tied to one location limited one's business opportunities. Take it online, however, and the world was your oyster – though he doubted Caramel Teeth Man had ever tasted one. He dialled the number and waited for Caramel Teeth Man to answer.

"Yeah?"

"I need a piece as discussed."

Luke heard a gurgling sound as Caramel Teeth Man took a long pull from a can, then a hearty belch.

"When do you need it?"

"Today."

"That's tight."

"That's tough."

Watch it, Luke.

Silence while the man thought. Then he said, "Tonight. Back door of the Pole. Still a Colt?"

While Luke didn't like the sound of the back-door situation, he couldn't be choosy at this late hour. "Yes, and a silencer. And ammo."

"Right. Don't want much on short notice, do you." More of a statement. "It'll cost you a bag, in twenties. And no one comes with you."

"A bag?"

"Yes, a fuckin' bag. A bag o' sand. A grand! You thick or somethin'?"

Luke winced at his mistake. Cockney rhyming slang and dodgy blokes weren't particularly his forte, though he was learning fast.

"That's more than I was expecting."

"Well, take it or leave it. I'm a busy man." Another glug filled his ears and Luke imagined the 'busy man' lying on a tatty sofa in a scruffy high-rise flat on the other side on Manchester, empty beer cans buckled and scattered around the floor. Luke had no choice and Caramel Teeth Man knew it.

"I'll take it, then. What time?"

"Make it ten. Like I say, I'm a busy man. And don't ring again 'cos I won't answer."

"I'll be there." Before he could say anything else, the line went dead and Luke was left staring at the screen of his burner phone. To himself, "Ten it is, then."

That gave him all day to do not much else but sit and worry that there'd be no trouble later on and he'd be home and safely in his bed by midnight, free of cuts and bruises. It wasn't ideal to be so late, but with limited options, that was what it was. Still, he wouldn't need to go through this again – or would he? He groaned as the realization hit him: of course he probably would. He'd not likely store a stolen gun that had been used in at least one murder, would he? A professional hit man would use their own weapons yes, but they'd be brand new, well looked after and safely stored someplace secret. Luke, on the other hand, was a wannabe entrepreneur trying to get a business off the ground and raising funds via a side hustle. Still, it would work.

He hoped.

Figuring he'd better fill Clinton in on where he was at so far, he dialled his number from his regular phone.

"Fancy a coffee? I've things to tell you."

"Oh?"

"Tell you when I see you." Luke glanced out the window to check the weather. It wasn't raining. "Meet you in the park by the swings. I'll bring coffee. Will an hour suit you?"

"Sounds secret squirrel, but yes, see you there in an hour."

Now all Luke had to do was hope Clinton saw sense and didn't go flying off his rocker. Last time he'd broached the subject, he'd started to come round to the idea and Luke hoped he hadn't changed his mind. It wasn't as though he had to *do* anything, really: Clinton was to be more of a back-up guy just in case, a bit of moral support and someone to find any holes in the plan that Luke hadn't foreseen. Clinton would be his wingman and share the driving. Easy.

Nearly an hour later, Luke was on his way to their rendezvous, two takeaway coffee cups in his hand. Heading for the swings, he could see Clinton up ahead of him not far from their chosen spot and he watched him settle into the seat to wait. Two young boys squealed with glee as a woman pushed them both on the swings. Happy days.

"Here you go," he said handing over a cup and settling himself into an adjoining swing. They both watched the youngsters for a moment before Clinton spoke.

"So what's up?" Clinton took the top off his cup and sipped.

"I wanted to tell you where I am up to, where *we* are up to."

"Ah, I see. I should have known it was about that. Go on, then. Enlighten me."

There was exasperation in Clinton's voice, but Luke tried to ignore it. Luke himself was the one driving this and Clinton needed to buckle in. He told him everything – and Clinton listened. When he'd finished, the two men sat in silence, Luke willing Clinton to say something positive. Eventually he spoke.

"Right, then. So it looks like we're all set." Matter-of-fact. "This better work or we're both in the shit."

That was good enough for Luke.

Chapter Fifty-Seven

THE PICKUP HAD GONE without a hitch and Luke now had a Colt and silencer wrapped up in an old T-shirt safely inside his backpack as he walked. He'd borrowed his dad's car, not wanting to risk the walk in such a rough neighbourhood again or risk travelling on public transport carrying his purchase back home. And of course, he might have needed a quick getaway if Mr. Caramel Teeth had decided he wanted to keep the cash *and* the gun.

He trotted along the pavement at pace and hoped the car was still where he'd left it − and that it still had all four wheels attached. Turning the corner, he spotted it up ahead. All looked in order. It was lucky his dad didn't own a Jag − it would have stood out like Pinocchio's nose. An Alsatian barked angrily nearby and a woman's voice screamed after it. She sounded harassed, and her skilful expletives would have been funny on any other night.

But not tonight. Luke made his way to the car past boarded-up windows and curtainless dark glass; the only light came from the few remaining streetlamps that hadn't been smashed.

He kept checking behind him to be sure he wasn't followed, but no one was interested, it seemed. He hoped Mr. Caramel Teeth was too busy counting his loot to bother with anything further. The man could buy more than a few cans of beer with what Luke had given him, enough to cover his sofa and the floor with empty cans.

Luke picked up the pace and jogged over to the driver's side of his car, unlocked it and slipped inside, then immediately locked the door. While he'd liked to have rested and caught his breath a while, he needed to get out of Dodge – and right now. The ignition caught, and the tyres struggled for grip as he accelerated rapidly out of the estate towards the main road and home. Next, he needed a quiet place to inspect his purchase, a purchase he was still unsure of how to use properly. While he'd hoped to get a client or two, he hadn't expected to get one so soon, but he had, and he'd have to do the best job he could under the circumstances. Tomorrow was D-Day, which left him only a few hours to get some practice in. His plan on the day was to get in nice and close as the man lay asleep; if all went to plan, it would be a doddle. What could go wrong? A child could shoot a sleeping man at close range and not miss.

He went back through his plan as he drove.

"First, he's at the hotel on Purley Way. Second, he'll be asleep because we're going in after midnight. Third, I can get right up close, and fourth, no one else will hear a thing – I've got a silencer. Fifth, exit out the window then back to the car and home. That's it, isn't it? I don't think I've left anything out."

Satisfied he had thought of everything – because after all, he'd been thinking of not much else since this started – he slowed to a more reasonable speed and relaxed his shoulders. Getting caught speeding could be tricky if they asked to look in the bag – after all he was dressed in his 'thug' gear.

The bag. It seemed to glare at him from the passenger seat and Luke glanced at it from time to time on the journey back, hoping everything he needed was inside. And what if it wasn't?

Then he was in the shit.

Luke slunk in through the back door and headed straight upstairs, avoiding the lounge where his parents were probably engrossed in a movie. His mother called out anyway.

"That you, Luke?"

"Yes, Mum, only me. Be down later."

When he was inside his room, he rammed a chair under the doorhandle to stop either parent from entering unannounced. He used the same trick when he was getting changed. A small bolt would have been just as effective, but neither he nor his parents had got around to doing it. The chair worked well for now. Sitting on the edge of his bed, he opened the bag and removed the T-shirt with the gun and its accessories wrapped in it. It was surprisingly heavy. The silencer rolled loose and thumped to the floor. A small box of about a dozen bullets finished the inventory.

Picking the silencer up and examining it, Luke sat thoughtful for a moment. Suddenly everything felt very real. Pressing a button on a laptop had felt final, but that was nothing compared to holding an actual gun, bullets and a silencer in his hand. He was about to use this weapon and take someone's life – for a measly £12,000. How many other lives had this particular piece snuffed out like candle flames? he wondered. How many people's lives had been ruined because of it? He attached the silencer and examined the piece in its entirety, feeling the weight and size of the whole thing in his hand.

A knock at his door interrupted his thoughts and he fought to keep himself from jumping.

"Yeah?" His voice sounded wobbly to even him.

"I'm making hot chocolate. Do you want some?" It was his mother.

Luke let out the breath he'd been holding and couldn't help smiling. If she could see what he had in his hand on the other side of the door, she'd have a flying fit.

"Please. I'll be out in a minute," he called back. He wrapped the gun up and stuffed it along with the bullets under his pillow for the time being. Where he'd store it permanently he'd no idea, but there was time to figure that out.

Or was there?

Tomorrow morning he'd head off somewhere quiet and practice, though with only twelve bullets to his name and no way of getting any more at the eleventh hour, he couldn't afford many practice rounds. It was far from ideal, but he'd have to make it work. Satisfied of the temporary hiding place, he left his room to join his parents downstairs for hot chocolate.

As he sipped his drink and chatted cosily with his parents, he was struck by the contrast between the two worlds he currently inhabited. And tomorrow night, things would get about as far from cosy as they could ever be.

Tomorrow night, he was a hit man for hire.

Chapter Fifty-Eight

"THANK THE LORD FOR THAT," Amanda said, putting her brush down on the paint can lid. "I thought it'd never end."

Ruth came up behind her and put her arm around Amanda's waist, snuggling in close.

"Looks great, though, doesn't it? A nice shade of blue, if I say so myself."

"Well, you did pick it, so I hope you do like it. But yes, it's a nice shade all right. The room looks much fresher now it's all done. It was worth the effort."

Amanda stood with her hands on her hips admiring their handiwork. "Room one down, another five to go."

"Yes, the thought is exhausting, isn't it?"

Amanda nodded, frowning.

"We should consider getting a pro in to finish the rest. I hate the turmoil everything is in. We can't do it any faster and I'm not taking valuable holiday to damn well decorate."

Ruth looked thoughtful. "I agree with the turmoil and not taking holiday time to do it. I wonder how much it would be to hire a professional. This really isn't a good use of our precious down time together.

I'd much rather be enjoying a movie with you than you painting the walls. Perhaps I'll look into it and see."

"You've just reminded me of something I wanted to ask you. And since you're a techy, you might know the answer."

"How may I be of service, Detective McGregor-Lacey?" Ruth bowed deeply, hiding her cheeky grin.

"Do you know of any apps out there that allow someone to preload them with money, then place an order for a product and use that money, but do it all anonymously, so that it's untraceable? So, for instance, you could buy drugs from a food truck by placing an order for a bacon sandwich with 'special sauce'" – she made air quotes – "then pay a hugely inflated price for said sandwich and receive a little packet of oxy with your bacon butty."

"A baggy and a butty, eh?" Ruth couldn't help but laugh. "It rolls off your tongue, doesn't it? Butty and a baggy, baggy and a butty," she repeated, trying the two combinations out for fun. "Baggy and a butty, I think. Perhaps I should have been in marketing, not building websites and apps. I'm obviously wasted."

"Are you going to tell me the answer, then?" Amanda picked up the paintbrush and held it threateningly in her hand. Ruth ducked, feigning horror. "Or have I got to find someone else in the know?"

"I dare you." Ruth smirked, egging Amada on.

"If you don't tell me the answer by the time I've counted to three, I absolutely will." A beat passed, "One. Two..."

Ruth stood her ground, grinning. Amanda moving a step closer, brandishing the brush.

"Three." Amanda struck, the brush leaving a trail of pale blue down the front of Ruth's shirt, but not before catching her on the chin first. Ruth spluttered with laughter. Her hand went to her chin and she wiped the blue away with the back of it, but that left her with the problem of where to wipe that.

"I warned you," Amanda stated, "and you dared me."

With paint on the back of her hand and Amanda still with the brush, Ruth lunged in an attempt to wipe her hand on Amanda. But Amanda was too quick for her: she thrust the brush out in front of her as the two connected, pasting more pale blue onto Ruth's arm. Both women shrieked, and Ruth turned, quick as lightning, and wiped the back of her hand into Amanda's blonde hair.

"Oh, not nice."

"You started it, Missus," Ruth said still smiling. "Probably time to get it cleaned up, though, before that dries," she said pointing. "You have blue on blonde. I'll go and turn the shower on."

"So do I get the answer now?" Amanda asked, following her down the hall.

"The short answer is yes, it can be done. The long answer is it's tricky. Obviously, the vendor needs to see the product has been paid for, and the purchaser needs to prove he's paid in order to pick up, but for someone looking in, like the police for instance," she nodded to Amanda, "that's the tricky part. How do they keep the transaction away from law enforcement? They'll not want to get caught. In that sense, it's riskier than cash."

"I'm thinking Bitcoin or similar?"

"I'm thinking I'll double check with Valance tomorrow and let you know, eh? He's a couple of steps ahead of me on that stuff, particularly the slightly illegal as you know."

Amanda had first met Valance Douglas a few months back. He was an acquaintance of a vigilante victim she'd found herself working with as part of a sting that had gone so far off track she could have lost her job. Luckily, Plan B had come along and saved the day – in the form of tech whiz Valance Douglas. He and Ruth had stayed in touch afterwards; he'd proven to be a talented techy and private investigator. You never knew when you might need such a person. Like now.

"Right now, though," Ruth said sternly, "that paint is drying, so get in the shower and get scrubbing."

"Yes, Miss," Amanda said chastely, and did as she was told.

Chapter Fifty-Nine

AMANDA'S HEAD had gone into overdrive after her chat with Ruth the previous night. She'd thought about up, getting out of bed and making a mug of warm milk to try and ease her overactive brain but didn't want to disturb Ruth in the process. She'd finally dropped off sometime around 2 a.m., and it had felt like she'd been asleep for five whole minutes when the alarm had pierced the quiet of their bedroom. In a deep sleep, Amanda had ignored it, but Ruth had leapt bolt upright. Worse, the clock was on Amanda's side of the bed.

Six a.m. She would normally be out running by now, but since the decorating had cut into their relaxation time together, she'd not run for nearly a week. Maybe that was why she was feeling a little tetchy.

"Amanda," she called from under her pillow. "Amanda!" She tried again more urgently, but it seemed nothing was getting through. Brute force was next. Lifting the pillow off her head, Ruth sat up and shook her wife by the arm in an effort to awaken her from a near comatose sleep.

Finally, a grunt from the blonde head.

Then movement as the noise became clearer and, as Amanda finally realized what it was, she reached out to turn the noise off.

Silence fell on the room once again. Ruth tossed the covers back and headed to the bathroom, muttering to herself.

"I may as well be up running now. So much for a bit of extra sleep," she grumbled. After splashing water on her face, she made her way downstairs to make a mug of tea for each of them, hoping Amanda would have surfaced and shown herself by the time it was ready. She yawned. And yawned again. Maybe they would have to get someone in to finish the rest of the house after all; the extra workload was half killing them.

There was a shuffle at the doorway as Amanda entered, wearing her pink robe. Her blonde wavy hair stuck out at all angles.

"The tea will stir you into action," she said. "Did you sleep well?"

"Hardly at all, actually," said Ruth. "Though I must have towards the end. I think the last time I looked at the time it was nearly two a.m. and I still hadn't gone off by that stage. I nearly got up but I knew I'd start bloody Googling stuff for work and then there'd be no chance of sleep. So instead, I lay there with my brain whirling round like a Catherine Wheel. I may as well have got up for all the use it was. Might have cracked the case, even."

Amanda yawned loudly, her face contorting. The kettle came to the boil and Ruth smiled at Amanda's optimism. Cracking a case via Google was rarely that easy. She poured boiling water onto tea bags and grabbed milk from the fridge as Amanda slumped into a chair at the kitchen table.

It was still pitch-black outside. There were a few upstairs lights on in other houses nearby, probably commuters getting ready for another day in the city. Ruth was no different; her office was in Green Park, not far from the tube station, though as the boss, she wasn't on someone else's time clock, only her own. And that's the way she liked it. Adding milk to the tea, she passed Amanda a mug and sat with her.

"You're as tired as I am, so let's get the decorating finished by a pro, eh? I couldn't care less about the cost at the moment. Neither of us likes doing it, and both of us are sick of the mess so I'll see what I can come up with."

Amanda nodded her agreement. "Great idea. But anyone worth

their salt will be booked up, so we'll have to wait a bit to get it started. I guess there's no real rush, though."

"I agree. Well, that's settled, then. I'll get someone round to look at the job. You're busy, and I'm busy, so it's the best way." Ruth sipped on her tea, gazing over the mug's rim towards Amanda. "You're out tonight, aren't you?"

"Yes. Jack and I are taking a DS from Manchester for a curry. Duncan Riley. He's a nice bloke, actually. We're hoping he can throw a bit of light on the prescription drug and distribution scene. There may be a connection to his contacts up there. They seem to be spreading their network outwards down here a little. When might you speak to Valance? It would be good to get another viewpoint on things before we meet him. Once again, cyber at this end have no bandwidth to speak of, pardon the pun. They only work with the big stuff, or those in immediate danger, not a few 'baggies and butties,' as you called it last night." Amanda smiled as she said it; it *was* mildly amusing.

"Well, on that, I must have been figuring things out subconsciously because I remembered about Bitcoin and what I knew," Ruth said. "It would work, I bet, the app aspect, though I'll still talk to Valance and double check. I seem to remember some article of recent saying Bitcoin wasn't as reliable as it once was in terms of anonymity. And as smartphones go to run the necessary browser, I'm pretty sure the iPhone hasn't got the ability or the security. I'll have to check. But there'll be something else and some way else to fill the gap by now. I'll let you know." Ruth got up to rinse her now empty mug. "I'm off for a very quick run, I think. Maybe just the one lap and then a shower. I'll go and get changed. Care to come with me?" Ruth raised her eyebrows suggestively but Amanda scowled her reply.

"My body wasn't meant for running, so I'll grab breakfast then hit the shower. Thanks for the invite though."

There was no way Amanda would ever go running, Ruth knew, but she teased her anyway.

Five minutes later Ruth was heading down the front path in her running gear. Amanda sat at the kitchen table, pondering. If an app could be loaded with funds and used for anonymous transactions, then all sorts of things could be traded illegally with no one any the wiser.

That left two questions bubbling away: first, how did the mobile van's customers know about a secret app if it was a secret? Second, how could Amanda and Jack get access to it too?

By the time Ruth came back, sweating like a horse, Amanda was dressed in her best suit, hair coiffed and make-up expertly applied. She had the bones of an idea.

"Wow," exclaimed Ruth, looking Amanda up and down. "I hope Duncan appreciates your effort, though aren't you a little early?"

"Ha ha. Very funny. I'm going undercover." Grabbing her bag, she pecked Ruth's sweaty cheek as she passed, calling 'Wish me luck' over her shoulder as she went.

Chapter Sixty

SAM HAD CHECKED her messages from 'him' and was thrilled to see he'd received the funds without a hitch. She'd followed his instructions to a T, so why she was surprised she'd no idea. But reading the short confirmation text sent a tingle of excitement through her body, like when something exciting you'd been looking forward to for ages was suddenly upon you. It reminded her a little of her wedding day, and the excitement and anticipation that had consumed her for weeks before the event took place.

The day had been perfect in every way, from the sunshine to the ceremony and the party that evening. It had gone smoothly, and for the first few years they'd both been blissfully happy, bringing two delightful girls into the world and enjoying every moment they spent with them. When it had started to crumble, exactly, she couldn't remember, but Duncan's job hadn't helped. It had begun taking up so much of his time and his attention even when he was actually present at home.

Still, she pushed the thoughts away and tried to clear her head. What was done was done: there was nothing to be gained by rehashing it all. It no longer mattered whose fault things were, who had said or done something. It was all water under the bridge. Best to just let it wash out to sea.

The kitchen looked like a TV studio waiting for a celebrity chef to arrive. Several bowls sat with prepared ingredients in them. Pastry was resting in the fridge and flour dust covered every surface, including the floor. Anyone looking would think the two girls had had a flour fight, not that a grown woman was making pastry, but Victoria and Jasmine were safely at school, out of harm's way.

Satisfied that she had everything ready, she took the pastry out and began to roll it, lining individual circular sections of the tray to create the bases for the mini-quiches. When the tray was filled with twelve perfect-looking pastry bases, she began to fill them with the finely chopped ingredients from the bowls. In the bottom of each went tiny slivers of green potato skin topped with tiny bacon pieces, chopped tiny potato eyes, chives, cheese and herbs. Then she poured the eggy mixture over each one to fill the tartlets to the top and sprinkled a little more grated cheese on top. When the poisoned pies were complete and she was satisfied she hadn't forgotten anything, she placed them in the hot oven to cook. There was an air of satisfaction about her as the golden oven light glowed over her creations. During her research, she'd learned that the active ingredient could be a little bitter, and she hoped the bacon and strong cheese would mask any flavour issues. The last thing she wanted was for Duncan to spit it out and be fully alert when his evening visitor came to call.

Twenty minutes later, the delicious-looking treats were done and the homely smell of fresh baking and cooked cheese filled the kitchen – she was almost tempted to try one herself. After placing them all on a wire rack to cool, she dug into the back of a kitchen cupboard for a suitable travel container. The oven clock read 1.15 p.m. Duncan had said he'd come by about 2 p.m. to grab his overnight gear before heading down south for the night, and that he'd be back late Friday night.

Or that was the intended plan ...

She'd already laid his toiletries out along with his hold-all and pyjamas; somehow, he always managed to forget these when he went anywhere overnight and would end up sleeping in his underwear. Idly she wondered if he'd be wearing them when the time came; it seemed an odd thing, sad almost, to wear for his demise. But what would be better, a suit and shirt? His running gear? Jeans and a T-shirt, perhaps? What was the preferred attire to be wearing when your time came? Sick patients lying in bed wouldn't have any choice in the matter, so Duncan would be in their company as his spirit left this life – wearing just his PJs.

She stared at the stripes on the bottoms, blue and purple, and touched the soft flannelette fabric, though she resisted lifting them to her face. To do that would mean she still cared for him, and really, she didn't. Anger started to bubble in her stomach like toxic gases. She could still feel the sting of his words like the slap of an elastic band her your arm – so cruel and unnecessary. He'd started her down this road she'd taken – *he* had! He was to blame for what was about to happen next. Yes, it was all his doing! Sam was getting wound up now, anxiety rippling through her chest, heat coursing over her skin, scalding tears filling her eyes.

A door slamming shut downstairs brought her to attention and she hastily wiped her eyes with the back of her hand. Duncan's voice rang out. "I'm home, Sam." It was kind of sing-song, happy even, not like his usual stressed, dull tone.

Sniffing fiercely and wiping her eyes again, she called down to him, "I'm in the bedroom."

His heavy footsteps climbed the stairs and he popped his head around the doorframe, a smile in his eyes. He seemed so happy.

"I smell baking," he said with a tone of happy accusation.

"Guilty as charged," she replied, then winced inwardly at her words – was that slip up an omen? Changing the subject for the moment, she added, "I thought I'd get a few things together – you know, the things you might forget." She held up his pyjamas and he smiled knowingly. "Can't have you cold. You'll need these in your room. What if there was a fire alarm in the night? You'd be stood there half-naked and freezing to death."

She knew she was rambling on about nothing, talking for the sake of it, but it helped. Why hadn't she taken a couple of pills this morning to steady her nerves? Wasn't that what they were there for? If only her bag was nearby, she could easily have sneaked a couple from the side pocket and slipped them down. But it was hanging at the bottom of the stairs where it always was. So, gibbering on was the next best alternative. It took her mind off what was coming.

Duncan walked into the room and started to fill his bag with the other items he'd need and she stood back and watched him. "Not sure if I mentioned but I'm meeting them from Croydon station for a curry at seven p.m. so I need to get going. There's a case they're working on that might be linked to a case of ours, so I'll call you when I get in if it's not too late, okay?"

"Oh, don't worry about me. Do what you need to do. I'll probably have an early night anyway. I'm nearly at the end of my book so I'll finish that off and that'll be it. I'll text you before I go to sleep."

It was all part of the plan.

"Okay." He looked around the room to see if he'd forgotten anything, then hoisted up his packed bag. He was almost ready to go.

"I've made you something to nibble on for your journey down," she said as she headed for the kitchen. He followed her down, bag in hand. He watched as she put four mini-quiches into a container and handed it over.

"I thought you'd like these more than sweet brownies – they're much more substantial. Now don't eat them all when you set off. You'll appreciate them late afternoon when you get the nibbles." Timing was important, but she could only suggest.

"Thanks, Sam. That's nice of you. I appreciate it."

Their eyes caught for a moment and she smiled. He'd always had beautiful eyes... He leaned in to kiss her, their lips touching briefly for the last time.

When he walked out the front door, she'd never see him alive ever again.

It was a sobering thought.

She needed a drink.

Chapter Sixty-One

SHE LOOKED every part the businesswoman. Her smart navy suit fell a little below her knee; a deep cream blouse with a plunging neckline set off her blonde hair perfectly. The look was completed by a pair of large pearl studs in her ears and a swipe of pale peach lipstick – she was aiming for classy.

Funny how a change of style of clothes could make a person feel so different about themselves. Amanda's normal attire of work suit and Doc Martens was functional, though certainly not what you'd call stylish. High heels were impractical on the job for many reasons; really, it was only TV cops who wore them, women who, incredibly, managed to sprint over gravel and climb chain-link fences without difficulty when the time came. No ankles were ever broken in the making of those episodes. Away from television and back in the land of reality, of course, it was a completely different story, so she'd head back home to change out of her Wonder Woman suit after her assignment.

Kodaline sang about all she wanted while Amanda drove down Purley Way, headed towards a bacon sandwich and a spot of early morning surveillance over a Styrofoam cup of tea. Thinking she'd better tell Jack what she was up to, she directed Siri to call him. Kodaline and her song faded down and a loud ringing tone.

"Morning, Lacey-McGregor, or McGregor-Lacey, or whatever you're now called," he teased her, chewing loudly and following up with a slurp.

"I gather you're still finishing breakfast."

"Yes. Full English this morning, too. Mrs. Stewart came early specially to make it. Good of her, eh?"

"Yeah, great. Send her over when you've done with her. I have a few chores that need doing. But right now, I thought I'd fill you in on where I'm headed."

"Oh? And where's that?" Another slurp. Amanda envisioned him with his mug, a brown sauce-stained plate in front of him.

"I'm a businesswoman with a need for something to calm me, so I'm going to order a bacon sandwich with a side order of special sauce. I want to see what happens, and who makes it happen. All being well, I should have something to report back when I get to work. If I'm not in by ten, it's gone horribly wrong and you'll probably find me whacked and tied up in the bushes somewhere nearby."

"Cheery thought, Lacey. Righto, then. Thanks for letting me know. You be careful, and I'll see you a bit later."

"Never thought of that, Jack, but will do," she said, rolling her eyes. Though he was only a handful of years older than her, he treated her like the daughter he had never had. And for the most part, she let him; in many ways, he was the father she had never been close to.

The line went dead, and Kodaline's soft, eerie voice again filled the car. Up next was Meghan Trainor. Perfect; Amanda was in the mood for something quietly soothing.

Ten minutes later, she swung the car into the layby, and parked at the furthest corner, as out of sight of the van as possible. Satisfied that the staff couldn't see her, she turned the engine off and pretended to be searching her bag for something. Compact make-up mirrors were one of the best surveillance tools, she'd learned: they looked completely natural yet were small enough to see around without looking obvious – unless you were a man, of course. Amanda took hers out and pretended to preen a little, all the time watching the front of the van and who was doing what. Even though it was still early, there were already a couple of people queuing. Both were wearing business suits, and both had their phones in their hands. To the uninitiated, there was nothing wrong with the picture but Amanda stayed put, watching and pretending to adjust her make-up.

Her phone rang. It was Ruth.

"I have something for you that may be of use."

"Oh? What is it?"

"I've just spoken to Valance and run a hypothetical at him, and he came back with how it could be done. I say *could*, not *is* – that's up to your team. The detectives."

"Come on, then – spill the beans," Amanda said. "I don't need a disclaimer statement attached."

"Crypto currency could be used easily, and there are various forms now –loads, in fact, not only Bitcoin. In fact, he says it's unlikely to be Bitcoin because it's way too valuable. He mentioned Monero and Dash and a couple of others, but here's the thing." Ruth took a breath then carried on. "Anyone can do it, and it still runs off the Onion browser, but money can be added to the app. But it can't be done on an iPhone: Apple doesn't support crypto apps. So Android would more than likely be the one to use. Have a look at which phones customers are using if you can. From what he says, you won't find an iPhone amongst them."

"Nice work, Detective McGregor-Lacey. Does he have any idea how money changes hands through the app?"

"He said he'd do some checking, but his initial thought was what he called a 'pooled wallet,' where value is assigned to an account but no specific currency is associated with it. It basically means funds are harder to track. To purchase, the buyer would then wire the currency to the app, and hey presto! – transaction almost complete."

"Nice one, Ruth. Thanks. I'd better go and see what's what, then. Wish me luck."

"Stay safe, eh?" Sheesh – first Jack, and now Ruth. Amanda rolled her eyes heavenward. Well, at least they cared.

"Will do. See you later." Amanda rang off and glanced over to the food truck. The queue had grown to four people waiting.

"May as well get going," she mumbled as she made her way across the uneven ground in heels she wasn't used to. Little pieces of fine gravel pinged as her heels caught the loose covering and she was thankful it was a clear morning. Holding an umbrella and balancing at the same time might have been a problem. Amanda joined the back of the queue, eyes and ears on high alert. Immediately she noticed a couple of things: first, no one was talking at all, although that wasn't necessarily cause for alarm; these people were probably all strangers. Second, each person had their phone in their hand – again not all that uncommon, but on further inspection, she noticed that not one of them was an iPhone. Again, that on its own wasn't startling, but given Ruth's intel and her own suspicions about what went on at this partic-ular food van, it was a glaring indicator.

Amanda watched carefully now. As each person placed their order, they put their phone on the serving hatch, screen up. Someone not paying attention, someone who was there solely to get a sandwich and nothing else, would probably not have noticed this. Intrigued, Amanda moved forward in the queue, watching closely without seeming to watch.

Her main question now was how such an operation could be marketed to those looking to shop, because the suppliers, the two men inside the food van, could hardly hang their sign out, could they?

There were a couple of ways to find out more. And Amanda was going to try them both.

Chapter Sixty-Two

THE MAN directly in front of her had turned his head as Amanda joined the back of the queue and given her a smile of admiration – as well as a rather obvious top-to-bottom look she could have done without. "Too bad, buddy. I'm taken," she thought gleefully. Still, it was good to know she could still pull, even if it was a man.

"Good morning," he drawled when he'd finished browsing.

Play nicely, Amanda …

"Morning," she said, acting friendly. She was keen to chat with Mr. Smooth if she could.

"The best bacon sandwiches this side of Watford Gap, wouldn't you agree?"

"Yes, the best." Another bright smile from Amanda.

"Do you come here often?"

Amanda groaned inwardly. Seriously, did he have nothing better? That was the cheesiest chat-up line in the book, though there could have been a double meaning to his question. "I've just come a couple of times," she said, "but as you say, they are the best. They give me a bit of a buzz, actually. Love the special sauce."

She watched his face and waited. His eyes flicked across hers, searching for her own double meaning, she assumed. At last he nodded slightly. No doubt about it: he knew exactly what she was referring to – and it wasn't the bacon.

He held his phone out – an Android – and waggled it in the space between them, like a secret being shared between two friends.

Amanda smiled knowingly. "What currency do you use? Monero or something else?" She wore a natural, easy-going smile, as if they were two friends discussing laundry powder.

Mr. Smooth was definitely eager to chat, although he clearly thought he was getting somewhere with the classy-looking woman behind him.

"Yeah, I started with Monero," he said self-importantly, "though I use Dash now. I've tried a few, actually, but in the interests of keeping it away from prying eyes, I juggle things a bit." He touched his nose and gave her an exaggerated wink. "And you?" he enquired chummily.

"Same as you, actually," she said, smooth as butter. "Seems to work."

The queue shuffled forward, and another man joined in behind Amanda, phone in hand.

Amanda turned back to Mr. Smooth. "How did you find this place?"

"Probably the same way you did. A friend told me I should try their sandwiches if I wanted a little stress relief. I thought they did 'massages'" – he made air quotes around the word – "until I figured it out. Wasn't sure if I was going to get a helping hand or a hand job when I first came."

He threw his head back and laughed at his own wit, and Amanda did her best to join in. The man in front of him turned around and scowled, but Mr. Smooth ignored him. "But it's all done so nicely," he went on, lowering his voice. "No one who didn't know about it would be any the wiser."

Amanda smiled. "Yes, extremely clever, and neat too." Lowering her own voice even more, she asked him, "How many outlets are there? Any idea?"

They shuffled forward again. Mr. Smooth was up next.

"I don't know of any others myself," he whispered, "but there must be, right? To set it up like they have. It's not like the days when ice cream vans first started serving alcohol from their fridge instead of Mivvies. My guess is the queues of blokes waiting for ice cream gave the game away on that one." He made air quotes around "ice cream." "None of that here, though," he went on, glancing around him. "Just a few folks lining up for breakfast, you and me included." He gave her another sickly wink and then moved forward to place his order.

She watched discreetly as he set his phone on the counter, screen up. She could see an app page open, waiting. It happened so smoothly that anyone not in the know really would be hard pushed to notice; she had to admit she was impressed. From her current position, Amanda was now able to see what was happening inside the van. One male was cooking and putting bacon sandwiches together. A second male slipped a serviette and sachets of special sauce into the bag, along with what looked like a sachet of salt. Except Amanda knew it wasn't salt; it was something a lot more relaxing than that. And who in their right mind put salt on their bacon sandwich, anyway?

Mr. Smooth moved off with his order, waving lightly as he walked back to his car, and wished her a nice day as he went. Smiling, Amanda stepped up and placed her order for a bacon sandwich and a cup of tea and waited. How very vanilla of her, considering the present company.

It was extremely clever, Amanda mused. Nobody would suspect the white sachets had anything sinister in them and, as no large cash notes had changed hands (she had used only a few coins paying for the sandwich), there had been no obvious transaction either. To the casual observer the men in the van were simply selling and serving bacon sandwiches.

Damn clever.

So, who was the mastermind behind this venture? Maybe DS Duncan Riley could shed some light on that later.

Chapter Sixty-Three

Amanda hadn't gone home to change before heading back to the station, figuring she'd be ready for dinner with Duncan later that day so what the hell.

She soon wished she had. The first wolf whistle landed while she struggled to climb out of the car without exposing too much thigh in the process.

"Oh, for hell's sake," she mumbled as her heel caught on the floor mat. Cursing, she yanked her shoe off and set one stockinged foot on the ground, looking for all the world like a hippy celeb staggering out of a limo. The observer whistled again and was rewarded with a swift middle finger from Amanda.

With both feet on the ground and once again contained within their shoes, she clumped off towards the station, noticing the backs of a couple of the men as they scurried inside ahead of her.

Jack swivelled round in his seat as she approached and his face lit up with a cheeky grin. "I didn't know you cared, Amanda. I'd have dressed up a little if I'd known." He rearranged his tie theatrically.

"Not you too, Jack," she groaned, and feigned a swat at him. "Can't a woman wear nice clothes occasionally?"

"Oh, that she can. And you should do so more often – you scrub up rather well."

She cocked a brow at him. "Hardly practical in our job. I'll be back to functional tomorrow. And my feet are killing me already in these shoes. Where's my Doc Martens when a girl needs them?" She slipped her shoes off under her desk and rubbed the side of her foot. "But it worked, though. I now know what's going on."

"Really? Go on, then."

"I will, but I need coffee first. You want some?"

They set off for the kitchen, and as they waited for their coffees, Amanda filled Jack in on what she'd learned from chatting with Mr. Smooth and her observations on the inside of the operation.

"So, the salt packs aren't salt at all," Jack mused. "I wondered why they weren't printed when you found them in that rubbish bin, but I thought no more about it. And they wouldn't get mixed up with the real salt because that *would* be in printed sachets, I'm guessing."

"Precisely."

"But we still don't know how many vans are operating, do we?" Jack said thoughtfully. "And I suspect it's more than one. How the hell do we find out, do you think? This could be nationwide or just a local network."

"Quite, but I think the first place to start is van ownership. We loosely traced this one back to one of Duncan's contacts, so we could do the same with any others on our patch. See what we're dealing with ourselves before taking it further afield."

"I'm on to it. Shouldn't be too hard to get a list of license holders from the council. I'll get Raj to give me a hand." Jack drained his coffee mug and thumped it down with satisfaction. "That, Lacey, was a good cup of coffee."

Amanda smiled at his back as he returned towards his own desk and work. It seemed she'd been dismissed.

"Well, I guess I'd better tell Dopey what we've got going on," she said, and padded off barefoot towards DI Dupin's office. He was seated at his desk engrossed in a document in front of him, his bald patch more prominent than ever, it seemed. She knocked on the doorframe with a knuckle to get his attention.

Without looking up he said, "What is it, Lacey?"

"How'd you know it was me, sir?"

"You forget I'm a detective too, Lacey, and to answer your question, first of all I saw you, and second, your perfume."

Immediately Amanda wondered if she'd been putting too much on.

"And no, you haven't. Put too much on, that is."

Dear God, he was a mind reader, too.

Finally, he looked up from what he had been reading and smiled at her. Dopey Dupin didn't have a mean bone in his body, which was one of the reasons the team took the piss. Every DI needed mean bones occasionally.

"What can I help you with?"

While he wasn't what you'd call an attractive man, he had a nice smile and clear eyes, and had always been decent to Amanda.

"It seems we've stumbled on a prescription opioid distribution racket, through mobile food vans. Selling codeine and oxy to the business community, from what we've seen so far." She explained the rest – the salt packets, the app, the clientele.

Dupin sat quietly for a moment before he spoke. "What's your plan?"

When Amanda explained what they intended to do and that she and Jack were meeting with a DC from Manchester later, he nodded approvingly. "Keep me up to date. I may need to go regional if it's more widespread, and why wouldn't it be?"

Amanda nodded her understanding, and Dupin resumed reading his document, indicating she was dismissed.

When she'd left his office, he picked his phone up and dialled.

Chapter Sixty-Four

M1 or M40? That was the question facing Duncan as he skirted around Birmingham heading south towards Croydon. If he hadn't needed a car he'd have taken the train, caught up with some reports or read the paper, listened to a podcast or something – all much less stressful than afternoon traffic on the Midland's motorways. Google and Siri told him the M40 was the quickest option, though not by much. He yawned, glanced at the clock on the dash and estimated the time to a service centre he might want to stop at. He dimly remembered that Oxford was the one to aim for, though in truth most of the motorway network's service stations were pretty grim. Torn seating in the food court areas, filthy toilets, and the general décor and state of repair of these over-used locations left a lot to be desired. Millions of people went through these places every year, so much so they were like small towns, on the move 24/7. Some had designated truck stop areas, some caravan areas, but they all had one thing in common – huge volumes of cars and bikes at any given time. Unfortunately, this meant that refurbishment was almost out of the question.

He made a mental calculation to the stop at Oxford and dreamed of a hot coffee to stir him up with; travelling so far on his own was tedious work. Then he remembered the mini-quiches Sam had made and, driving with his right hand, slipped his left into his bag on the seat and rummaged for the tub.

"Got you," he said as he wrestled the lid off and removed a little pie. The lightly browned cheese on the top made them look quite delicious and he took a bite from one, sinking his teeth into the soft filling and fresh homemade pastry. He groaned at the taste of them.

"Sam, you've outdone yourself, my girl. Absolutely delicious."

Shame she wasn't there to hear his praise....

Crumbs fell down his front and he brushed them away before taking another bite, the act of eating relieving the monotony of driving in a straight line for so long. When both pies had been devoured, he savoured the cheesy taste on his lips before calling her to say thanks. She answered almost immediately.

"My God, Sam, those little pie things were delicious. You'll have to make some more of them."

"Have you eaten them both already, then?" she enquired.

"I was going to leave one for later, but the first one was so good I thought, Sod it, I can only eat them once." He heard Sam giggle a little at his praise and enjoyed the sound of it. It was a shame they'd had to go about getting back on track the way they had, but he felt sure she was changing back to the Sam he had loved and married.

"Well, I'm glad you liked them. I hoped you would. Listen, I'll send you a text later before I go to sleep, all right?"

"Okay. Give the girls a kiss goodnight from me, won't you?"

"Of course, and enjoy your meal out. Drive safely." Sing-song. Then she was gone and Duncan was back to the solace of a mind-numbingly boring drive down to Croydon.

It was almost 6 p.m. when he pulled into the hotel car park after four hours of snarl-ups and roadworks, and he parked up below one of the available street lamps for extra security. The amber glow gave his car an eerie finish, changing the colour from navy to almost green. He grabbed his bag and headed inside to check in, feeling dog-tired and wishing he was staying in for the evening rather than going out for a curry. But he'd agreed to go, so that was the end of it, though his stomach didn't much feel like a curry. Something plain would perhaps ease whatever was going on in there. He put it down to too much coffee and sitting scrunched up for too long.

"Duncan Riley checking in," he said to the receptionist, an older woman with perfectly coiffed hair. She reminded him of a TV sitcom wife from the 80s. But efficient was her middle name, and within a few moments she was handing over his key and directing him to a room on the first floor. She wished him a good evening.

Duncan skipped the lift and opted for the stairs. His room was near the far end of the first-floor corridor. Silently, he let himself in and browsed around the functional room. Bathroom immediately to the left, bed further in to the left, desk and chair at the foot of the bed against the wall opposite. TV screen, tea- and coffee-making equipment to his right. A piece of nondescript art hung over the bed. The computer-generated image matched the décor colour of green and oxblood almost exactly. The scent of air freshener from a can lingered in the room, probably to mask that someone had smoked there recently; an underlying whiff of tobacco was still evident. He opened the window a little to recirculate the odour back outside, and a cold draft blew into the room. Still, he gave it five minutes to clear.

His head was starting to ache a little as he unpacked his bag and took his toiletries through to the bathroom. Since he wasn't being picked up for at least thirty minutes or so, he turned the taps on and ran a bath, pouring the little bottle of shower gel into the running water. White bubbles formed and grew upwards while he shaved and stripped. Then, satisfied with the temperature, Duncan slid into the tub. The warm water felt good on his body, the tiring drive easing out of his muscles, and he began to relax a little. His thoughts drifted to Sam and the change in her, her thoughtfulness baking the mini-pies, and he wondered if they'd turned a corner. Perhaps they should go away somewhere soon, the two of them, somewhere warm; maybe the south of France or farther afield even. It wasn't like they couldn't afford it, and the girls always enjoyed staying with their grandparents.

His phone rang back in the bedroom and dragged him away from his thoughts, though he didn't get out of the bath, not yet. Whoever it was would wait or leave a message or call back soon. He closed his eyes a moment and floated somewhere between Sam and work. His phone rang again.

"Sod it," he grumbled and stood up, letting water and soapy suds run down his legs onto the floor. He wrapped a towel around him before heading to the bedside table.

"DC Riley here."

"Ah, were you sleeping?" A woman's chuckle followed, but Duncan didn't recognize the voice or the number that flashed up.

"It's DS Lacey, Amanda. Dinner?"

"Yes, sorry. Miles away. Is it that time already?" He glanced at the clock on his phone. 6.40 p.m.

"We're early, so I called on the off chance, but if you're sleeping . . ." She let the words hang with a touch of jovial sarcasm.

"Give me five. I'll be down shortly." He disconnected the call, quickly dried, and dressed in jeans and a clean shirt with a jacket over the top. With hair that was still ruffled and damp, he left his room to meet his dinner mates, letting the door swing closed behind him.

All three slipped into Amanda's car, Duncan in the back.

Parked on the other side of the car park were two men in disguise and on surveillance.

They were not detectives.

Chapter Sixty-Five

IT WASN'T FAR to the restaurant. Parking directly outside was impossible unless you were happy to be towed away, and even detectives weren't exempt from that carry-on. And bus drivers got tetchy if you parked in a bus stop. Amanda drove past Chat House and pulled up in a nearby side street with plenty of room. Duncan's head was now throbbing and he wished he'd stopped at a chemist for Paracetamol on the way. Amanda caught the look of pain on his face and asked, "Are you all right?"

"A headache, that's all, though I couldn't tell you when I last got one. I don't suppose you have any painkillers, do you?"

Considering the topic they were about to discuss over dinner, it was fitting, Amanda thought. She rummaged in her bag and produced a packet with four left in it.

"Life saver – thanks," Duncan said, and removed two from the individual blisters, popping them straight into his mouth.

"There'll be water inside," added Amanda. She handed him the rest of the pack. "Here, take the rest in case you need them later."

Duncan nodded his appreciation and followed them both into the restaurant. The warmth was welcome; even the short walk from the car was cold enough to require hat and gloves. The smell of rich tandoori spices and garlic filled the room. For a weekday night, the place was busy, and the clientele was heavily male. Amanda wondered where all the women were; perhaps these customers were all on a boys' night out? She imagined the women doing the same someplace, a wine bar maybe.

A man dressed in black and white showed them to their table and handed out menus.

"Can I get you something from the bar?" he enquired.

"A half for me," ordered Jack.

"Mineral water, thanks," Duncan said.

Amanda ordered a white wine, not caring that it was a school night.

With the waiter on his way, Jack took up the small talk. "How was the journey down?"

"The usual. I don't think I've ever driven straight through without roadworks somewhere along the way. I reckon they only need a home for their cones, so they lay them on our motorways." He rubbed his temple and poured a glass of water from the jug to speed the pills up a bit. A light sheen of sweat had formed on his top lip. It glinted slightly, enough for Amanda to notice. She didn't say anything.

"Well, I'm famished," declared Jack, and stuck his head in the menu. "I don't know why I'm looking because I know what I'm going to have." He beamed around the table. "Chicken Jalfrezi."

"Same here," said Amanda. "Lamb Jalfrezi for me." She placed her menu back down on the table.

Duncan didn't fancy anything spicy, "I think I'll stick with chicken Korma. I fancy mild tonight." In reality, he fancied a boiled egg and soldiers at home with his girls, but that was a world away. His head was pounding.

The waiter returned with their drinks and Jack placed their order. Poppadums and chutney appeared in front of them and all but Duncan tucked in. He was beginning to feel quite unwell. He figured he should tell them what he knew, then grab a taxi back to the hotel and go sleep off whatever this was. He cleared his throat.

"Tell me where you're up to, then, and I'll see where I can fit some missing pieces, perhaps."

Amanda began with a rundown. "We know now they are using an

app, prepaying with crypto currency so no cash changes hands at the van. It seems they place their phone face up with the app showing on the screen, and that's a signal for the dealer to glance and see the prepaid order. Tabs are disguised as salt packets and slotted into the bag with the bacon sandwich. I've also heard special sauce mentioned – a code word, I expect. That's as much as we know. But we figure it could be wider than our patch because of the technology."

She sipped her wine and looked at Duncan. He was quiet. More sweat had surfaced on his upper lip and brow. Suddenly, in one swift movement, he leapt from the table and raced towards the back of the restaurant, looking for the toilets. Jack and Amanda sat speechless, looking at one another.

"He really didn't look too well," Amanda said. "His top lip was all sweaty. I think you should see if he's okay."

The waiter was approaching the table with their food, but Jack dutifully followed Duncan, hoping he wouldn't be too long. He'd been looking forward to chicken Jalfrezi all afternoon. He entered the gents' toilets and heard Duncan before he saw him. The retching sounded like it was coming up from the basement drains of the building.

"Hell's bells. Are you all right?"

Duncan spat saliva into the bowl and wiped his mouth with toilet tissue. The room smelled of vomit. Jack waited.

"Yeah, I'm okay," Duncan said weakly. "I think. Maybe it's a migraine." He started to get up from his kneeling position but his legs were wobbly. He grabbed on to the tissue dispenser, ripping it from the wall as he stumbled backwards, sending it crashing to the floor. Another wave of nausea coursed through him and he retched again, this time missing the toilet completely and vomiting onto the floor. Jack stepped out of the way, but not before the splashes hit him.

"I think we'd best get you back to your room. Can you stand up?" He put his hand out and Duncan took it gratefully. Once Duncan was on his feet, Jack dampened a paper towel and handed it to him to wipe his face with. Beads of sweat coated his forehead. When Jack was satisfied Duncan was stable on his feet, he slowly led him back out to the restaurant and towards the front door. He caught Amanda's eye but she could see all was not well. She set her napkin aside and hurried up to them.

"Best get him back," Jack said uneasily. "Where's your keys?"

"Hang on – I'll drive," Amanda said. "Let me go and settle the bill and I'll meet you out front. Can you bring my car around?"

Jack nodded and took her car keys from her. Turning to Duncan, he said, "Wait here. I'll be back in five."

When Jack pulled up out front, Amanda was waiting with Duncan. Some of the colour had returned to Duncan's face. He and Amanda both got inside.

"I'm really sorry about this," Duncan said. "I've never experienced anything like this before. If it's a migraine, I never want another." He rested his head against the headrest, grateful it was only a short drive.

"It's no bother, as long as you're okay," said Amanda. "We'll catch up by phone, maybe in the morning? I hope you'll be all right for your training tomorrow."

"Me too. Sleep will do me good."

Amanda pulled up at the hotel entrance and Duncan climbed out, looking only slightly steadier than he had a few moments ago. They said their goodbyes and both watched him go inside before driving off.

"Hell, I hope he's all right," said Jack anxiously.

"He'll be fine. If he's got a migraine, he'll more than likely be fine now he's vomited. A nice dark room and sleep is what he needs right now. It's still early yet, so hopefully he'll feel better in the morning. I'll call him then."

"You're a regular Mother Teresa, aren't you?" chided Jack. He was remembering back to when he had had appendicitis a while back and had vomited lavishly all over Amanda and his own car. To her credit, Amanda had looked after him like a champ that day.

He pulled out into traffic and they headed back to work. Neither of them noticed the surveillance vehicle that was still parked in the car park. But the two men inside noticed Duncan had returned.

Somewhat early.

Chapter Sixty-Six

 Never before had he felt so ill, had such a splitting headache or been so violently sick. He'd made it back to his room, washed his face, and got straight into bed, leaving his clothes where they fell. It was darkness and peace he craved. The hotel curtains were thick and well fitted, so not even a chink of light from outside could get through. Still, he kept his eyes firmly closed.

But behind the blank canvas of his eyelids was a place for the devil to dance, and he was only just warming up. Imaginary insects, sounds outside his door, smells drifting from under it were all fighting for places as the devil took over. A beetle with hundreds of legs, like a millipede but with a hard oxblood red and green shell, crawled up the inside of his leg. Duncan reached down and pushed it away, sending it flying across the room towards the bathroom door where it righted itself and raced back to the bed. Only this time it was bigger. Much bigger. Duncan yelled out as he watched it grow in size then sat on the bottom of his bed and laughed at him. But it was gone as quickly as it had appeared, leaving a lingering odour in its place. Had someone burnt something? Was the hotel on fire?

On and on they went, torments in all shapes and sizes making him cry out in distress. With his eyes tightly closed he thrashed about, sweat beading on his face and chest as the hallucinations drove on and on. Duncan was oblivious to the world around him, floating in another dimension, unable to escape the pain as the devil played with his mind for his own pleasure.

Duncan was in a hell of his own.

At 9.30 p.m., Sam texted Duncan goodnight, a short message followed by a handful of kisses. But Duncan was oblivious. In fact, he was barely conscious and lying drenched in his own sweat, the soaked sheets knotted around him. By 12.30 a.m., the worst had passed, and he rolled onto his side in the wet bed, exhausted and drifting in and out of consciousness.

He didn't hear the light click of the lock as his door opened and two figures entered, standing in the short passageway by the bathroom door. He didn't hear their heavy breathing; he didn't hear or see anything – just the remnants of the devil dancing inside his skull.

They waited for any movement, for their target to call out on hearing them enter, but any sound they had made had not disturbed him. The two men ventured the short distance forward towards the bed, one with an arm outstretched holding a gun, poised ready to fire, the other man slightly back out of the way. The long shape lying in the bed was only just visible in the darkness. A long moment passed and nothing happened. The man stood still, his arm outstretched and ready to shoot. Then, at last, the man lowered his arm and Luke turned to Clinton.

"I can't do it," he whispered. "You'll have to do it."

Clinton gasped. "What? No way! Get on with it!"

"But I can't!" Luke's voice was quiet and urgent as he tried to make Clinton understand.

"Too late. Pull the damn trigger and let's get out of here! Come on!"

Luke turned back towards the bed and his target, who lay under the covers sound asleep. It had seemed a good idea at the time, an easy way to earn a few quid, but now as he stood in the darkened room, he wasn't so sure. A slight movement followed by a groan from the bed made him jump. The target was coming round.

"Get on with it!" urged Clinton. "Take him now!"

But Luke was frozen to the spot. That was, until Duncan rolled over fully onto his back and groaned again. What Luke couldn't see in the darkness was whether the target's eyes were open or not, whether he was staring up at him. Oh God – perhaps he could see him. That would never do. Being identified was out of the question. It was all he needed to spur him into action. Raising the gun again, he pointed it directly at the man's chest and fired. But his intended victim had other ideas, rolling quickly off the bed onto the floor at the far side.

Luke had missed.

"Shit!" he cursed. Duncan must have seen him; otherwise, why roll so quickly? There was no way he could leave the job half-finished now. It became a mad scramble.

"And again!" urged Clinton as Luke moved like lightning and fired again at the man, who was now lying on the floor. Even with a silencer, the noise of the gunshot filled the room. It was nowhere near as quiet as he'd assumed it would be, he thought, as though from a great distance. He peered across the bed. There was no way he could have missed from such close range. Duncan lay face down, not moving and not making a sound. *He had to be dead.*

Not wanting to risk the noise of a third shot, Luke shoved the gun into his waistband.

"Let's go!" he urged.

Clinton didn't need telling twice and both men bolted towards the door. Grabbing the Do Not Disturb sign as they left, Luke fastened it to the outside handle, then softly closed the door behind them. They slowed their steps now and walked briskly, as casually as they could, down the hall and into the nearby stairwell.

Neither Luke nor Clinton said a word until they were safely in their car. They'd left it parked a little way down a side street out, of the glare of any streetlamps or cameras. Adrenaline rushed through their veins, but both men were grimly silent. Luke started the engine and moved off down the side street, away from the main entrance of the hotel, as a precaution. Clinton looked back through the passenger wing mirror for activity – lights turning on or someone outside the entrance looking, perhaps, but there was nothing. It was a good ten minutes before either of them spoke.

"Are you sure he's dead?"

"Yes."

At least, Luke hoped so.

Chapter Sixty-Seven

HE'D BEEN SHOT. Duncan lay face down on the floor, a bullet hole through his right shoulder. It must have gone right through because it had pierced his hand, which had been trapped beneath him during the fall. Being shot at point-blank range stung like all hell, he realized with a strange sense of detachment, but there had been little time to do much about it. Right now, he was grateful he was still alive and breathing, though he wondered if they'd be back to finish him off. He'd heard them leave. He'd also heard them whispering earlier, or had he imagined that part?

After a few moments, he figured it was safe to move. He tried to get himself back upright, or at least on his hands and knees, and call for help, but his head sloshed about like a wave pool and the pain in his shoulder and hand was excruciating. Nausea rolled over him again and he felt a fresh urge to vomit, but he knew there was nothing but bile left in his stomach. Everything else was on the curry house toilet floor.

Slowly, using his uninjured hand, he managed to get himself back up on to the bed and steady himself for a moment. Blood seeped down his front from his shoulder wound and mingled with the blood from his hand. Although it was good that the bullet had exited, he didn't hold up much hope for his hand to work properly ever again – there were likely too many small bones damaged. He knew he needed to find his phone urgently before he passed out again, but the room was also a crime scene and he was aware he could be contaminating it by moving. But he had to get help or he would die, he told himself sternly, and since he hadn't finished with his life yet, he'd risk contaminating the scene.

He took several deep breaths and then held the last one in his chest as he moved around the bed towards the desk. He knew he'd left his phone there earlier as he'd collapsed into bed. The pain was piercing, but he pushed through it with gritted teeth. Nothing seemed to work properly, but with his left hand, he found the table lamp and managed to switch it on. The pale lamplight felt like fire on his sore eyes and he squeezed them shut, groaning. Then, gingerly opening one eye, he spotted his phone and reached out with his good hand to retrieve it.

His hand shook as he struggled to unlock it. Blood made the screen slippery as he punched the keyboard icon and hit 999.

"I've been shot," he told the operator. His voice sounded like it was coming from another room. He heard himself give his location and room number, asking if she might be able to locate DS Lacey or DC Rutherford from Croydon station.

He set the phone down on the bed and activated the speakerphone. There was a whooshing sound in his ears now. Dimly, he heard the operator instructing him to put pressure on the wound. He raised his left hand and pressed it onto his right shoulder, but the blood kept flowing. *Well, shit*, he thought. He was grateful for the soothing comfort of the operator's voice. She sounded kind, taking his mind off the pain as best she could. Then at last, he heard the distant sounds of the ambulance coming for him – at least he hoped it was, because he was in danger of losing consciousness again, fighting the urge to lie back on the bed and never wake up again.

He closed his eyes and suddenly saw his girls, all three of them, dancing on the inside of his eyelids, giggling together, enjoying a game. Then Rochelle joined them, but she wasn't dancing and giggling with them. She was off to the side, a look of concern on her face, watching Sam. What was Rochelle doing there? Then came whispered voices, a man saying he couldn't do it, and Rochelle crying. And all the time his girls laughed and giggled and danced . . .

He tried to open his eyes again, but Mother Nature clearly had her own agenda for him right now. He slumped back and let her take him to wherever she had planned.

When Duncan awoke some hours later, he was in a hospital bed, wired up and bandaged up but still alive. A nurse hovered like a honeybee, working on his chart. She gave him a bright smile as he came to. His mouth felt like the bottom of someone's old trainer, his throat raw where tubes had lain earlier. A drip was attached to the back of his good hand, fluids to ease his pain and fight off infection. He'd obviously been in surgery.

"Good morning Mr. Riley. It's good to have you back with us." What a killer smile she had, Duncan thought. Then he figured he must be okay if he'd noticed that.

Always the hot-blooded male.

Duncan tried to talk, but his throat wasn't working. He uttered a hoarse croak and then gave up. Instead, he matched her smile with one of his own, though not as dazzling.

"Your throat will be a little sore, but only temporarily. Just nod or shake your head to my questions, okay?"

One nod.

"Are you in any pain?"

One shake.

"Great. You shouldn't be. We operated earlier to stop the bleeding and stitch you up front and back, and your hand has been set, though it may take another procedure or two to get that finally fixed up. Time will tell, but you're still with us – that's the main thing." Another dazzling smile. She went on, "There are a couple of detectives waiting to talk to you, but as you can't talk at the moment, I'll tell them to come back."

One shake.

"Are you sure?"

One nod.

"All right, I'll send them in when I've done with you." She handed him a glass of water with a straw sticking out the top. "The more you can drink, the better for you." Duncan drained the glass. God, he was thirsty. She refilled it and set it down on the side table. With a quick rearrangement of his pillows and one last smile, she left the room.

He closed his eyes for a moment. That moment turned into half an hour, and similar visions filled his head again: Sam, the girls, and Rochelle.

Rochelle.

Pre-offence behaviour.

"A spouse that has a sudden and unexplained change in behaviour towards their partner. A significant change in a partner's behaviour can mean the partner may have already begun to plan for a change in the status quo. Textbook stuff."

It was like thick fog inside his head, but Rochelle's words filtered through and started to make a modicum of sense.

When he opened his eyes again, Jack and Amanda were stood together at the side of his bed looking at him with concerned faces. He tried again to speak, to clear the frog that was preventing him from doing so.

"Shhhe. Wan. Mme. De."

Each word was laboured and slurred, but Amanda understood immediately what he was trying to tell them. Only moments ago, she had spoken to DS Rochelle Mason, who, once she'd got over the shock of the terrible news, had told Amanda a theory all of her own.

And she was now en route.

Chapter Sixty-Eight

JACK'S EYES nearly popped out of their sockets. Rochelle had made the journey in record time and was standing with them beside Duncan's bed now, her crash helmet in one hand, dressed in black leather from head to foot, catching her breath as Amanda brought her up to speed.

Jack motioned her to one of the vinyl chairs by the bed, but she shook her head.

"I've been sat down long enough. Thanks, though."

She gave him a strained smile, and Jack was willing to bet that, under different circumstances, it would be a knee-trembling one. He also bet she was a ball-buster; her sheer presence in the room changed the vibe from low-key to supercharged. He wouldn't want to mess with her. He smiled inwardly, musing.

"Jack? Jack!" Amanda was speaking to him but he hadn't heard a word.

"Sorry. Yes, Lacey. I was miles away."

"I know you were. Welcome back." Amanda suspected exactly where he'd been. "I was saying about last night – how ill he was with his headache and what he was like when we dropped him off."

"Yeah, he said he was all right, needed an early night. He was looking forward to his training, so we left him at the door. I can't believe what's happened to him since. It's unreal."

"Sure is," said Rochelle. "Do they say when he'll be allowed home, and has anyone told his wife yet?"

"He's probably only in for a couple of days, but they're looking to move him to Manchester when it's feasible. To my knowledge, his wife hasn't been told yet, particularly in light of what you've said. Thought maybe it would be best coming from you or one of your team." Amanda hated notifying next of kin at the best of times; it reminded her too much of when she'd had to tell Ruth's father that his wife had died. Ruth had been too shocked and upset to tell him herself.

"In that case, I'll get Rick – DS Black, I mean – to go round now that I know what state he's in. Has he said much?"

"No. His throat is too sore yet, so it's head nods and shakes when he's awake. He tried to write some notes but his right hand is shattered, so that's awkward too. He managed to say he'd been dreaming a lot, imagining things. If it was a migraine, that could be the cause of the strange visions, though that's usually visual disturbances, not hallucinations. He didn't eat anything at the restaurant; he was as sick as a dog in the toilet before our food came. He was really sweaty, though. I remember seeing it on his top lip before he ran for the loo." She checked her notebook. "Apparently the hotel housekeeping had a master key card go missing during the night, so we're assuming that's how the culprit got access. Easy enough to garner a room number if you're intent on getting one."

"He must have been ill because when we found him, the bed was soaked. I remember thinking how unusual that was," added Jack. "Forensics are at the scene now pulling evidence together, but Amanda tells me you might have an idea who's behind it?"

"It's loose, but the pieces seem to fit. I don't think I'm *making* them fit. That's why I'll get DS Black, to go round to their house. He can watch her reaction if he knows what we're looking for, see if it's genuine shock or shock that he's still alive when he shouldn't be."

"Jesus, that's rough, isn't it? Your missus planning your demise and she's shocked you're *actually alive* when she's likely paid good money to have you bumped. I'd like to be a fly on *that* particular wall." Jack shook his head in disgust.

Rochelle dialled a number and left the room to make the call so Duncan couldn't hear if he woke up. Even though he'd already mentioned the possibility, she didn't want to rub it in any further; they'd only just been discussing it in front of him.

Amanda and Jack raised their eyebrows at each other and waited in silence. Nothing stirred from Duncan's bed. Jack's phone vibrated.

"Hopefully a clue," he said, picking up his phone.

Amanda listened to one side of the conversation and picked up that they'd located two bullets from a Colt 45, a gun easy enough to get hold of if you knew the right people. Since nobody had heard the gunshots, the gunman would have used a silencer and that alone pointed to someone more organized. This was not a random hit, and probably not a retaliation from someone Duncan had put away, though uniform were checking recent releases from prisons in case there was someone after him.

Then there was the strange fact that he had been shot in the back, through the right shoulder, and left for dead. Gangs, organized crime and experienced criminals tended to be a great deal more accurate – and thorough.

So, the person or persons they were looking for were sloppy. The burning question was, *who* had wanted Duncan dead? Was it his wife? Or was it someone else entirely?

A nurse stepped into the room and gave them both a disapproving look.

"The rest will do him good, as would the peace and quiet. Perhaps you can wait in the waiting room until he wakes. He's not going anywhere for a while," she said. It was more an order than a request. Amanda and Jack both rose to leave, but a croak from Duncan stopped them all, the nurse included.

"Try again, Duncan," Amanda said soothingly, avoiding the nurse's warning look.

"Looook a Saam. Speak ta Saaam."

"We'll speak to Sam. Rochelle is here and understands. Anything else? Did you see anything?"

"That's enough for now," interjected the nurse sternly. "He must rest. Please, the waiting area?"

Obediently, Amanda and Jack decamped to the waiting room. They met Rochelle as they moved rooms and she followed them along.

"Rick is going round now and will inform Sam. He knows what to look for. Then we'll take it from there. Still asleep, I assume?"

Jack explained what had gone on and Rochelle rolled her eyes impatiently.

"I know Duncan well, and he'd be wanting us to get on with this before too much time elapses. It must be frustrating for him if he's aware, though he is pretty sedated."

"Why don't you stay here and wait? We'll head back to the room, see where forensics are at, ask some more questions, check footage again. We're doing no good here."

"That's fine by me," Rochelle said. "Maybe I'll get a cup of that horrible hospital coffee before I face Nurse Ratchett again."

"I'd be interested in Rick's observation when you know," Amanda said to her.

"So will I," Rochelle said, narrowing her eyes. "So will I."

Chapter Sixty-Nine

AFTER THE CALL, Rick stood for a moment, thoughtful, looking at his phone. Really? Sam a suspect? Rochelle had not mentioned anything before now, but then why would she? That was between her and Duncan, and she wasn't one to gossip. Still, if Sam was involved somehow, they needed to find out. He hoped she wasn't.

"I'm off out. I'll be back shortly," he shouted across to a colleague, who nodded. With Duncan in hospital and Rochelle down there with him, his department was a couple short. Others were out investigating cases of their own, leaving only a couple of civilian clerks to carry on with case research in their absence. He grabbed his jacket off the back of his chair and a half-filled takeaway cup of coffee from his desk and headed outside to his BMW. He swung out of the station gates in the direction of Duncan's home, a place he'd been to many times but not like this, not to deliver news and dig at the same time.

His automatic windscreen wipers came on as the first signs of moisture hit the windscreen, tiny wet dots the size of pinheads glistening like diamonds. *Whoosh. Whoosh.* The rain increased in intensity until it was pouring heavily, bouncing off the car bonnet as he drove the few miles and parked up outside Duncan and Sam's house. The street was a dark, sodden grey, making everything look more depressing than it was on a brighter sunny day; rain had a habit of doing that. It was like Manchester was crying at its own pain. He glanced up at the front window of the house hoping she was home, not wanting to have to psych himself up again to deliver the news later.

Sam. He hoped this was all a big mistake. What motive had she got? What reason could she possibly have to want her husband, her loving Duncan, dead? And who had she organized to do the deed? Sam certainly didn't mix in those circles. Maybe he didn't know Sam at all. And maybe, just maybe, she wasn't even involved. Maybe this whole thing was the product of an overactive imagination on Rochelle's part. But a sudden and unexplained change in behaviour was not something to take lightly, he knew. It was a well-known 'tell' that something was adrift; a well-known FBI profiler had figured it out some years ago, and it was now taught as part of advanced police training. He wondered about motive again. Maybe the change was to do with something else?

There was movement at the window, a curtain then a face, briefly.

"Let's get this over with," he said, and lifted his jacket up over his head before stepping out into the pelting rain. He dashed up the front path and knocked, grateful there was an overhang to shelter him. He ruffled his hair back into shape and put a weak smile on his face ready to greet her. The door opened, and Sam stood there, a smile on her own face, looking as normal as ever.

"Hi, Rick. Come on in out of the rain," she said cheerily.

He was noting everything she said, every miniscule movement she made, and adding it to the imaginary notepad in his head.

"Thanks. It wasn't even raining when I set off."

"Want a cuppa? I'm just making one."

"Please, thanks." Why hasn't she asked immediately why I'm here? he wondered. I've never been here without Rick unless I'm picking him up. He added this to his mental checklist.

He followed her through to the kitchen. The place looked spic and span; nothing, it seemed, was out of place. He watched from behind as she put tea bags in two mugs and reached for a packet of biscuits. Still no question as to the reason for his visit. Finally, the tea was ready and they sat down at the kitchen table. Rain pelted the window outside. The wind had picked up, adding to a wild day.

Finally, she asked.

"So, to what do I owe this unexpected visit? Duncan is down in Kent somewhere."

He watched her sip her tea, looking over the rim of the mug at him. "Well, that's why I'm here Sam. I have some news. There's no easy way to tell you, but I'm afraid Duncan has been shot and is in hospital in Croydon."

He waited, handing the floor over to Sam to make the performance of her life. And make it convincing – to them both.

"What?! How bad is he?" she asked, shocked. Her mouth hung open.

"He's doing okay. They operated earlier this morning. He was shot in the shoulder, but he was lying on his hand so the bullet went straight through and into his hand. He'll need more surgery to get his hand working properly again, and he lost a lot of blood, but other than that he's a lucky man. He'll live." He waited for a twitch, a tell, something at the deliberate words 'he'll live.'

Sam took a deep breath in and out, which could have meant anything, but other than that, there was nothing obvious.

"I need to see him. Let me organize the girls overnight, and I'll grab a few things and head down." She looked at the clock, and Duncan waited while she made some calculations before speaking.

"They will be transferring him up to Manchester as soon as they can, but I don't know when that will be. It's maybe worth a call to the hospital before you dash down there."

"Yes – good idea."

She sat silently and Duncan again watched, wondering what was actually going on inside her head. Would a loving, caring wife with a husband in hospital a good four hours away really wait, or would she dash off no matter what? Noted again. He sipped his tea and took a biscuit, more for something to do in the strange atmosphere than anything else. Rick was eager to learn as much as he could, and as with any suspect (if she was one), he was prepared to let her talk and ramble on; that's generally where they slipped up. Too much detail equalled a set-up alibi; too little was clever and cagey but didn't necessarily mean guilty. It only meant smart.

When Sam spoke again, it wasn't quite what he expected to hear.

"Right, then. Well, thanks for coming round and telling me. I really appreciate it. I'll give them a ring and see what's what." She managed a smile – a weak one, but a smile nonetheless.

Rick stood to leave, adding her last comment to his imaginary notepad along with a couple of other observations: no tears, no pain, not much shock and not a great deal of concern about seeing him any time soon. As far as Rick was concerned, there was more digging to be done before Sam was completely eliminated as a suspect. And that disappointed him immensely. She was not the woman he'd thought she was.

Chapter Seventy

"I'm assuming that's us done as hit men?" Clinton enquired as they both sat in Luke's tiny room, Clinton in the chair, Luke on the bed. They'd got home in the early hours after leaving Croydon in a rush around 1 a.m. It was safe to say their little foray into being killing machines hadn't gone so well; Luke's bottling it at the last minute had been awkward. Clinton would never have been able to take over if Luke hadn't found his balls in time before the target had woken up; thankfully the strength had found him somehow.

Or the stupidity. Or the sheer dumb luck, depending on your view.

As it was, they were forced to dissect what had gone wrong and how it might affect them from today onwards. And was the guy even dead? Clinton seemed to think so, Luke thought; otherwise he wouldn't be talking like he was. Luke had not yet voiced that concern. He sat silent, listening as Clinton went over the details.

"There shouldn't be any footage of us. There weren't any cameras in the corridor – of that I'm sure – and we both kept our heads well down, hoodies up, so there'd have been nothing to be seen even if there had been a camera. It would simply show two figures, hoods up, caps on, heads down. No one saw us enter or leave or nick the master key card.

"And the beauty of a hotel such as that one is the transient clientele, passing through for a night on business," Clinton went on. "They'll all have gone back to where they spend their days and nights now, no one the wiser. I bet most of them spend the evening catching up on work, have a drink or two then watch a porn movie before an early night."

Luke marvelled at how calm and reconciled he sounded and wished he felt the same. He wished he knew whether their target was still alive or not. He sat quietly on the bed, giving the odd grunt to show he was listening and agreeing. There was no point mentioning his concern until he knew for sure.

The guy's body must have been discovered by now, though surely? A quick look online hadn't returned any reports of either. Gunshot wounds would be newsworthy either way, Luke knew, so he could only take from that the body – if there was one – was still to be discovered.

He looked at his bedside clock. It was just coming up to noon, which meant housekeeping would find the guy any minute if someone else hadn't in the last hour or so. Word would soon be out – and he hoped it was the right word.

He rubbed his eyes with the heels of both hands and tried to clear his head, to push the stress out of his brain and think about something else. But how could he when he had no clue what the problem was going to be? Attempted murder or murder – both held hefty sentences. The only difference was that with murder, the victim couldn't give evidence.

But a target who was still breathing could.

Luke got to his feet. "I need to sleep. Why don't we meet up again later? I can't think straight right now." He rubbed his eyes again and yawned dramatically, more for effect so Clinton would leave.

"Me too. I'm wasted," Clinton declared. "Okay, I'll be off, then. Come round to mine later? The parents will be at bingo so we can talk uninterrupted for a couple of hours."

"Yeah, great. Let's do that."

Luke got up to show his friend out, not that he didn't know the way. It was manners, the thing to do. He stood watching from the front window as Clinton disappeared from view, then retrieved his laptop, went back up to the sanctuary of his room and logged back on to the website. There was a message waiting for him. A surge of dread ripped through him. He hoped it wasn't a new enquiry; his days of being a hit for hire were over. He'd frozen when the time had come, and that had been dangerous. He couldn't risk that happening again, and more to the point, he didn't want the stress that went with the job, money or not. Whoever this was, he was no longer open for business.

But wasn't a new enquiry – it was an angry customer.

Nausea washed over him, replacing the dread. The words were clear:

You fucked up. He's still alive. Get it sorted.

Head in his hands, Luke wasn't sure how or if to respond. He'd received the money and he wasn't about to give it back, but he was – *they were* – counting on the second payment. Six thousand pounds wasn't to be sniffed at. It was a tidy sum of money and the whole reason they'd started the damn venture. He groaned to himself, wondering what the hell he was going to do now – loose ends, an angry customer and his own lost nerve wasn't a helpful mix. His fingers hovered over the message to hit reply, but his head was pulling him back. If he said the job would be finished, how was he going to do that exactly? If he apologized? Well, that wouldn't likely fly in a situation like this. Or he could ignore it, keep the first payment and leave it at that – they were still £5000 to the good. There was no way the customer could find out who they were and hunt them down, just as he had no idea who the customer was. Nor had he any desire to know, so in that respect they were safe.

His fingers still hovered. He had to do something, make a decision, and deal with it, and even if the decision was not to reply, that was still a decision. Luke's room was deathly quiet as he sat on his bed, digging deep for his gut instinct, because in this case, that's all he had. In a tricky business decision, Clinton would force him to go by the data, the numbers, read what they were telling him and go with that, because without data, it was merely an opinion, he'd say. Well, in the absence of data, gut opinion was all he had now.

The answer seemed obvious now: ignore the message. And delete the site before anything could be traced to him. And on the upside, in the unlikely event that he ventured into the dark web again, he now knew how to build a shop window.

So that's exactly what he did. When he was satisfied the files had been deleted he sat back and sighed, pleased with his decision. With the website now gone, there was no means for any angry customer to reach him.

He was out of the hit-for-hire business – for good.

Chapter Seventy-One

SAM FELT like she'd been the one shot in the chest, not Duncan, and it wasn't a pleasant feeling. Who knew disappointment could be so painful. She'd been ready for the knock at the door, been ready for one of Duncan's colleagues to deliver the news, but not like this, not *this* news. She'd practiced her reaction in the bathroom mirror, acting it out over and over again, not wanting to overdo it but still be the shocked and distraught wife, overcome with grief at news of the death of her soul mate. What she hadn't practiced for was the news that he'd been badly injured and was still alive in Croydon. She wondered now if she'd passed the test, pulled it off after all – in the end, her shock had been real, not acted.

Rick had only been gone five minutes and still she stood in the hall-way, frozen to the spot, thinking. What happens next? she wondered. This was not going to plan so far – she should be spending the day being consoled at his death, perhaps even thinking about funeral arrangements, drinking sweet tea or sipping brandy.

She took a deep breath in, then let it stream out slowly through her nose, like a toke of cannabis, only not as relaxing. Inside she was revving up, anger starting to boil in the pit of her stomach. What could have gone wrong? And the money! Six thousand pounds gone to waste. Well, they'd have to give her a refund, wouldn't they?

"Good luck with that," said a mocking voice in her head.

Deciding she needed a drink to settle her down, she paced rapid steps to the kitchen, flung open the freezer section of the refrigerator, and grabbed a cold bottle of vodka she kept there. Not even bothering with a glass, she unscrewed the top and tipped the bottle into her mouth, taking a couple of large gulps. The icy liquid burned the back of her throat but it felt good, numbing her from the inside in an instant. Gasping, she caught her breath again then repeated it, clear liquid escaping from both corners of her mouth as she gulped greedily, trying to anaesthetize something inside her, screwing her eyes up against the pain of the freezing cold liquid.

When she was done, she stood motionless in the room. There was not a sound coming from anywhere or anyone, and for a moment she felt totally alone in the world. Tears sprang to her eyes without warning, her mouth contorting as she stood and sobbed, letting them flow. She heard herself wail in pain – pain that Duncan was still alive, and not because he lay injured in hospital after being shot.

Suddenly she stopped in mid-sob as the realization struck her that there'd be an investigation, and a large-scale one at that. Everyone knew that when an officer got hurt or killed, the police would leave no stone unturned to bring the culprit to justice, send the full force of the law slamming down on them.

And that could be her.

She needed to think, to work out what to do next, but there was a bigger pull – the pills in the side pocket of her bag. Her head swam; the vodka she'd gulped was swimming alone in her empty stomach, making her woozy. Grimly, she fought for control of her fluid mind.

"Sit down, Sam," she told herself sternly, "and think. Think what to do next." But the lovely white pills filled her vision, egging her on to take just a couple, to blot out all thoughts of Duncan, erase the memory of his face from her mind. They bobbed about tantalizingly, even when she closed her eyes to clear the vision. It was no use; she knew she'd succumb.

She ran out into the hallway, grabbed her bag off the banister end and dived into the side pocket. She clutched a handful of pills and shoved them greedily into her mouth, not bothering to physically count them, desperate for the relief they would give her. Slowly, forcing herself to breathe evenly now, she walked back to her spot in the kitchen and filled a glass with water to wash them down properly. Yes, that was better, just knowing they were inside of her, that the soothing feeling would follow in a moment. But she needed to think; there were things she needed to do to keep herself away from any suspicion. She forced herself to think about what any other woman, a woman still in love with her husband, would do in such an instance.

She'd call the hospital. Yes – I need to call the hospital.

She scrambled for her phone, her hands shaking with booze and nervous energy, and Googled the hospital in Croydon. She punched the number in and asked to be put through to Duncan Riley's room. After a few rings, a nurse answered and told her he was doing okay under the circumstances but was groggy from the painkillers. They expected to move him to a ward later today, she said, all being well.

Sam thanked her, making sure the nurse knew she'd called, and checked the task off in her head. What next? What would she do next?

Ring a friend, tell her the bad news. Right.

Anika answered after a couple of beats and Sam told her the news.

"I'm on my way – you shouldn't be on your own," Anika said, alarmed.

"No, I'm okay now I've got over the initial shock, and I'll have to get the girls soon. I just wanted to let you know. Stay where you are, but thanks."

The last thing she wanted was Anika being a well-intentioned friend when there were things to be done – like get in touch with the man she'd organized to do the job in the first place. She needed a refund or the job finishing, not left dangling as it was. If Duncan lived, he'd find out about the loan and expenditure for sure, and that was something she'd have to address convincingly. Being married to a detective had its drawbacks.

Her head was beginning to feel sleepy, and Sam regretted the tablets on top of the vodka. How many had she taken anyway?

"I need food," she said. She walked over to the toaster and slipped a couple of slices of bread in, not because she was hungry but to soak up the alcohol. While she waited for it to toast, she opened her laptop and found the relevant site. She posted a message for 'him.'

"You fucked up. He's still alive. Get it sorted."

She hoped he'd see it soon and respond; she'd log on again in an hour or so. She wondered how he'd play it, what he'd do to make their contract right. All she could do now was wait until it was time to get the girls, then explain to them what had happened.

Tomorrow, she'd drive down to Croydon and play the dutiful wife – she'd better be convincing.

Thoughts of the Cornish coast were slipping away . . .

Chapter Seventy-Two

BACK AT THE hotel and scene of the crime, Amanda was talking to the doctor on call, Faye Mitchell. She'd worked with Croydon for more than five years and was one of the best in the business. Never one to speculate before she had the facts to deal with, she often found herself at odds with detectives who wanted to get on with the job of detecting. But Dr. Mitchell could never be swayed – ever. Amanda stood waiting patiently in the doorway of the room Duncan had stayed in overnight, watching the last of the technicians finish their job. Faye raised her head and gave a brief smile, knowing what Amanda was thinking.

"All in good time," she quipped. A moment later, she stood from the spot on the floor where Duncan had fallen before being shot through the back of his shoulder.

"Two bullets: one in the bed, one in the carpet. But you already know that. From point-blank range, too. He was damn lucky there wasn't more damage to him than what he has. Any ideas your side who may have wanted him dead?"

Amanda stepped further into the room. "We may have a rather loose person of interest, and if it pans out, it would be a sad state of affairs, I'm afraid."

"Oh? That sounds ominous."

"It is. It's also a bit left field, not what we normally come across in cases involving a shooting. We're more used to gang-related hits. I'll tell you more when we know more. We've only an inkling to go on, nothing concrete, so the more you can add to that, the better." Changing the subject slightly, she asked, "Any DNA or fingerprints from the shooter?"

"There's plenty – it's a hotel room, after all – but from the shooter I couldn't say yet." Faye looked at the bed cover and added, "God only knows what and whose will be on that."

The thought rolled Amanda's empty stomach. "I'd hate to be the one to work the bathroom plughole contents."

Dr. Mitchell went on. "The tough bit will be eliminating those with legitimate reasons to have been in here in the recent past. The hotel has a transient clientele, as you'd expect. They could live anywhere and everywhere, but that's over to you and yours. It seems the hotel's cleaning team aren't that thorough, given the amount we've recovered to work with so far. Let's see whose fingerprints are on file, eh? A print is only good when it can be matched."

Amanda rolled her eyes. "Thanks, Captain Obvious," she thought. Mitchell was renowned for remarks like this.

"Any usable camera footage?" the doctor asked her.

"Yes, but not much use. Two figures, presumably male from their stature, were seen leaving the back exit and headed off down the street on foot, not in any hurry. Dressed in what look like jeans and hoodies pulled up tight, but it was a cold, damp night. Could be coincidence, since it was around the right time, or they could have been visiting someone. Either way, they went down a side street. Jack and a couple of uniforms are talking to the neighbours down there, but it was the dead of night. Most of them were probably in bed. So we're hoping you have better luck finding something for us to work with."

"No pressure, then?" Dr. Mitchell smiled wryly. "And how's our man Duncan?"

"Stable now, still groggy from the anaesthetic and painkillers, but we'll talk to him again later when he's a bit more compos mentis."

Amanda looked at her watch. "Right, well, I'll leave you to finish off. Call me as soon as you hear something I can use."

"Of course. You'll be the first to know."

As Amanda left the building, heading towards her car, her phone rang. It was Rick.

Amanda went straight to the point. "How'd she do?" There was no point dressing it up.

"Mixed, I'd say. Put it this way: she didn't seem in any hurry to get to him, but then there are the two little girls to think of."

Amanda grunted, not entirely convinced. There were ways to have the girls taken care of if she had wanted to dash off.

"She put on a pretty good act if it was one," Rick went on, "but I saw a couple of holes. I've arranged to get her phone and bank account records, the usual, see if anything pops up. I'm also owed a favour up here. I'll see what the word on the street is for a possible hit."

"Someone with a grudge?"

"There's always someone with a grudge when it's an officer, isn't there? One of the lads is checking recent releases, but I'm not aware of anyone from that side of things. Any news on transferring him up here? It would be great to see him."

"Not that I'm aware of, but I'll see Rochelle shortly. His groggy state will be wearing off soon. She's with him now."

"Good. At least a friendly face will be there for when he wakes up properly, eh?"

"Let's hope he can tell us a bit more than he's managed so far."

They said their speak laters and hung up, promising to do just that.

Two hours later, Rick was at his desk when the first of Sam and Duncan's account details hit his desk. He surfed through her mobile phone bill, followed by the house landline bill. There wasn't much on either, nothing to use his highlighter pen on so far. Calls and texts to a regular number that turned out to be registered to someone named Anika, a friend of Sam's, he assumed. He called it to confirm and then hung up before she asked any questions. If Sam did have something to do with Duncan's attempted murder, he didn't want her friend forewarning her of her involvement in the investigation. There was also a text sent at 9.32 p.m. the previous night from Sam to Duncan's phone, a number Rick knew well. He had looked at Duncan's phone and had read the loving message from Sam saying goodnight. He asked a colleague to see where exactly the phone had been when that text was sent. Other than that, there was nothing noteworthy.

He turned his attention to the bank statements for the last six months. There were the usual deposits and store transactions, but he did note a pattern of regular £100 and £200 withdrawals from cash machines, and not the same one each time. Most people used their bank cards these days, didn't they? Weren't they all becoming a cashless society? Maybe she liked to use cash when shopping, unless she was using it for something else. Still, it was to be noted as somewhat unusual.

He turned to the last page.

"Hello, hello," he said to himself.

There in black and white was a transfer of £20,000 into Sam and Duncan's joint savings account. And that was closely followed by the sum of £6000 leaving it. Rick was not aware of the couple having planned any home improvements or nice holidays. His heart slumped.

"Oh dear, Sam. What have you been up to?"

Chapter Seventy-Three

IT WAS AROUND 4 p.m. when Duncan's throat worked a little better and he was finally able to put a coherent sentence together. Though he was still hoarse, he was sounding remarkably better than when he'd first come to and was glad to see a friendly and welcoming face as he struggled with one hand to sit himself up in bed a little more.

Rochelle was by his side as his eyes fluttered open

"Here, let me give you a hand," she said brightly, rearranging his pillows behind his head. "Welcome again to the land of the living. How are you feeling now? You've been asleep for ages."

"Sorry to have kept you." Duncan smiled as he slumped back heavily into the softness of them. "And quit the hand jokes, please."

Rochelle smiled and offered him a glass of water with a straw. He sucked greedily on the end, draining the glass again.

"Feel up to some questions, then?" It wasn't a question that warranted a 'no,' no matter how he was feeling. She needed to push for some answers before more time elapsed and evidence evaporated. Duncan knew the drill. She dived straight in.

"Let's start with what you know, then we'll move on to theory, okay?"

He nodded his approval, saving his voice for real sentences.

"From the top, then. Let's hear it."

And so Duncan recited all he could remember about travelling down, checking in, Amanda and Jack picking him up, being ill and getting into bed back at the hotel. There were some blurry bits about the night, how ill he'd been and the visions he'd had, which had made it difficult to decipher what had been real and what was a figment of his imagination.

Intrigued, Rochelle probed about the visions.

"I'm sure I heard hushed voices at one stage," he said, struggling to think. "Otherwise I wouldn't have rolled off the bed and thrown myself on the floor, would I?"

Rochelle narrowed her eyes. It was a good question. "That roll could well have saved your life because that's where the first shot was found. The bullet lodged in the mattress over to the right side of the bed. If the intruders had been over you and aiming for your heart, we wouldn't be talking now."

It was a sobering thought for them both. In the gap in conversation, there was a gentle knock on the door. Amanda walked in.

"Welcome back!" said Amanda. Duncan rolled his eyes and, croaking, said, "if anyone else says that I swear I'm going to slap them."

Amanda turned to Rochelle and said, "Nothing wrong with his sense of humour, then." Both women smiled at each other.

Rochelle filled her in from the notes she'd scribbled on her pad, and Amanda made her own notes as Rochelle spoke. Even though it was Amanda's investigation, Rochelle was a close colleague of Duncan's and she knew she needed to tread respectfully here.

"So can you remember what the voices said?" Amanda asked Duncan now.

"It sounds almost comical now, lying here, but I'm sure one said he couldn't do it, and the other person told him he had to. They were definitely both male voices – if they were there at all. But like I said, why else would I have rolled?

"What did the other voice say?"

"Told him to get on with it. Then I rolled and got shot. I couldn't do much else, so I pretended I was dead. I don't remember anyone touching me, though I might have blacked out. Then I got to my phone and called it in. It was so dark and like I say, I wasn't well. Migraine or something nasty."

Both women scribbled in their notebooks for a moment, and then Rochelle broached the subject of what he'd said on first coming to.

"Do you remember what you said earlier, about Sam?"

Duncan stayed silent for a couple of beats, considering.

"Maybe I had that wrong," he said at length. "She wouldn't do something like this, and she'd have no idea how to find someone either. It's not her. Sam loves me and the kids. Where is she, anyway? On her way down?"

The two women looked at one another and Rochelle took the question.

"Rick told her this morning, but with the kids, she may not make it down today. But they're looking to move you to Manchester, so there may be no need for her to travel all this way." Rochelle hoped she'd sounded positive and convincing that all was well on that front, that Sam did care.

Changing the subject away from Sam, Duncan asked about what they had so far.

Amanda took over. "By all accounts there's a few prints to follow up but CCTV doesn't hold much apart from a couple of grainy figures with hoods up. But we're making the most of what we have, so we should know something a bit later. DC Rutherford, Jack, is talking to neighbours in the area where the figures headed off to. We'll find whoever is responsible for this, Duncan, no stone and all that."

She beamed at him, but he seemed to be somewhere else as she said it, deep in thought, remembering back to events of the previous night, maybe. Rochelle looked at Amanda who shrugged her shoulders, also wondering where he'd disappeared to in his head.

Would Sam have done such a thing? Could she be capable of finding a hit man to take me out? And if so, why had she? We were getting on so much better —she'd turned the corner, had sorted herself out, was taking an interest in life again. I've been worried about her for a time, worried for the kids, and after their adventure that day, ending up at that elderly woman's house — a woman with a past, albeit from years ago − I'd nearly torn my hair out. I've never told her about that part, not letting her in on the fact the woman had done time, had been convicted for her part in a paedophile ring, not wanting to offload any more stress into her life when she was just getting it together.

But the change in behaviour raised a flag in my mind and Rochelle had voiced her opinion about that too − the status quo was about to change, she said.

And from where I'm sitting, it already has.

He pretended to be asleep while he thought it through, not willing to give Sam up to his colleagues yet. He could be wildly off track. No, better to let them do their jobs and follow other leads, and if that didn't pan out, he'd perhaps say something.

But not until then.

Chapter Seventy-Four

RICK BLACK SAT BACK in his desk chair, deep in thought. If Sam had taken a loan out and used some of it for a down payment, there could be trouble brewing – Duncan was still alive, thank God, but that left loose ends. For instance, was there a professional hit man roaming around out there with unfinished business? That could mean another attempt on Duncan's life. Or at the very least, an angry customer – Sam.

But if Sam was behind all this, how had she got involved so deep, and who had she got to do the necessary?

He had to find out, and while it went against everything he stood for, he knew just the person who could help him shed some light on it.

Wilfred Day.

While Day wasn't exactly on his speed dial, it wasn't hard to get in touch with the man. He'd interviewed him many times in the past for various things. Rick looked up his contact number, dialled, and waited to be connected. He could almost hear the smile in Day's voice when he answered.

"And a grand afternoon it is. How may I help you, DS Black – or is it DI yet?"

If nothing else, the man had manners. Rick smiled despite himself. "Not quite. I'm working on it."

"And I've no doubt that'll be soon."

Duncan came to the point. "I'd like to buy you a G&T if I may, Wilfred. I could do with your help with a particular matter."

"How positively delightful and totally unexpected." He sounded like a delighted aunt, not a criminal yet to be caught and prosecuted. "Of course. When would you like to partake in this little get-together?"

"How about right now? Name the place, and I'll meet you there – if you're free, of course."

A moment ticked by, presumably while Wilfred checked his social calendar and thought of a venue.

"Meet me at The Washhouse; you know where it is. I'll see you there shortly, and I shall be in eager anticipation of how I might serve you, Detective Sergeant. It could be an interesting meeting." He chuckled.

"I'm on my way," Rick said, and hung up before Wilfred told him to have a fantastic day. It was time for a favour to be returned. Wilfred Day owed him. Years ago, Wilfred's twelve-year-old nephew had got himself tied up with a hit-and-run that had left a sleazy local drug dealer badly injured, and Day had persuaded Rick not to lay charges. The boy had been a decent kid at heart, though a bit of a tearaway. He shouldn't have even known how to drive, never mind actually *been* driving, but living the life he had been at the time, it was no surprise. Rick knew the lad would be better off learning a life lesson from Wilfred rather than being swallowed up by the system of corrections. Mr. Day had been grateful, and today Rick was going to capitalize on that.

Duncan pulled up near the bar, one of Manchester's secret though legal drinking places hidden in the back of a laundromat. Moments later, he saw Day's distinctive Bentley pull up. Day, clad in a diamond-patterned sweater, climbed out, pushed his fingers lazily through his tousled blond hair, and then set his sunglasses back on top of his head. On a cloudy Manchester afternoon, they really were obsolete but he wore them rain or shine. Rick fell into step alongside Wilfred as they headed towards the door, which immediately opened. They went inside.

At four in the afternoon, the place was deserted, which was probably why Wilfred had chosen it. They could talk without being overheard or seen together. When they were seated in a private booth with their drinks, Rick began to speak.

"DS Duncan Riley has been shot. He's stable but I need to know who might want him dead. Have you heard anything?"

Rick watched Day closely as he delivered the news. To his credit, the man actually looked shocked, which told Rick he wasn't anywhere near it.

"I'm not aware of anyone holding a grudge, and I'm sure you'll have looked at those fellows he's helped put away in the past who now have a bit of freedom again?"

"There is one person whose activities I'm hoping you can trace," he said.

Day smiled wolfishly. "Ah, and so we get to the real reason you called. You want me to find out how it was organized and with whom. And I'm assuming you can't go to your own cyber team for some reason, even though they'd throw everything they could at it since he's one of you."

Rick nodded.

Day went on. "And this is the favour you wish returned, I presume?"

Rick nodded. He could feel himself going red in the semi-darkness of the bar and was glad it couldn't be seen. There really was nothing more to be said. He took a sip of his drink and waited.

"So who is he? Who do you want me to snoop on?" Day tasted his gin and reached for a bowl of spicy cereal nibbles in the middle of the table. He tipped half of the bowl into his paw-like hand and took tiny amounts out with his other paw. Rick wondered how much pain those hands had inflicted on his enemies in the past and watched the nibbles slowly disappear.

"Come on, then – who hurt your friend? What's his name?"

Rick was silent for a moment. Once he'd spoken the words, there was no going back. Did he really want to do this?

"It's not a he, it's a she," he said finally.

"Oh." Day looked nonplussed. "I didn't think DS Riley was the type for a side piece." He nibbled some more snacks, smiling at his own double meaning. Then he stopped chewing as the name of Rick's suspect dawned on him.

"You think Mrs. Riley is behind it? Ah. Now I see why the cageyness. You want me to see whom she organized it with, so to speak. Am I correct? You'd like me to do some digging?"

Rick nodded. "Can you? She has never seemed the type to move in such circles, so I'm wondering ..." He let the sentence hang in the air.

"You want me to trace her online activities. I get it. But it's not that easy if you don't know where to start looking. Can you get her laptop for me? And give me a list of her regular movements and the places she goes? If she's been a buzzy little bee, she may have left me some breadcrumbs."

Rick ignored the mixed metaphor. "How long will it take you if I can?"

"That depends on the trail and whether she took precautions on public Wi-Fi or not. And of course, who's behind the operation when I get there, if anyone. Often, they shut up shop and move to another squat before the next customer comes along – helps keeps things secure. That's why there are still so many kiddie-peddlers still walking the street. If you lot could clean that up, you would, wouldn't you?"

He had a point there, Rick knew. It made him think of Duncan's two and their recent brush with Mrs. Skeen. Thank God she'd called it in before making an alternative decision.

"I'll get you the laptop and recent places of interest tonight. She'll be waiting for an update so I'll pop round and get what you need then. I need to move fast on this, though, Wilfred."

"I understand, my friend. Call my number later when you have what I need and we can arrange the drop-off. Now drink up, for tomorrow you'll know who shot JR." He threw his head back and laughed at his own joke. "Get it? Remember JR Ewing?"

"I've heard the story, though I'm surprised you know it. That TV show ended before you were born, almost." Rick wasn't in the mood for games. He tossed the remainder of his drink back and stood to leave.

"I'll call you when I have what you need," he said, then walked away, leaving Wilfred to finish the rest of the spicy nibbles alone.

Chapter Seventy-Five

"Still no bloody reply. What the fuck?"

Sam was getting more and more irritated as the evening wore on. Since sending her earlier message demanding to know what was going on, she'd heard nothing back, not a whisper, and she was fast losing patience. Draining the wine glass beside her, she poured another large one from the bottle of red on the coffee table and sat back to nurse it – and think. This was not what was supposed to have happened – her sitting there wondering. No, she should be making plans for herself and the girls and arranging a funeral for their father. Instead, she was worrying about whether her tracks had been covered enough to keep her out of trouble, keep her safe.

And keep her out of prison.

She slammed the lid shut and plugged the laptop in to charge the battery, deciding instead to watch TV and finish the rest of her bottle before bed. Her head was buzzing from the alcohol on an empty stomach and she knew if she didn't soak it up with something, her head would feel like someone had split it open with an axe the following morning. Padding into the kitchen, she turned on the oven, unwrapped a readymade pizza from the freezer, and placed it inside. There was time for a quick shower, so she headed up the stairs.

Halfway up, she heard a knock at the front door and, mumbling to herself that it was a bit late for visitors, she went to answer it.

It was Rick again.

"I was passing by and thought I'd see how you and the girls were doing."

His smile was bright, and he was unapologetic for the hour. He picked up on her disapproval. "I'll only stay a minute."

She opened the door wide and let him through.

"I was headed for the shower, actually, but how kind of you to drop by."

He noticed her forced smile and added it to his observations of her behaviour.

"Then you go ahead. I'll make a cuppa quickly. Would you like one?" He could smell wine on her breath but asked anyway, and he was already on his way through to the kitchen.

"No, thanks," she called after him, annoyed at his intrusion but not wanting to say so.

"You carry on. I'll make myself at home," he called.

Still annoyed, she carried on with her plan. It wasn't long before Rick could hear the shower running overhead as he stood in the little kitchen. He hadn't got long to act. He quickly moved back to the living room and scanned the surfaces looking for her laptop, then noticed it plugged in by the window. It was there for the taking. But would it be too obvious – him turning up and her laptop vanishing? Surely, she'd know he was investigating her, and that wasn't what he wanted – not yet. But it was tempting. The sooner he got it to Wilfred, the better.

He thought of Duncan lying alone in his hospital bed, an officer stationed on his door as a precaution, and suddenly he didn't give a rat's ass about whether he showed Sam his hand so soon or not. If she had set someone up to kill Duncan, Rick wanted to know about it now so he could do something about it. And he needed more evidence.

His phone rang, but he let it go to voicemail then called upstairs to Sam. Whether she heard him or not didn't matter.

"Sorry, got to go. Duty calls," he shouted, then quickly grabbed the laptop and cable and stuffed them inside his jacket. Out on the front step, he gently closed the door behind him and slipped down the path towards his car. He chanced a glance at the front bedroom window before driving off. The light was off. He assumed Sam was still in the bathroom.

Sam watched from behind a crack in the bedroom curtain, her hair wet and dripping onto her bare shoulders. What had he wanted so late? she wondered. Regardless, she was pleased to see him leave so early: there would be no awkward questions about Duncan, questions she might have tripped herself up on. The investigation would already be in full swing, she knew, with all possible resources engaged to find the attempted cop killer. Law enforcement stuck together, protecting one another, and Manchester was no different.

The smell of pizza cooking returned her thoughts to herself, and she quickly towel-dried her hair and slipped into her robe. The tension of his surprise visit was making her nerves jangle and she knew she needed something to soothe them. Wine alone was clearly not strong enough for the task. Tomorrow, she had to show her face at Duncan's bedside as the dutiful, loving and distraught wife, and that meant an early start getting the girls to Anika's – she would take them to school for her. The rest of the day? Well, driving down would be as boring as hell but it would give her time to rehearse her act. Convincing was going to be her new middle name.

Back downstairs, she found her bag and the rest of the bottle of wine and swilled down a couple of pills before starting on the pizza. It wasn't long before the potent concoction in her stomach started to take effect and a pleasantly drowsy state enveloped her as she dropped off in front of the TV. A couple of hours later, she groggily climbed the stairs and finally crawled into her bed.

Rick called the number he'd rung earlier and told Wilfred he had the laptop. A drop-off point was agreed to, and Rick thanked him again for helping him out with a delicate situation. Wilfred assured him that it had been no problem, that it was nice to be working with him instead of against him for a change. He'd take a look a little later and fill him in first thing. Rick detected the boyish excitement mixed with amusement in the man's voice but said nothing. They'd speak in the morning.

Rick hoped with all his heart he was wrong about Sam. A spouse organizing their partner's demise wouldn't do much for anyone's relationship. How do you move forward from there?

Chapter Seventy-Six

As Rick handed the laptop over, he said, "It would be great if you could return it before the morning so she doesn't suspect anything."

Anyone would think Rick had never dealt with Wilfred Day before; he was as nervous as a kitten in his company, but that was more likely the subject matter – a woman he knew, his partner's wife. He wasn't enjoying what he was doing.

"Not a problem. For speed, jot the address down and consider it done. She'll be none the wiser by morning."

Rick looked at Wilfred squarely and said, "I'm not stupid. I'm sure you can remember it."

Wilfred gave him a mock hurt look as Rick recited the address to him, storing it in one of his deep memory banks, no doubt. Rick hoped he went to the right address – not that Wilfred himself would be going, of course. Most likely he'd send a minion. Wilfred Day kept out of trouble himself; that was part of the problem, and the reason he was still operating like he was.

"Let's hope there's a trail of breadcrumbs for you to follow, eh?" said Rick.

"Most novices leave a trail. I'll be more surprised if there isn't one."

And that was the end of their conversation. Wilfred slipped back into the driver's seat of the ostentatious Bentley and waved like the Queen Mother as he pulled away.

Rick stood uneasily, watching him go. "This better bloody work," he said to the cold night. Not a star nor a sliver of moon was visible; there was just the hazy amber glow of the city lights above Manchester. Rick got back in his own car and headed home. It had been a long and stressful day, and he knew there were probably more to come.

It didn't take Wilfred long to get back to his place and start working on Sam's computer. Breaking in without her password was a stumbling block that took him mere seconds to overcome. He rubbed his giant hands together in glee like a child about to tuck into a banana split all to himself.

"Let's see what you've been up to, then, Sam. Are you a clever girl or a buffoon?"

It didn't take him long to find the first of the breadcrumbs as he worked, shaking his blond head occasionally at her mistakes. At least she'd had the good sense to use a Tor browser, but she hadn't the knowledge to use a secure connection. It seemed the public Wi-Fi in the café she frequented could have been the start of her downfall. From there, it was easy enough for a talented hacker such as himself to find out what she'd been up to and, as he was beginning to discover, it wasn't pretty.

The site she'd contacted for the job had since been removed, but again, that wasn't a problem to a man with his particular talents. Deleted files still left a footprint, one that he could follow, but he'd do that later. Right now, he concentrated on loading the cloning software so he could watch any further keystrokes she made from the privacy of his own system. He sniggered as he thought of privacy – privacy was on life support, almost like the man he was trying to help, in his own roundabout kind of way.

It wasn't long before he'd done what he needed but for good measure, he decided to check her regular web browsing history.

"Well, well, well, Sam, what have we here? I can only imagine what you've been buying from such places." He took a closer look and then sat back thoughtfully, tapping his fingers as he considered his findings. Depending on what DS Rick Black had in mind when he reported back, Wilfred could make use of this information to solve the problem of a naughty spouse. She'd never make the same mistake again, that was for sure.

He checked his watch. It was getting close to midnight. No matter – she'd be fast asleep now, tucked up in the marital bed more than likely. He turned his attention to the deleted files and the trail they'd left. Novices really should be more careful when dealing in areas they don't know much about, he mused. A few more keystrokes and he had another set of information he could use later on if it suited.

He'd been the top man in his field for more years than he could remember, and while his competition still chose to beat and maim their victims in order to collect on debts or ensure loyalty, Wilfred had always found his methods less invasive and just as successful. Fingers didn't get pointed, blame wasn't apportioned and snitches didn't benefit to their own end, and that was because he held the knowhow. He, Wilfred Day, was the talent, the untraceable hacker who could hit his enemies where it hurt the most.

He turned back to Sam's laptop. Now he had two lots of intelligence to work with that would prove valuable in both the short and long runs. But now, he had to get the druggie's laptop back to her lounge before she suspected anything was amiss. He called the relevant number and recited the address. By the time she awoke, her laptop would be plugged in again, sitting right where she'd left it – with a little added invisible software on board for good measure. He'd report back to DS Black in the morning, and then it was down to him to decide how to handle it.

Chapter Seventy-Seven

RICK WAS FINISHING his first coffee of the day and eating a slice of toast when his phone vibrated on silent. It was still early, just gone 6 a.m.

"Morning." He wasn't happy about associating with the very man he'd tried so many times to put away, but right now Rick needed the shortcut – and quickly.

"I hear today will be a beautiful day. What do you have planned, DS Black?" Wilfred sounded like he'd already been up for a couple of hours. Rick ignored his joviality and got straight to the point.

"What did you find?"

"Ah, patience, my dear man. All will be explained in due course."

Rick groaned inwardly but waited dutifully for Wilfred to say more

"First I have a question for you."

"And what's that?" *Patience, patience.*

"Since you can't use my evidence in court, how are you planning to handle this situation?"

Rick really didn't want to explain his plan to anyone until he'd spoken to Duncan, so he tried to evade the question. "I'm not entirely sure yet, so let me worry about that. What did you find out? Is she involved?"

"That she is, I'm afraid. As I've said before and will say again now, novices shouldn't dabble in this type of thing. It took me a handful of minutes to figure out what she'd been up to."

Rick groaned audibly now.

Wilfred went on. "Tell me, do you like this woman, or, more to the point, does DS Riley like his wife? Are they close?"

"She's not my favourite woman in the world but then I'm not married to her. I can't speak for Duncan, though I expect he'll be pretty pissed off when I tell him. Why?"

Wilfred ignored his question. "Will you arrest her? Do you have any evidence other than what I've found?"

"Not enough, I'm afraid." He sounded defeated to his own ears. What a sorry state to be in, and even more so for Duncan to be in. Rick could sense there was more to come. There was.

"Did you know of her habit?" Wilfred said. "Her predilection for pills, of the codeine variety? She likes to shop online, I expect to balance buying from the local chemists. That way she can always have a stash on hand, as it were."

"No, I didn't know that," Rick said wearily. "But that would explain a few things." He paused for a moment, then said, "Thanks, Wilfred. I think we're about square."

"Glad I could be of assistance. Let me know how it turns out. And have a fantastic day..." He gave a familiar chuckle.

They rang off, and Rick sat frozen in place, his head whirling with thoughts about what to do next and how to tell Duncan. He wasn't looking forward to the day ahead.

In truth, Wilfred Day hadn't yet been to bed since his discovery. One thing he'd learned early on in his career was that there was something to salvage from every situation, no matter how bad it seemed on the surface. Last night's discovery of Sam's activities, coupled with who she'd been involved with, had given him an idea, an idea that could be beneficial on several fronts. Once he'd found out who had been behind the hit, he'd spent time doing some homework, and it had paid off.

He liked both DS Black and DS Riley. He'd always found them easy to deal with on the few occasions he'd been interviewed officially, and he saw them both out and about regularly. He looked at the address he had jotted down, along with a man's name. A drive-by later was in order, but for now, it was time to get some sleep.

He had a busy day ahead of him.

Sam was almost ready to go. Anika had collected the girls and taken them both to school on her behalf, allowing her an early start down south – a journey she wasn't looking forward to and a visit she was looking forward to even less.

But there was no choice if she was to keep suspicion at bay.

Inside Sam was fuming; not only had there been no reply to her message, but the website had since vanished and with no clue how else to contact 'him', it seemed that was the end of that. What a waste of £6000. And with Duncan still alive, she knew she'd have some explaining to do about the transaction in the first place. Could she be planning a surprise vacation for them? Could that be her excuse? It might work; after all, why would someone suspect her of being behind the shooting. She was simply an ordinary, loving housewife. As she made her way out to her car, the sun was climbing the Manchester sky slowly, but would the day stay so bright?

She hoped so.

Chapter Seventy-Eight

Amanda and Jack were back at the station, rehashing what they knew over coffee. Mrs. Stewart had put two slices of chocolate cake into another plastic tub for Jack, and Amanda was halfway through her piece, dark brown crumbs resting in her lap. Jack hadn't yet passed comment, but who was he to talk about messy eating? She'd thought about banning him from eating sandwiches with mayonnaise in them, since it meant a greasy stain on his shirt every time. Still, he had someone to wash them now, she mused.

"Don't you think it's a bit odd we have virtually nothing to work with?" Amanda asked him, looking thoughtful as she ate.

"It's not that uncommon, Lacey. There are any number of unsolved cases that never get solved. We can only follow the evidence."

He was right, of course, but it did nothing to ease her agitation. "I'll call Rick. He may have some news. And maybe as time goes on, Duncan's account of what happened will clarify. It didn't help him being so ill, either. Also, we never did talk about the food van drugs. Maybe Rick can help with that now, too."

"I wonder what caused him to be so ill. Can a migraine really do that to a person, and so violently?" Jack licked his fingers clean of chocolate cream filling then wiped his hands down his trousers. Amanda glared at him disapprovingly.

"What?"

She stared pointedly at the napkin dispenser on the table before going on. "From my experience, severe headache, visual disturbances and vomiting are part of it, but it sounds like Duncan had severe hallucinations at the same time, and I've not heard of that before. I'll double check with the doc; she'll know for sure." Thinking again, she asked, "Did she do a tox screen?"

"Doubt it. He's not dead, so there'd be no reason to do one. Why? Do you think he ingested something to cause the hallucinations? He didn't eat anything at the restaurant."

"No, I know that, but the ferocity of the hallucinations he mentioned seems extreme. Worth checking if it's not too late. Right," she said, standing. The coffee break was over. "I'll call the doc and ask her to do a tox screen, and you check in with Rick. Then we'll head over and see how our man is this morning. I believe his wife is coming down."

Jack's antennae pricked up. "That should be interesting to see. Can't we plant a camera and mic and watch remotely?"

Amanda raised her eyebrows in a 'no.'

"Good idea, though, don't you think?"

"It's still no."

Duncan was sitting propped up in bed. Normal colour had returned to his face and he spoke with a more natural voice again, his throat having healed nicely overnight. He greeted Amanda and Jack with bright eyes and an equally bright smile as they entered. Clearly Duncan was feeling much better.

"Looks like I'll be heading back towards home soon. Just a couple more days in hospital and I think they'll let me go home." He sounded chipper for someone who had had the ordeal of his life a little over 24 hours ago. "Sam called me too. She's on her way. I could have saved her a journey." Again, his beaming smile. Amanda couldn't help wonder if he'd had a full change of heart about her. But given what Rick had found, and what they had yet to tell him, well, who knew how he'd react. She wasn't looking forward to it.

They pulled chairs up and sat down. Amanda took the lead.

"It's good to see you looking so much better, Duncan. You had us all worried there for a while."

"It seems like a distant memory now, apart from the throb in my hand. My shoulder doesn't feel so bad in comparison. They reckon I'll need another operation on it in a few days. Looks like I'll be desk bound for a while."

"Duncan, I need to ask you a couple of sensitive questions. Regarding Sam, actually."

"Oh?"

"Do you remember what you said when you were first found, along the lines of 'look at Sam'?"

They watched as the smile vanished from Duncan's face.

"I wasn't myself. I was hallucinating. Badly. God, I've never felt so ill as that night."

"I understand. But we had to check it out – run the normal account checks, telco, bank, etcetera. You understand."

"I'm guessing from your tone something came up." It wasn't a question.

Amanda pressed on. "There was a bank transaction, a loan taken out, of twenty thousand pounds." A flicker of surprise showed on his face. "There was also a withdrawal the following day of six thousand pounds. Would you know what those were for, by chance?"

Duncan's face was utterly blank now; it was clear he had no clue what the money meant.

At that moment, the door opened and in walked Sam herself, looking for all the world like the concerned wife of any man in. As she bent over the bed and brushed his lips with hers, attempting to give him a hug without hurting him, Amanda and Jack both discreetly rolled their eyes.

Jack mouthed, "Question her here?"

Amanda shook her head no. "Not yet," she mouthed back.

They stepped tactfully out of the room and waited in the family room until Sam had finished her doting wife routine.

Duncan would surely ask her about the money, Amanda thought. Wouldn't he?

Chapter Seventy-Nine

AMANDA AND JACK sat patiently in the waiting room, chatting waiting for Sam to finish her visit and clear off.

Amanda's phone buzzed. The caller ID showed DS Black. She hit answer and put the call on speakerphone.

"Hi, Rick. You're on speakerphone with Jack. Anything to report?"

"Hello to you both, and yes, you could say that. It's probably better you take me off speakerphone and relay back to Jack when we've finished. Let's say it's extremely sensitive and walls have ears."

Amanda and Jack exchanged a look, and Amanda clicked the speakerphone off again and put the phone to her ear.

"Go ahead. It's just me now. What's up?"

"First, don't ask me how I know this because I called a favour in. I now need evidence to back it up, evidence that we can use in court, because what I'm about to tell you won't fly on its own."

"Let's hear it, and then we can see what we're dealing with."

"Sam was behind the attempted hit. Paid six thousand as a down payment, likely another six on completion. The site she used is no longer operating. It closed up shop and moved on like many of them do. My source followed her trail easily. She left tracks, and because we were looking at an individual, the trace was easy enough to do."

He let that sink in and waited for her to respond.

"So Duncan was correct to begin with," Amanda said, "but now he's saying she wouldn't do such a thing. He either doesn't want her in trouble or simply doesn't want to believe it, eh?"

"Could be. But it gets worse. She's also been buying packets of painkillers both locally and online, more than the average household would use. My guess is, and it's only a guess, she will be getting other stuff as well. Maybe losing her job hit her harder than we realized."

"And my guess is Duncan doesn't know that part either."

"Correct, but it explains the regular cash withdrawals I found. They've been going back a few months. It won't be that hard to find out exactly where she's buying from."

"Well, that may be related to our news," Amanda said thoughtfully. "We've asked Faye Mitchell to run a tox screen because Duncan's hallucinations don't add up. I'm wondering if he took something without knowing it. It makes even more sense now we know Sam arranged for his death. We should get the results later today. And speaking of Sam, she just arrived a few minutes ago."

"Urgh, thanks. Let's see what the tox comes back with. We could maybe trace a positive result back to her. At least that evidence would stand up."

"Agreed. They're moving him tomorrow; will you tail her from your end? At least possession would be a start, and I doubt much will happen while she's down here."

"Will do. Oh, and until the results come back, don't say anything to Duncan. I'll do it later if need be. Buddy to buddy, as it were."

"Understood. He only knows about the loan, nothing more, and we'd just told him about that when Sam arrived, so I'll keep you posted. I need to ask you something else, though."

"What's that?"

"Remember when we talked about Wilfred Day and our suspected food van connection? Well, Duncan was going to go through what he knew just before this all happened. So it never got discussed. Perhaps when this is all over, we can go over what we both know in a bit more detail?"

"Absolutely. Any way I can help let me know."

"Great. Speak to you later."

Amanda rang off and then filled Jack in, though he'd already caught the gist of it. Sam Riley had balls, that was for sure. But would those same balls keep her out of trouble? That depended on how Duncan reacted to the news when Rick had a word sometime later.

Rick sat with his phone in his hand, unsettled by the mention of Wilfred's name again. He'd always thought he'd eventually get Day, that the man would trip up eventually, but now he wasn't so sure. Without Day, how else could he have found out what Sam had planned, and about her drug problem? By hacking in as he had, Wilfred Day could well have saved Duncan's life. Did Rick now owe Day, rather than the other way around?

Later that afternoon, Dr. Faye Mitchell sent a terse text to Amanda.

Drop by my office ASAP.

"Grab your jacket, Jack," Amanda yelled across to his desk, where he was busy writing up a report. "Faye has news."

Dr. Faye Mitchell's office was on the other side of Croydon, which, in non-rush-hour traffic, took only twenty minutes tops. It was however, rush hour and that meant double. By the time they'd arrived and parked, there weren't many people left in the red brick building. They hurried into her sparse second-floor office, which even on a hot sunny day gave Jack the chills. Faye seemed to like a cold working environment.

"Come in. Sit down." She directed them to the two chairs in front of her desk. "I thought it best to go through this in person rather than over the phone."

Jack and Amanda both looked at one another, excited.

"Ever heard of solanine?" she asked.

"Nope, can't say I have." This from Jack.

"Ever remember your mum telling you that green potatoes were poisonous?"

They nodded.

"I thought that was an old wives' tale," stated Amanda. "But go on."

"Our boy Duncan was more than likely poisoned, intentionally if the amounts of solanine in his system are anything to go on. Many of us have small amounts of solanine in our systems simply from the foods we eat, but Duncan's levels were over the top. I'd say given his reaction – the strength of his hallucinations, his extreme stomach upset and the lingering sore throat – he's lucky to be with us, never mind the bullet wounds. Someone tried very hard to kill him, it seems. Well done for thinking about the hallucinations, Amanda!"

Amanda didn't feel like celebrating, but the result did now give them real cause to talk to Sam more formally. Assuming Sam had given it to him, of course – that was the next hurdle. She needed to get Rick to look in the rubbish bins at the house and find whatever it was she'd given him. She hoped the bins hadn't already been collected and emptied.

"I need to make a call quickly," she announced, and stepped outside to speak to Rick. He listened closely and said he'd get on to it, but first he wanted to give Duncan a call since he was now more coherent. Perhaps a casual conversation would tell them what food they were looking for.

"Is Sam still there?" Amanda asked him.

"I don't think so. She said she had to get back for the girls."

Sitting back in her chair, Amanda felt excited and deflated at the same time.

What sort of woman would go to such extremes to get rid of her husband?

Chapter Eighty

RICK DIDN'T WASTE any time getting a team round to Sam's place.
He'd then headed out to the hospital to speak with Duncan again and
had learned that Sam had baked some delicious little quiches for his
journey down. Duncan had also told him what a change he'd seen in
her recently, how lovely she'd been to him and the girls. He was lucky
to have her, he said.

Rick had been puzzled by that; he wondered if Duncan was telling
the truth or just trying to convince himself of the opposite to what he
had already suspected himself. Reluctantly, he decided not to question
him about the bank loan; he had no wish to upset him further. It would
have to wait until later.

Sam had left just after 2 p.m., Duncan told him, so with a bit of
luck she'd be home before the traffic really jammed up.

That left Rick precious little time to get a warrant and find the
offending pies.

A short time later, Rick entered the Rileys' home accompanied by two
officers dressed in white coveralls. They quickly found what they were
looking for – the remainder of the home baking nicely tied up in a bin

liner and shoved halfway down the bin. Why she hadn't flushed them down the toilet instead Rick had no idea. If you were planning on poisoning someone, it seemed pretty obvious to him to dispose of any further evidence, but then that's why the prisons were filled the world over: they were filled with dumb pricks. He was, however, grateful that Sam fell into that category. Now they had real reason to question her formally. He was looking forward to hearing what she had to say on the matter. And soon.

Sam saw two cars parked outside her house as she turned into her street. The girls were in the back, chattering about their day and about how they'd had donuts with Anika after school. She only half-heard them now. One of the parked cars was Rick's; the other was a painted squad car. What the hell had happened now? And what did they want with her?

Pulling into her drive, she instructed the two girls to stay in the car for a moment while she went inside. She climbed out and almost sprinted up the path. She yanked open the front door and . . . silence. Where were they? As she passed through the house, she spotted them through the kitchen window: they were going through her rubbish. At that precise moment, maybe he sensed she was home because Rick Black looked up and their eyes met. And held. Suddenly it dawned on Sam what they were looking for exactly – and they were in that bin. Inside, she was screaming at her own stupidity.

Shit, she hissed – and saw Rick watching her face.

Sam wanted to bolt but that wasn't possible. They'd only give chase, making it worse for her in the long run. What reason would she give?

Think, think, think!

Sam stood stock still as Rick approached the back door, his eyes never wavering until he reached the step. Knowing the door was locked, he knocked politely and she went to let him in.

Act normal, Sam ...

"Hello, Rick. What's going on out there?" She hoped her smile wasn't too false; it was the best one she could muster under the circumstances.

"Hello, Sam. May I come in?"

She stood back and opened the door fully, then stood aside to let him in. He stood in front of the kitchen window, looking out at nothing it seemed, and then he spoke. Slowly.

"It looks like Duncan had been poisoned as well as shot."

She raised both hands to her open mouth in shock. That bit was real – how had they found out that nugget of info when they'd only just retrieved the pies?

"Oh my God! How?"

"Looks like something he ate that day; something was put in his food. But here's the thing – apart from a bowl of cornflakes and a canteen meal of egg and chips, he only ate one other thing before falling ill." He looked straight at her. "And that was your home baking – quiche, I believe."

She swallowed deeply. So they already suspected her. But did they know about the contract to have Duncan killed?

Rick moved on. "Sam, are we going to find something in the rest of those pies that, for some reason, you put in the bin? Something that would have given Duncan such a serious reaction?" He paused. "Poisonous potatoes, perhaps?"

They knew. And as soon as the pies were tested, they'd know it was her. There was no point in denying it. Sam took a seat at the table and put her head in her hands, hoping for a moment to think through the mess. As far as she knew, it was only the poisoning, nothing more. Waterworks might help.

"Looks like I've been rumbled," she said wearily. Tears welled in her eyes and she let them fall freely. "I only wanted to give him an upset stomach so he'd come home the next day and not go on the stupid course. We never see him anymore. It's all work, work, work with him, and when he is here, he's not really present. I didn't mean to do any real harm – you've got to believe that!" With each word she sounded more distraught, so by the end of her last sentence, she was almost shouting her innocence.

Rick stood silently, watching Sam's tear-stained face, which was turning pinker by the second. Had he got it wrong, then? Was this part as she said it was, and not actually an attempt on his life? But he knew about the contract, the one she herself – the woman sat in front of him, the wife of his work partner – had set rolling and paid good money for. Six thousand pounds, to be precise.

No matter that it was illegally obtained evidence. He couldn't let that go.

Chapter Eighty-One

THEY'D FINALLY LEFT her in peace. But had Sam been convincing enough? Would her spur-of-the-moment story fly? She mentally slapped herself for being so careless with the remaining pies. Why the hell hadn't she dumped them away from the house, in a public rubbish bin for the rats to feast on? But it was done and dusted now: they had the hard evidence in their bag and she'd had to admit as much as she'd sat there in the kitchen with Rick.

The big question now was, what would happen next? With Duncan in hospital for another day or two, there was precious little time to cover her tracks if they did look at her any further. The money was an issue, though, and one she knew they'd easily find out about, though she figured the crypto transfer aspect would be safe. Once she had a plausible explanation for the loan and the missing £6000, there was nothing else to tie her to his attempted murder. No, she'd been tucked up in bed when he'd been shot. The text she'd sent shortly beforehand would prove her phone had been used near to or inside their house. And her car wouldn't be on a CCTV motorway camera anywhere because she hadn't stepped out the door. No, she had been safely at home and safely out of trouble.

But the £6000 irked her, and the fact that she'd had no reply and no means of contacting 'him' irked her even more. She pulled her laptop close and began to search; maybe he had another site, another shop – though how she'd know if another was his, she had no clue. It was worth a try, though. The money needed returning and soon.

From the privacy of his knocked-through house, a G&T by his side, Wilfred Day followed her keystrokes as she did her best to search. He watched as she scrolled through other hit-for-hire sites, clicking, backing out, clicking the next one, backing out again. He raised an eyebrow. Good lord – was she actually searching for another hit man, someone to finish the job off properly?

"Feisty little minx, aren't you, Mrs. Riley?" He picked his phone up and dialled.

Rick stared at his phone as it vibrated. The screen said Will D, his own code for Wilfred Day in case someone was looking over his shoulder. He clicked accept.

"Thought you should know, she seems to be searching again, looking for another hit. It's over to you," Day told him.

"Thanks. I'll get a uniform on his door," Rick said wearily. After all this, was she actually stupid enough to come back for a second kick at the can? He made the first phone call, and then sat back, shaking his head. That settled it; Rick had no choice but to tell Duncan what was going on. What happened then would be up to him.

It wasn't a conversation he was looking forward to.

The following morning, after she'd dropped the girls at school, Sam took a detour home – first to a chemist on the outskirts of town for some everyday help, then over to Beswick to visit the tea lady. With everything that had gone on in the last 24 hours – the finding of the poisoned pies, her own lame story to Rick, and her growing anguish over the £6000 and her vanished 'employee' – a few Paramol were not going to do the trick today. No, Sam needed something far stronger, and the £200 in her purse was going to provide it for her. With no one in the house all day but her, she'd spend the rest of the day looking after *herself* for a change and not worrying about anyone else. Some people drank, some spent money they didn't have. What Sam chose for her stress relief was no different, really, she told herself huffily.

It took an age to get to the house; the traffic was backed up on the A57, adding to her nervous, irritable mood. But finally, she parked up outside the grubby little house and almost wept with relief. There was no one else about, no smartly dressed woman with a racy red Mini parked nearby, no one to bother her while she made her purchase. In her agitation, Sam didn't bother pulling a cap over her hair – which really, needed a wash, come to that – before getting out the car and approaching the door.

It opened just before she knocked. The woman must have seen her approaching on a security screen – either that, or someone had notified her of Sam's arrival. She slipped gratefully inside. The woman looked the same as she had on Sam's last visit – four inches of dark roots, the same fitted black pants and pretty blue blouse with little flowers on it, the same clinking gold bangles.

"What kind of tea would you like?"

"Something nice and strong, please."

Sam felt her pupils dilate in anticipation as the lovely little balsawood tea box came out. She watched as her hostess removed the top layer and exposed the variety of little bags underneath.

"How strong would you like it?"

The woman allowed Sam to scan the contents and select two bags. They were £80 apiece, Sam knew. Thinking of the £200 burning a hole in her purse, she tried her luck for a discount and picked up another bag, making it three in total. The woman raised her eyebrows and held her hand out, reminding Sam to show her the money. Sam met her eyes and held out the four crisp £50 notes. The woman paused for a moment and then, nodding her silent agreement to the discount, quickly pocketed the money. She closed the tea box and put it safely back in the cupboard as Sam slipped her purchase into the side pocket of her bag.

The transaction was over as quickly as it had begun, and Sam stood up to leave. There were no thanks today. Sam's mind was preoccupied with bigger problems than the possibility of someone listening in to the trade going on. If she ever got caught, she knew, it would be her first offence and a slap on the wrist would cover it. If the tea lady got nicked, though, she would be in for a good deal more, and Sam couldn't care less.

Once back inside her car, Sam hit the accelerator harder than was necessary and spun out of the quiet cul-de-sac like her life depended on it, headed back to the quiet sanctuary and safety of her home. She resisted the urge to swallow a tablet on the way, fighting it hard like an alcoholic fighting a beer stood in front of him. She could almost feel herself drool at the thought of the relief ahead.

When she hit the return traffic on the motorway, her resistance crumbled. She had no strength left. Figuring there was no point in delaying the inevitable, she reached across to the passenger seat and fiddled around the inside pocket of her bag until she felt what she was looking for. With a sigh of relief, she swallowed it dry.

By the time she got home, the edge of her problems would be sanded clean off, as smooth as a pebble from the bottom of a riverbed.

Wilfred Day traded in information. From long experience, he knew that almost all information had a value to someone, somewhere, and that meant he could leverage it for his own gain. And in the last short while, Wilfred had gained some very interesting information indeed. The tracker he'd ordered placed under Sam's bumper when her laptop had been returned that night showed a familiar address. He'd been there himself many times, but not for the same reason Sam and most of the others dropped by. No, Wilfred really did stop in for tea, and to catch up with one of his most valued employees, one he'd set up in business after he'd helped her out of a sticky situation with her violent ex-husband. He chuckled to himself as he realized the similarity between the two women: they had both wanted their husbands out of their lives, though for rather different reasons.

Chapter Eighty-Two

BY THE TIME she was putting the key in the door, Sam could barely see straight. How the hell she'd managed to drive back unscathed she had no clue, but how long would the gods, or the angels, or whatever they were, look out for her from this point forward? Throwing herself on to the couch, she kicked off her boots and lay face down without moving for a good five minutes, thinking, a little drool leaking from her open mouth onto the cushion. There were no cares in her world when there was oxy floating around her system, and the feeling of utter lethargy was divine.

The sound of her phone ringing shattered the quiet of the empty house and forced her back into a hazy semblance of reality. It was Rick.

"Yeah?" Even that one word was a struggle.

"Sam, are you okay? Only you sound half asleep."

"Yeah, a bit under the weather. Taking a nap."

"Oh, okay. I won't keep you. But I thought you should know they aren't transferring Duncan to hospital up here any longer. He's going straight home instead. They say they'll schedule his next hand operation from hospital here. Good news, eh?"

That got Sam's attention. Struggling, she managed to sit up straight, head lolling on the sofa back.

"Great news! When will that happen?"

"Should be tomorrow if all goes to plan. I can pick him up if you like. Might be easier with the girls and school. I'm not sure yet what time it's likely to be. Then I can drop him off at your place. Will that work for you?"

Sam was too fuddled to think straight. Her eyelids kept falling closed as the oxy rushed through her system, trying to pull her down to oblivion.

"Sam? Are you there?"

"Yeah. Sounds great. Thanks, Rick," she slurred, and pressed end.

On the other end of the call, Rick stood in the station car park staring at the phone as if something was going to jump out of it. Sam had sounded so drawn out, like she was in a deep slumber. She'd told him she wasn't feeling too good, though, so maybe that was it. She *had* been through quite a lot lately.

Still, Duncan would hopefully be home the following day. *Home.* Rick sat up uneasily. Maybe, given the circumstances, he'd have Duncan stay at his place for a couple of days while the dust settled. He needed to have a long talk with him before he went home to Sam and the girls.

He was still stood in the car park thinking things through when his phone buzzed. Wilfred Day again. What could the man want now? He pressed answer.

"Another call? People will get the wrong impression about us," he joked.

"You're not my type, actually, but that's another story. I bring news to your ears."

"Oh?"

"Your friend Sam likes the stronger pills too. In fact, she has just made a purchase. Can't tell you where, but my source said three oxy tabs. Strong ones. Our young lady must be feeling stressed over something." He gave a sing-song tone to the last word – *something.*

Rick let out a loud sigh. Would Sam never cease to surprise him? A few packets of painkillers were one thing, but oxy? That was something else. He thanked Wilfred and hung up, wondering why the man had bothered to call him with that tidbit. Rick was grateful for the intelligence, of course, but if Day was working on getting a copper in his pocket, he'd have another think coming.

My source says. . .

Rick blinked. Had Sam inadvertently bought her drugs from one of Day's outlets?

Well, there was no time to find that out now. There was work to be done, and since Rochelle had been out of the office for a couple of days and Duncan was laid up in hospital, he needed to get to it.

So that's what he did.

Chapter Eighty-Three

ALL SAM WANTED to do was sleep. But the news that Duncan could be home the following day fought for space in her head and brought her problems so much closer. Now she had not even 24 hours on her own before he'd be back in her life.

And he'd know her secret

He'd know she'd poisoned him, at the minimum, because Rick undoubtedly would tell him. He had searched her rubbish bin, for heaven's sake. But would he believe her cover story about the loan, the one she'd settled on – that, as a surprise, she was planning on buying a caravan for family holidays and weekends away with the girls when he was working? And taking him and the girls away for a fantastic holiday abroad, somewhere warm, after his big case? Could she fudge it without raising more questions? It seemed plausible in her mind, but then her mind was as dull as the sky outside her window. A tear slid down her cheek and she let it roll without wiping it away.

"I'm so tired of this, so tired of him. So tired of everything," she moaned to herself, her voice trailing off as the tears slid untouched down her hot sticky face. Thoughts of ice creams on the Cornish coast with the girls were now gone, her happy dreams rolling away like her tears. Was she strong enough to face him if the truth came out? Could she be that woman? Did she even want to be?

In her half-conscious state, she wondered about leaving it all behind. About taking the remaining two tablets that were hidden discreetly in the side pocket of her bag, swallowing them down with ice-cold vodka, never waking up again. The blessed relief of her wrong-doings being forgotten.

To leave everything. Find the peace she so desperately craved.

And that's exactly what she did.

Chapter Eighty-Four

WILFRED LIKED it when things turned out well, especially the unplanned – because that meant fate had intervened and something was destined to be the way it was. And that's why making this particular house call was going to be the start of something special.

His meaty hand rapped surprisingly gently on the front door and he took a step backwards to wait. There was the sound of footsteps getting closer and then the door opened, revealing a man in his mid-twenties with brown, poodle-like hair. Luke said hello.

"Good morning. I'm looking for Luke Montgomery."

His brighter-than-bright smile always put people at ease. Wilfred knew he was a likeable character, and that people found it hard not to fall under his charming spell. Luke was no exception. He smiled back.

"I'm Luke. What can I do for you?"

"Well, Luke, my name is Wilfred Day and I hear you've been looking for finance to get a food van business off the ground. Can we talk somewhere private?"

Another flash of perfect dentistry; it did the trick.

As the man's words registered, Luke's face lit up, his smile as big as Wilfred's but a lower wattage. He stood to one side of the door and signalled for him to enter. "My parents aren't home right now so there's no one here. We can talk in private. Can I get you a coffee? Tea perhaps?"

Wilfred followed him through the house and out to the back where most people's kitchens were and helped himself to a seat at the central island. He admired the set-up.

"Tea, thanks. One sugar." He took a slow look around. "Nicely done," he said casually, taking in the whole room. "Modern with a dash of antique," he added, nodding his approval.

Luke busied himself with the kettle and tea bags as he spoke. "My parents travel extensively. That's why I'm house-sitting for them."

Wilfred let the fib lie, realizing the young man was putting up a front, not wanting to admit he was broke and living in his folks' back bedroom. It made what he was about to offer him all the more tantalizing, and he wanted Luke to want it, not simply do it. Having skin in the game, so to speak, bred loyalty, and loyalty made good business.

"Good for them. It's life's experiences that make the person, not material objects. Those are of relatively little value."

Luke hadn't noticed the Bentley when he'd opened the door but knew the man sat in his kitchen wasn't short of a bob or two. His Rolex was a giveaway, as were the perfectly capped teeth.

"So, who do we know in common, then?" he asked the stranger. "Who put you on this doorstep?"

Wilfred chuckled to himself, then replied, "Well, that's the thing. I don't think you know her at all. Actually, let me correct myself: you only know her online. She's a woman called Sam Riley, lives around the Manchester area."

Luke handed him a mug of tea and joined him at the island, looking thoughtful as he tried to remember who Sam was. Maybe he and Clinton had presented their business plan to her at some point, but no. Wilfred had said online. He really couldn't place the name.

Wilfred could see his brain doing a search and coming up blank. As he would expect him to.

"Can't say I can recall," said Luke at length, "but I guess it doesn't matter."

"Well, actually, Luke, it does rather matter. It's vitally important, actually, how you know Mrs. Riley, because she's key to this business relationship moving forward." His casual smile was still lighting his face up, causing no sniff of concern. But clearly Luke hadn't the faintest idea what he was driving at. He took the opportunity to explain. "Well, allow me to explain who Mrs. Sam Riley is, and then we can talk about how I can help finance your venture."

"I'm listening."

"Luke, Sam Riley is the woman who booked you and your partner to kill her husband a couple of days ago, in Croydon. You may remember that night?" Still the smile remained, and then it turned into a light laugh at the look on Luke's face – all colour had drained from it. Instead of the happy, healthy-looking young man of a moment or two ago, he was now the colour of a Dairylea triangle. Wilfred gave him another moment to compose a reply.

With a bit of a stutter, Luke asked, "Who are you?"

"I'm a businessman. I'm not the cops or MI5 or any other agency you might wonder about. I'm Wilfred Day. And it's my business to know about other people's business. So, when I was helping an acquaintance out recently, I came across your enterprise, the one on the dark web specifically. And on that, you could have been a little more careful, I must say. If I found you so easily, others could as well if they chose."

Luke gulped but said nothing.

"Still, it looks like I'm here first, and that's a good thing for you and for me. And quite by chance – and you should believe in chance if you don't already – you want to launch a food van business. And, since I have a fleet of my own, I can offer you advice as well as funding."

Luke couldn't believe what he was hearing.

"What about the website and Mrs. Riley?" he stammered. "If you're not the authorities, what is in it for you and why are you really here?"

"Glad you asked – and your secret is safe with me, by the way. I also notice you haven't denied anything so far. I like that. If we're going to be working together, trust is vital in our game."

"And your game is what exactly?"

"I told you, I have a fleet of food vans, except we offer a particular product with our sandwiches that has proved extremely popular with the locals. And it's all high-tech, all done via an app. And untraceable."

Wilfred was enjoying himself immensely, explaining how things were going to work from now on, even if Luke didn't fully realize it yet. "So, I'm willing to fund you a small string of vans, to start with anyway, as long as you sell my product and use my technology for payment. Simple, eh?"

He drained the rest of his tea as Luke took it all in. He'd barely touched his own. Wilfred looked at his Rolex. "Look, think it over and I'll be in touch so we can chat more. But just so you have the alternative side of things, remember I know what you and Clinton did. And I can prove it."

The smile was gone now. Luke swallowed hard.

"I'll call you again tomorrow about this time so we can iron out any details," Wilfred said smoothly. "And look at it this way: you get your own fleet, a dream you've had for some time now. And it can all become a reality, making you both rather wealthy young men." He gave Luke's shoulder a light slap as he stood and walked towards the front door. "I'll let myself out. Have a fantastic day!" he called to him.

Fantastic day, thought Luke, his heart pounding. More like unusual day.

Chapter Eighty-Five

"WHO THE HELL tipped them off, then, do you reckon?" Jack asked the room.

Blank faces stared back at him, and Amanda took the opportunity to speak up. It was better coming from her, as detective sergeant, rather than Jack. She noticed that Dupin was watching the proceedings through his office window.

"Jack is right to be pissed, as we all are," she explained. "It seems as soon as we figure it out, they've moved on. Where to, we've no idea, but my guess is they are still operating in some form – this gig is far too lucrative for them not to be. Our friends in Manchester warned us Wilfred Day was slippery, and the link between him and the vans here was tenuous, to say the least. But since we don't believe in coincidence, somehow in all this he's been tipped off. I doubt we'll see vans distributing on our patch any more now. That doesn't mean they won't get caught somewhere else, but it won't be by us. Drug squad have now taken an interest, so it would have been taken out of our hands soon enough anyway.

"In other words, don't be despondent about it. You all worked diligently with the case and the shooting of DS Riley, who's back at home

"

again now, by the way." Amanda paused for breath. She saw that Dupin was stood behind her now, listening to her every word.

"Would you like to add anything, sir?" She stepped aside and let him take over.

"I think DS Lacey has covered it nicely. If Day was behind it, he'll slip up one day, and drug squad will be ready to swoop, mark my words. But excellent work anyway. Excellent." There was a pregnant pause as all eyes remained on Dupin, waiting for him to go on, but it became obvious he hadn't anything else to say. Eventually, chairs and bodies turned back to their desks, and a low hum of conversation resumed.

As they walked back to their desks, Jack looked at Amanda and gently shook his head in defeat. He hated it when a case ended on such a low. In a quiet whisper, he said, "I'd like to know who the leak was. I'm not going to forget this. If it's someone in this room, I'll find them. They'll not do it again."

Amanda was taken aback by the vehemence in his voice and couldn't help but wonder why. Why this case? What was so special about it or the slippery Wilfred Day? No doubt he'd tell her when he'd calmed down – she'd wait until then.

"I hear you, Jack," she said, then added, "Listen, why don't we all get take-out from Wong's tonight? You, me and Ruth. Sweet-and-sour pork balls will cheer us up, eh? I'm buying."

Amanda knew Jack couldn't resist a meal from Wong's. She smiled as he accepted the invite, though it was obvious he was still annoyed.

"Sounds perfect," he said. "I'll bring a bottle. Or two."

"Well, if you're bringing two, you'd better bring your toothbrush or be prepared to leave your car and taxi it home. I suspect between us we'll easily polish them off. Come round for seven o'clock?"

She smiled brightly, trying to lighten his mood. It must have worked. Jack smiled back.

"Great, and I can check out your decorating standards at the same time."

She knew he was only joking. His idea of decorating was re-gluing loose wallpaper edges back down so that they'd be good for another ten years. She checked her watch. It was nearly time to leave for the evening anyway. She called Ruth and told her they had a guest for dinner.

Chapter Eighty-Six

One week later

They were all in attendance. Sam's parents, Anika, Victoria and Jasmine, and a couple of aunts and uncles alongside supporting one another as the casket was lowered into the ground. Duncan watched on with Rochelle and Rick, his two best friends in the world, beside him for support on what promised to be an exceptionally sad day.

Rick placed his arm around his friend's shoulder; Rochelle took his right hand in hers as the service drew to an end and handfuls of soil were sprinkled on top of the casket. Slowly the crowd dispersed, most in search of sherry and sandwiches at a nearby pub. Had either of them been paying attention, they'd have noticed the hulking blond man in the long caramel-coloured coat at the edge of the cemetery watching the proceedings and then returning to his tan Bentley and driving away as the service drew to a close.

Duncan felt numb to the bone, though it wasn't the weather making him feel so. For a change, the usually weak winter sun shone brightly high in the sky, casting a strangely summery glow across everything it touched. Duncan had barely said a word to anyone, and people had mostly let him be, figuring he was too distraught at Sam's suicide to speak much. But he had already grieved that loss while he lay injured in hospital. What he was doing as he stood there, as others moved on, was all for show. He'd already said all he needed to say. Though Sam would never hear it.

When talking is too painful, experts say, it often helps to write a letter to whomever is causing your anguish, but never send it. The process of putting thoughts down on paper helps to take the burden off your own shoulders, gets the thoughts and feelings out in the open and allows the healing to begin. So, before they'd closed the casket lid for the last time, Duncan had slipped the letter inside. It read:

Sam,

It was very nearly me in this casket right now.

It pained me to find out you wanted me dead. After all these years and two wonderful children I was surprised, to say the least, but it all fits together. It was your sudden change in behaviour that raised the question initially, though in Rochelle's mind rather than my own – I was a bit slow on the uptake.

But here's the thing: when I heard these two novices that night, arguing about who was going to kill me, I knew she'd been right – no self-respecting criminal would have gone with such an amateur route. But an actual amateur would. And they were almost successful, because I was incapacitated – something I suspect was your own handiwork. The thoughtfulness of the little pies escaped me at the time. I should have known it was all part of it. How silly I've been.

Rick never said a word to me; still hasn't. Knowing Rick, I guess he's protecting my feelings because, now you're gone, it wouldn't do any good to bring it all up. He's good like that, and that's why I cherish him as a friend and work colleague as much as I do.

You're gone yourself now, and in a way I'm glad, because it means I don't have to face you and what you did. How could we ever go back after that? You made it impossible.

We won't be meeting in an afterlife, because I'm not going where you're already headed — a special place reserved only for you. So, the girls and I will pick up the pieces of our lives, and we'll find happiness once again, though it will take time. Thankfully, we have plenty of that.

Maybe you'll be happy now. You certainly weren't when you were here.

Duncan.

He'd poured it all out, cleansed his soul, scraped back the scales and prepared himself for life as a single father with two wonderful girls. Where he'd take them he didn't yet know, but it would be tough to stay where they were, in the house they'd all shared together, where she'd been found. He'd never forgive her for that. The girls didn't need to have witnessed their mother lying dead, face down on the sofa, with an empty vodka bottle beside her. Where had she got the drugs that had eventually killed her? How had he missed her having a problem? Maybe he hadn't known her at all.

In time the girls would get over it — they all would — but for now, he had to be there for them, support them through the years ahead and give them everything they needed, everything a single dad could muster.

Perhaps he'd buy a caravan, move to the Cornish coast where the weather was warmer and the ice creams were plenty. Maybe that's what she'd meant for them when she'd left the brochures and magazines nearby. A note would have been nice.

But she hadn't bothered, so Duncan had written his own note, which, along with the truth, was now buried with her forever.

The day was, indeed, done.

Also by Linda Coles

If you enjoyed reading one of my stories, here are the others:

The DC Jack Rutherford and DS Amanda Lacey Series:

The Controller

It takes courage to change sides.

They're making big money. When a group kidnapping dogs for ransom hits South London, local detective Amanda Lacey investigates after an acquaintance alerts her she isn't the only victim of the upsetting crime.

But what starts out as a way to make quick money for the gang, quickly turns sinister when a local hard-man gets involved. And Pete didn't sign up for what happens next. With a past record, can he put his personal fears aside and involve the police before it's too late?

Hot to Kill

Just how many deadly pranks can one woman get away with?

Approaching 50, Madeline Simpson is totally hacked off and the English summer heatwave isn't helping with her hot flushes. While it was never her intention to kill, the body count increases as she doles out retribution to those that rub her up the wrong way.

Alerted by similarities in local deaths, someone close to home is hot on her tail to put an end to the carnage.

Often humorous and regularly deadly, read ***Hot to Kill*** to find out how one woman discovers the identity of a local sex offender while wreaking havoc on a carefully crafted mission.

A quirky and humourous story of life, revenge, dead bodies and a good few bottles of Bombay Sapphire Gin.

The Hunted

The hunt is on...

They kill wild animals for sport. She's about to return the favour. A spate of distressing big-game hunter posts are clogging up her newsfeed. As hunters brag about the exotic animals they've murdered and the followers they've gained along the way, a passionate veterinarian can no longer sit back and do nothing. To stop the killings, she creates her own endangered list of hunters. By stalking their online profiles and infiltrating their inner circles, she vows to take them out one-by-one. How far will she go to add the guilty to her own trophy collection?

Dark Service

The dark web can satisfy any perversion, but two detectives might just pull the plug...

Taylor never felt the blade pressed to her scalp. She wakes frightened and alone in an unfamiliar hotel room with a near shaved head and a warning... tell no one.

As detectives Amanda Lacey and Jack Rutherford investigate, they venture deep into the fetish-fueled underbelly of the dark web. The traumatized woman is only the latest victim in a decade-long string of disturbing—and intensely personal—thefts.

To take down a perverted black market, they'll go undercover. But just when justice seems within reach, an unexpected event sends their sting operation spiraling out of control. Their only chance at catching the culprits lies with a local reporter... and a sex scandal that could ruin them all.

One Last Hit

The greatest danger may come from inside his own home.

Detective Duncan Riley has always worked hard to maintain order on the streets of Manchester. But when a series of incidents at home cause him to worry about his wife's behaviour, he finds himself pulled in too many directions at once.

After a colleague Amanda Lacey asks for his help with a local drug epidemic, he never expected the case would infiltrate his own family...And a situation that spirals out of control...

Hey You, Pretty Face

An abandoned infant. Three girls stolen in the night. Can one overworked detective find the connection to save them all?

London, 1999. Short-staffed during a holiday week, Detective Jack Rutherford can't afford to spend time on the couch with his beloved wife. With a skeleton staff, he's forced to handle a deserted infant and a trio of missing girls almost single-handedly. Despite the overload, Jack has a sneaking suspicion that the baby and the abductions are somehow connected…

As he fights to reunite the girls with their families, the clues point to a dark secret that sends chills down his spine. With evidence revealing a detestable crime ring, can Jack catch the criminals before the girls go missing forever?

Scream Blue Murder

Two cold cases are about to turn red hot…

Detective Jack Rutherford's instincts have only sharpened with age. So when a violent road fatality reminds him of a near-identical crime from 15 years earlier, he digs up the past to investigate both. But with one case already closed, he fears the wrong man still festers behind bars while the real killer roams free…

For Detective Amanda Lacey, family always comes first. But when she unearths a skeleton in her father-in-law's garden, she has to balance her heart with her desire for justice. And with darkness lurking just beneath the surface, DS Lacey must push her feelings to one side to discover the chilling truth.

As the sins of the past haunt both detectives, will solving the crimes have consequences that echo for the rest of their lives?

Butcher Baker Banker

Two deaths. Three extraordinary problems. Questionable ways to fix them.

A trio of individuals weave in and out of each other's lives without realising they have a connection. But they do.

Baker Kit Morris will do anything to keep his family business alive. Desperate for cash, he hatches a risky plan that lands him in trouble. As he struggles to stay out of prison, Kit forges an unlikely friendship with a tough man.

Local thug Ron Butcher rose to the top of London's gangland by "fixing things". But even his extensive crooked connections are useless when death knocks at his own family's door.

And where does the CEO of a high-street bank fit into all of this?

As DS Amanda Lacey and DC Jack Rutherford investigate recent deaths, Jack receives a last-minute history lesson and is left wondering where it all went wrong.

The Chrissy Livingstone series:

Tin Men

She thought she knew her father. But what she doesn't know could fill a mortuary...

Ex-MI5 agent Chrissy Livingstone grieves over her dad's sudden death. While she cleans out his old things, she discovers something she can't explain: seven photos of schoolboys with the year 1987 stamped on the back. Unable to turn off her desire for the truth, she hunts down the boys in the photos only to find out that three of the seven have committed suicide...

Tracing the clues from Surrey to Santa Monica, Chrissy unearths disturbing ties between her father's work as a financier and the victims. As each new connection raises more sinister questions about her family, she fears she should've left the secrets buried with the dead.

Will Chrissy put the past to rest, or will the sins of the father destroy her?

Walk Like You

When a major railway accident turns into a bizarre case of a missing body, will this PI's hunt for the truth take her way off track?

London. Private investigator Chrissy Livingstone's dirty work has taken her down a different path to her family. But when her upper-class sister begs her to locate a friend missing after a horrific train crash, she feels duty-bound to assist. Though when the two dig deeper, all the evidence seems to lead to one mysterious conclusion: the woman doesn't want to be found.

Still with no idea why the woman was on the train, and an unidentified body uncannily resembling the missing person lying unclaimed in the mortuary, the sisters follow a trail of cryptic clues through France. The mystery deepens when they learn someone else is searching, and their motive could be murder...

Can Chrissy find the woman before she meets a terrible fate?

About the Author

Hi, I'm Linda Coles. Thanks for choosing this book, I really hope you enjoyed it and collect the following ones in the series. Great characters make a great read and I hope I've managed to create that for you.

Originally from the UK, I now live and work in beautiful New Zealand along with my hubby, 2 cats and 6 goats. My office sits by the edge of my vegetable garden, and apart from reading and writing, I get to run by the beach for pleasure.

If you find a moment, please do write an honest online review of my work, they really do make such a difference to those choosing what book to buy next.

If you'd like to keep in touch via my newsletter, use this link to leave your details:

http://eepurl.com/gwfVqL

Enjoy! And tell your friends.

Thanks, Linda

Keep in touch:
www.lindacoles.com
linda@lindacoles.com
Follow me on BookBub

Also by Linda Coles

Jack Rutherford and Amanda Lacey Series:

The Controller

Hot to Kill

The Hunted

Dark Service

One Last Hit

Hey You, Pretty Face

Scream Blue Murder

Butcher Baker Banker

The Chrissy Livingstone Series:

Tin Men

Walk Like You